COMMAND A[illegible]NTROL

⊝ KNOCKIN' BOOTS ⊝

ANGIE DANIELS

ISBN-13: 978-1-941342-48-0

For questions and comments about the book please contact angie@angiedaniels.com.

Caramel Kisses Ink

DEDICATION

I want to thank all my loyal readers for their love and support over the last nineteen years. Happy Reading!

To the men and women who have served in the United States Air Force, past and present, I proudly salute you!

1

MEEKS

The ringing of the doorbell interrupted my evening romance.

I rolled out from beneath Blake's beefy arm, then reached for the fluffy, pink robe draped over a chair near my nightstand. I covered my naked body and padded downstairs to the living room, tying the belt on my robe. When I opened the front door, I found a short, dark-skinned woman standing on my porch with arms folded beneath her breasts.

"My husband here?" she asked with a knowing tone.

I startled and stared.

"Look..." She blew out an impatient sigh. "His BMW is out front, so I figured he's either here or the townhouse next door, but seeing that you're his type, I bet he's upstairs asleep."

She knew her man.

"You want me to wake him?" I asked because, at this point, what else could I say?

She shook her head, sending her sister locks swinging. "Nah, I'm just dropping off his dinner." She held out a red lunch pail. As soon as I took it, she turned and walked away. However, before she reached a blue Toyota 4-Runner that was double-parked and blocking my car, she swung around and said, "Just so you know, if I come by tomorrow and my husband is over here instead of at work, I'll be dropping off a lot more than just Gatorade and a bologna sandwich."

ʘ ʘ ʘ

As soon as Blake's wife left, I woke that fool up and kicked him out my house. I changed my bedroom sheets and made sure there were no traces of him left. Thirty minutes later, Blake had the nerve to come back knocking at my door because he'd forgotten his lunch pail.

Feeling sorry for myself, I took a long, hot shower then laid in bed and cried while thinking about all my failed relationships. At some point, I fell asleep.

I woke up, eyes red, and continued my pity party, which felt even more depressing being that it was my thirty-fifth birthday.

By the time I made a pot of coffee and was seated at a small, round, birchwood table near a bay window, I needed someone to talk to. Three minutes into the call and I was starting to regret calling my sister.

Layla managed to get out, "That's what you get for trying to find love on the internet," between laughter.

I momentarily held the phone away from my ear before saying, "How else am I supposed to meet anyone? Remember, I'm new to the area."

"Do it the old fashion way. Bump into him on the street. Matter of fact..." I heard a snap of her fingers. "I was watching one of those talk shows and the host said one of the best places to meet a man is at—"

"Church?" I replied between sips.

"No. Home Depot." Her response made me laugh. "I'm serious. A lot of handy men hang out in DIY stores."

"There are also a lot of *husbands* who spend the weekend checking off their wife's Honey-Do list. No thank you. I'll take my chances online."

"Whatever. I told you Faze has a friend he'd like you to meet," she reminded for the umpteenth time.

"Uh-uh. I'm not interested in any hook-ups." Mostly because I didn't trust my sister's taste in men. Her husband, Faison King, was cute in a nerdy sorta way. "At least when I'm viewing profiles online, I can swipe left if he's scary looking."

Layla drew a dramatic breath. "Suit yourself. You've never listened to your big sister before, so why start now."

My sister needed a man to screw in a light bulb. I do not.

"I listen to you all the time. Just not when it comes to men."

"And look where that has gotten you," she mumbled under her breath.

"I heard that," I warned.

"You need to learn to trust."

Here we go again. "How can I trust when I keep hooking up with someone else's husband?"

"Technically, that's not your fault. You just need to start asking the right questions. You remember what mama always used to say."

"Trust but verify," we said in unison.

I gave a laugh that ended in a rude snort. "That's because our father was a ho and Mama is bitter. Nope. That's just too much work. If I have to do all that questioning and verifying, then I don't need him." I changed the subject. "Speaking of Mama, have you called her yet?"

Her answer was a rude snort.

I drew a huge sigh. It was my fault. When Layla and Faison were having marital problems, I accidently mentioned it to Mama. Of course, negative Rhonda jumped on the bandwagon, bad-mouthing and bashing Faison. By the time the couple worked out their issues and salvaged their marriage, Mama was livid. Layla had every right to defend her husband, and the two haven't spoken since.

"I'll call Mama if you call Daddy."

It was my turn to grunt. I gulped down the last of my coffee and glanced at my watch. "Would you look at the time? I better get out of here before I'm late. The boss has been on my ass lately."

"Ha-ha. You think you're slick."

I couldn't help but laugh because my sister knows me better than anyone.

"Well, cheer up. Your prince is out there." There was a pause. "Maybe you need to reconsider your decision not to date—"

"Uh-uh, bye, Layla."

She giggled. "See ya later, Day, and happy birthday!"

"Thanks, sis." I ended the call and padded through the house and up to my bedroom. I wasn't reconsidering anything. I'd made my decision about love and I wasn't settling for anything less.

As I stepped into my room, I stopped in front of a full-length mirror that was mounted to the wall. I turned side-to-side, striking poses. I took in all my womanly curves and smiled. I'm five-foot-eight and in phenomenal shape. I work out at least three times a week, have a small waistline, thick hips and thighs, but I'm far from fat. I also have a generous set of D-cups that look delicious in a *Victoria's Secret* bra and have yet to be a victim to the gravitational pull.

I'm cute. Hell, better than cute. I'm a WOW with a brown sugar complexion and long, dark hair. So why am I single? I wish someone could tell me because I don't understand the problem. Maybe there aren't any good men left. The ones I meet are broke, between jobs, just got out of jail, don't have a car, or married. Sometimes I wondered if maybe Mama could be right. Growing up, she used to tell us, "Day…Layla…listen to me when I tell you, there is no such thing as a good man." She also told us we were stubborn and stupid, and setting ourselves up for years of heartache, and yet, I wasn't willing to accept that as my truth.

I stepped into the ensuite and moved in front of the vanity mirror. I reached for my mascara and brushed the liquid contents across my lashes. Within seconds my chestnut-colored eyes looked large surrounded by eyelashes that were dark with luminous volume. As I stared at the woman in the mirror, I shook my head because I just didn't get it. Is there a plague sweeping the country that I'm unaware of? Or maybe it's just my city, which would be a shame considering I went to a lot of trouble to relocate after my last heartbreak.

Grabbing my MAC lipstick, I puckered and spread my favorite shade of soft pink across my lips, then blew myself a kiss. Yes, I looked *that* good. However, as I stepped back into my master bedroom, I couldn't shake the despair I felt as I thought again about being thirty-five and still single.

Happy birthday to me...

I would be celebrating alone. Well, that wasn't completely true. My sister had invited me to have dinner at her house this evening. I would be the guest of honor and she would make all my favorite dishes. And then I would be forced to watch her and my brother-in-law slobber all over each other, which would only remind me that I didn't have a man to call my own.

Such a shame because I have a lot to offer. I'm educated with a Bachelor's in Business Administration with plans to pursue an MBA in the spring.

With a long sigh, I dragged the dull brown cotton t-shirt over my head while I thought about my most recent relationship that lasted all of two weeks.

I had met Blake at the 24-hour gym near my townhouse. He was often there after work just as I was, sometimes a few treadmills away. One evening, he took the one right beside me. We jogged at a reasonable pace to strike up a conversation. The following evening, we went to dinner, and a few more occasions thereafter, until I finally invited him to my place. He worked the night shift at one of the shipyards, so he always left around eleven. I thought it was cute that he spent his evenings with me. However, I should have known that something was going on because if I called him during the day his phone always went straight to voicemail. On weekends, he could never stay overnight, and any time I asked him to take me to lunch he always had an excuse. The dick was good and maybe that's why I preferred to ignore the signs. But when a wife comes knocking at my door, I don't care how hooked I was on that D.

Boy, bye!

I moved out the room and back to the vanity mirror to deal with my hair. I reached for my hairbrush, sweeping it up into a hair tie. I prepared one thick braid then twirled it around into a neat bun and secured it in place with another small, black hair tie. With my hair swept away from my face, the diamond studs in my earlobes shimmered. I wear minimal makeup. I'm hoping that if I kept is simple, I might meet a guy who wouldn't feel intimidated by my beauty and step to me like a man.

Yeah, right.

I slid on a pair of long, green socks, then walked over to the closet where I removed a lightly starched jacket and pants. I slipped my pants on, slid my arms inside my jacket, fastened the buttons, then took a seat on the edge of the bed and reached for my boots.

Loosely laced.

I slid on my foot gear, laced them up.

Tightly laced.

I rose and moved back to the full-length mirror and smiled proudly. The Air Force Battle Uniform looked good on me. The large chevron on the sleeves that proudly signified my rank looked even better.

Senior Master Sergeant Dayana Meeks.

With an about-face, I moved toward the stairs and grinned because I already knew—I looked damn good strutting in green combat boots.

2

HOWARD

"Howard, come watch me school this young Airman," Retired Chief Lawson called out when he saw me stroll into the room. It was happy hour and the crowd was just starting to gather at the All-Ranks Club.

"You better watch it," I warned the staff sergeant. "He likes to cheat at cards." The other retirees at the table laughed and cosigned my response. Grinning, I kept walking and headed over to a long mahogany bar that took up most of one wall. Stools were all around it, most were occupied.

"What's happening, Chief Howard?" Senior Master Sergeant Gideon Ryan greeted with a head nod. He had a Heineken in his hand, and I wanted the same.

I smiled and gave him a fist bump. "Another long week. I'm ready for the weekend."

"I know that's right. Your team ready for the upcoming exercise?" He was the unit deployment manager for Operations Group and responsible for ensuring our pilots were ready to fly at a moment's notice.

"We still have a few that need self-aid and buddy care training, but I think we're good to go." I'd been working all week so the last thing I wanted to do was spend my Friday night talking shop. I signaled Harmony, the bartender, and pointed to the beer in Ryan's hand, ordering the same. Within seconds, a bottle slid in front of me.

"You want to start a tab?" she asked. Harmony was cute in a ratchet kind of way with long, platinum weave; thick, fake lashes; and purple talons that were so long I don't know how she managed to pop the cap off my bottle. She was married to a technical sergeant in the Logistics Readiness Squadron. They were good people.

I nodded and reached inside the pocket of my Airman battle uniform pants and handed her a credit card. "Ryan, I'll holler at you on Monday." I gave him a fist bump and headed across the room while sipping my beer. It was just what I needed.

"Bruh, you late," Chief Master Sergeant Gage Taylor said as he glanced up from the table. He was involved in a serious game of bones.

I pulled up a chair beside the table and looked down at the domino chips. "Commander caught me before I could get out the door."

Taylor shook his head. "He's got way too much time on his hands."

"That he does." My commander was going through marital issues and, because of it, had been working a lot of long hours. The problem was he expected everyone else to do the same.

I glanced at the other dudes and then reached across the table to give them each dap. Master Sergeant Clint and Lanes, and Chiefs Cole, Taylor, Reid, and Tell. In the military we all refer to each other by the name stitched over the left pocket of our uniforms.

"I'm spanking that ass tonight," Cole said.

Taylor scowled as he looked over at me. "I already won the first round so I don't know why he's trying to blow smoke up your butt."

Cole chuckled. "Howard, your boy over here is tripping." He slapped a double onto the table, and I watched the disbelief on Taylor's face before he went back to studying his chips.

"You working this weekend?" Reid asked.

I gave an eyebrow lift that went without me saying, *hell no*. "I plan on scooping up my daughter tomorrow and taking her shopping."

Tell tilted the bottle and finished it before saying, "A teenager in your pocket? You about to be broke."

"Ain't that the truth." What Ava's mother didn't take in child support; my daughter took during our weekends together. But she was the apple of my eye and there wasn't much she couldn't have.

Moisture from the bottle dripped onto the table and I took a half-hearted swipe at mopping it away with my fingers, then allowed my eyes to travel around the room. The deejay was over in the corner setting up the dance floor. He had Marvin Gaye cooing through the speakers, which always brought a smile to my lips and soul. Mama's favorite. Just thinking about her made me realized it had been a minute since I'd last visited. I was going to have to give her a call later and make a trip home soon to Wilmington, Delaware to see her.

"Yo, Howard, take a look." Reid nodded in the direction of the main entrance.

I looked over to see three women standing there in dresses that screamed "come and get it". Since they weren't wearing a uniform it was hard to tell if they were in the service, military wives, or women wanting to get an ID card. Whatever the case may be, I'm a man and far from dead. While I sipped, I watched the trio saunter into the club. I wasn't the only one. In fact, they had all our attention. I was willing to bet that every man watching them had a serious hard-on, me included.

"That's Giselle, the female I was telling you about," Taylor said.

It took a moment before I remembered he had told me about the new training coordinator working in the education office. She was a civilian and a federal employee. Giselle was cute. Bright-skinned and skinny with straight, light-brown hair. When she spotted Taylor, her eyes lit up with recognition. She tapped the other two on the shoulder, pointed, and headed our way.

"Hey, Gage," she said once she was standing next to our table.

"Giselle, how's the wing treating you?"

"I'm taking it one day at a time." As her eyes circled the table, she waved. "Everyone… I'm Giselle Wade and these are my sorority sisters Cretia and Kayla."

I gave the other two a swift glance. They were both attractive. One chocolate. One caramel. Both wearing too much weave on their heads for my taste. I liked my women natural. Like Giselle. Her hair—at least it looked like her hair—was pulled away from her face with a pair of sunglasses.

"I haven't seen you in here before," Taylor said as he placed double sixes onto the table.

"These two wanted a tour of the base so I thought we'd drop in for a drink before we hit the nightclubs," she explained.

I liked the way her lips moved when she spoke.

"I'm Keim Howard," I said, holding out my hand.

Her eyes lit up with knowing. "Chief Howard in maintenance? Yes, I've heard about you." She shook my hand. Her fingers were just as long and slender as the rest of her.

"Hopefully good things."

She blushed. "Yes, absolutely. Several of your Airmen have come into the education office saying you sent them my way. So, I thank you."

I raised my beer and said, "You're welcome."

The rest of the group was introduced, and I could see the game of bones was practically abandoned. Nothing could pull them away. Except for a beautiful woman.

"Would you like a drink?" I asked.

Giselle nodded.

"And your sorors, too." I flagged down the bartender and ordered another round for everyone. While her friends were distracted by Cole and Reid, Giselle pulled up a seat beside me. I shifted the chair to give her my undivided attention. Women appreciated that. "I hear you're new to the base."

She blushed openly. "Not that new. I've been here since October. I was at Fort Bragg for almost four years and was ready for a change."

"I feel you."

We continued to chat, but at some point, the game started again, and we all got caught up in the excitement. After Taylor lost, Giselle and I went over to the corner of the room and played a game of darts while others started shooting pool. The buffet was laid out with wings and finger foods. We ate, talked, and had a good time, which was why I come on Friday evenings to unwind and release the bullshit of the week. By the close of the evening, I would walk away leaving the stress behind until Monday morning.

Giselle was cute and educated, which was always a good sign. I guess her and her girls hitting a nightclub was probably not happening any time soon, considering the two were grinding on the dance floor with Tell and Cole.

"So, what's your story?" Giselle asked while I licked buffalo sauce from my fingers.

"What do you mean?"

Her lips curled in a mysterious grin. "I mean, are you married? Seeing someone?"

I reached for another wing. "No, I'm not married. I date but no one serious at the moment." I saw the way she reacted to my response. Eyes sparkling... She was feeling a brotha.

"Why is that?" she asked. She leaned in close and I saw ample cleavage spilling out the top of her dress. "Are you picky?"

Moving closer to her, I kept my voice low. "Actually I am. I don't want just anything."

Giselle arched one perfectly sculpted eyebrow. "And what is it you want?"

I studied her smooth complexion before I shrugged and replied, "Don't know, but I'll know it when I see it."

"Well..." she began in a soft voice. "If you see something in front of you that interests you, give me a call."

"I can do that." I locked her number into my phone and then punched Talk so she'd have mine.

Leaning forward, she pressed her cheek to mine while affecting an air kiss. "I look forward to hearing from you," she whispered.

After that, I went back to focusing on the game. I was next up at the dominos table.

I watched as Giselle rose and joined her friends who both grabbed their purses and looked ready to leave for the club. Giselle waved, and I watched the sway of her hips as she left. She might be skinny, but the girl had plenty of assets.

I'd already decided I would call her. We would do lunch. But I wasn't sure if it would go any further than that. I was looking for my happily forever after. I wanted to marry again. Only do it right this time.

Sherry and I married right after I had graduated from basic training. I was twenty and too young to know what the hell I was doing, but when Sherry got pregnant, I knew I had to do the right thing, or my old man would have kicked my ass. Back then I had been stationed at Travis AFB, California and barely bringing home minimum wage. Hell, we qualified for food stamps, we were so poor. But Sherry and I stuck it out until Ava was almost four. I came back to our apartment one evening to find both Sherry and my daughter gone. She wanted a different life. Not as an Air Force wife. I remembered being both sad and relieved. Since our divorce, I have done everything I could to be an active part of my daughter's life. Relationships came and went. Most women just kept my bed warm at night, but for a long time Ava was the only thing stable in my life. I used to be okay with that, but now I wanted more. However, I rarely met anyone with even the slightest bit of potential and, when they did and I thought it was time to make them wifey, they'd do something to fuck the shit up. After a while, I stopped even looking and decided if it's meant for me then it would be. But one thing for sure, I wasn't just settling for anyone just so I could say I had someone. I'd seen too many of my friends dealing with unnecessary stress. And I wasn't having it.

I hung around long enough to play two games. I won and lost the other to Tell. I made it out to my car and started the engine of my Lincoln Navigator when I saw two fine ass women getting out of a silver Lexus and sauntering across the parking lot. A thick sista with short, blond hair turned my way and when her eyes met mine, I felt my loins instantly heat.

"Damn." One more beer wouldn't hurt.

I shut off the engine and rushed inside.

3

MEEKS

With earbuds in my ear, and SZA singing "The Weekend" I waited until the fitness monitor raised the stopwatch into the air, gave the signal, and then took off into a slow jog behind the dozen or so Airmen ahead of me. Within seconds the men in my unit were several feet in front of me. I didn't even let it freak me out; instead, I listened to the beat of the music, paced myself, and jogged. One foot in front of the other, breathing in through my nose and out through my mouth.

I get so worked up. Fitness tests were annual. I've never failed and don't know why I always worried that I would. I was too competitive for that. I completed thirty-five push-ups, maxed out on the sit-ups with fifty-five, and I had a perfect twenty-nine-inch waist. All I needed to do now was run under fifteen minutes and I wouldn't have to do this bullshit again for another year. Failure just wasn't an option. It never was and I wasn't about to start now.

I take him on the weekend.

I really need to update my playlist. Every time I listened to this song flashbacks popped in my head as I remembered my time with Dame. Command Chief Master Sergeant Carlos Dame. Originally, I had been his Monday through Thursday because he was spending the weekends with his family. The sneaking around had been so hard because I wanted him all to myself. He was gorgeous, confident, and he wanted me. The couple had been having problems for months. At least that's what he'd told me, and I believed him. When he moved out and got his own apartment, I was ecstatic because I knew that eventually he would be all mine. Soon I became his weekend girl. His everything girl. Our affair lit up like a torch between us. We spent all our time together except when he was spending time with his two children. He was a good father. I never stood in the way of that, but then his wife started needing him as well, and before long he was spending his weekends with them, at the gorgeous house they had bought together with his VA benefits.

I rounded the corner and as I passed one of the fitness monitors, he raised up a single finger letting me know I had just completed the first lap.

Five more to go.

He was kind of cute. Great body, evidence of spending hours in the gym. But he was military. Been there. Done that. When I decide I'm ready to date again, I wanted a regular man in my life. Well... at least one that wasn't married. It had been a month since that idiot's wife had popped up on my doorstep. I've had one date since, but he'd stood me up.

I scowled and replayed sitting at the Green Turtle waiting for Maze to show up. How hard could it have been for him to text me and cancel? It would have saved me from spending forty-five minutes waiting for a date who never came. Since then I haven't met anyone worthy of my time or attention, so I decided to take my sister's advice into consideration.

"As soon as you stop looking, he'll find you."

Layla was probably right, but patience had never been

one of my strong suits. I wanted companionship. Someone to take me to dinner, a man to fulfill my sexual needs.

Kanye West started singing in my ears. I kicked it up a notch and finished the second lap under four minutes. Most of the runners were way ahead but there were a few that lagged behind. *In through the nose and out through the mouth,* I mentally chanted as I jogged at a comfortable pace.

New unit. New attitude. New adventures. New relationships... One can only hope.

I'd been in Virginia a few months now and was getting used to the new area, but I wasn't quite sure if it had been the best decision. But all I could think about was getting away from Dame and his perfect life and lovely wife. Being at the unit and not being able to see him had been next to impossible to bare. I was desperate for a change. Moving closer to my sister had been the perfect solution, so when a position became available for a Superintendent, I jumped at the opportunity. By the time the government-contracted moving company came to pick up my household goods, I felt like I was finally escaping. I had spent that last night in my apartment with a sleeping bag and a bottle of wine ready to toast new beginnings. But he'd come. The Air Force community is small. Dame discovered I was leaving and he had come knocking.

I rounded the corner and the monitor held up three fingers. I was halfway done.

Ella Mai was singing, "Boo'd Up." I listened to the words of the song as I thought about the last time I'd seen him.

The moment I opened the door and saw Dame standing there, in that instance, I realized just how much I still loved him. It was wrong. I knew he was trying to fix things with his wife and kids; he had moved back in with them and yet I didn't care. All I wanted was for him to hold me. Once he put his arms around me and held me close to his chest, I felt whole again.

"I've missed you. I missed you so much," I moaned between kisses.

"I know, baby. I couldn't let you leave without letting you know how sorry I am." He slipped his tongue inside my mouth and I was a goner. Dame always had a way of making me feel like no other could.

"Don't go," he said. "Please stay."

"I can't. You're back with your family and I don't want to be around if I can't have you."

"I know. I understand."

It wasn't what I wanted to hear, but it was the truth. And I respected him for being a great father and doing everything he could to make his marriage work. That's what I wanted. A man who was willing to fight for me and our love. Only in this case, his love for his family was much stronger, so I had no choice but to respect that. Nevertheless, nothing was going to stop me from spending one more evening with him. I led him over to my sleeping bag, undressed him and myself and then we slipped inside. Dame made love to me for hours and I took everything he had to give because I knew that was it. There would be no more. We rested, and then were at it again. Sucking and fucking. Moaning and screaming. I utilized every second that we had because tomorrow, once I cleared the base and turned in my paperwork, I was on the road, heading to my new destination. He stayed all night with me. At least that was something. He didn't care if he angered her. His cell phone rang but he didn't answer it. The evening was all about me and I savored every second. By morning we said our goodbyes. No regrets. I didn't cling or beg. I knew it was over. And within hours,

I was on my way to Virginia.

I pulled my thoughts away. As I crossed the line, the fitness monitor held up five fingers. One last lap to go.

It had been seven months since he'd broken my heart and four months since I'd relocated. Dame was history. Out of my life and he should be out of my head, too. My heart was open. I was ready. I just needed to meet the right man. He would come. Despite every negative word my mother had ever said about men, I was certain of that. I was just as certain I was
about completing this test in under fourteen minutes.

I glanced down at the stopwatch on my arm and my mouth tightened. Thirteen minutes and sixteen seconds. I rounded the last curve. Drawing in a deep breath, I took the last stretch in a full-fledged sprint with energy I didn't know I still had. As I crossed the finish line, I grinned knowing in my heart, everything was going to be alright.

4

MEEKS

I passed my test, then treated myself to pancakes and hash browns. I made it into the office by nine and had been doing updates in the personnel system when I looked up from my desk to see Staff Sergeant Alicia Bailey standing in my doorway. I smiled at the sight of the Airman. She was a hard worker, dedicated to servicing the men and women of the 176th Wing.

"Come in," I told her, and she proceeded into my office. I pointed to the chair in front of my desk and waited while she took a seat. I have an open-door policy and have always tried to make sure I was available to meet the needs of the Force Support Squadron.

"What's going on?" I asked, giving her my full attention. If I allowed my eyes to stray to my emails, I would immediately be distracted by the endless number of requests from our squadron commander, Major Fallon Michaels.

A bleak expression lit the back of her brown eyes. "I have a deployment briefing scheduled today with Maintenance and Ops at fourteen hundred."

"That's today?" I looked over at the calendar on my computer. Clear as day it was schedule for fourteen hundred. "Okay, so why the long face?"

She cleared her throat. "The maintenance deployment

manager is out sick today."

"And?" I said, urging her to continue.

"I'm still waiting on him to sign the electronic deployment folders for his unit," she replied with a southern accent.

"How many are you waiting on?"

Her expression hardened. "About forty. I've been telling the UDM for the last two weeks I need time to review them, but maintenance still doesn't have them done." I now understood the long face. I reached for a notepad and pen and began taking notes.

"Have you conducted an initial review of the folders?"

She nodded gloomily. "Yes, and they're missing so many things. Total Force training, information assurance; two members don't even have a current security clearance."

This was a training exercise so it wasn't necessarily a requirement; however, this was supposed to be a mock deployment so everything needed to be checked off by the unit deployment manager just as they would have if the unit was really being mobilized.

"Did you give the UDM a suspense?" Establishing deadlines is crucial.

Bailey nodded. "Yes, close of business yesterday."

I uncapped the water bottle and drank deeply before answering. "Okay, so I'll call and let the UDM know you need those folders signed before the briefing."

"He's out sick today," she reminded with a lift of her shoulders.

"Oh yeah, you did say that."

"I was going to remind the UDM at the briefing, but now that's not going to happen." She hesitated before saying, "I was thinking about speaking to the maintenance chief, but I think it would probably come across better if it came from you."

I loved dealing with Chief Master Sergeants. I respect the

chain of command; however, most chiefs were cocky and full of themselves. A beat passed before I said, "No problem. That's why I'm here." I saw the relief that curled her lips.

"Thank you. He can be very intimidating."

I couldn't care less about him being intimidating. "We have a mission and I don't want to see any discrepancy reports just because maintenance isn't doing what they're required to do. Don't you worry, I'll take care of it," I said and hoped my smile reassured her.

"Thank you, Senior Master Sergeant Meeks."

I put the pen down and stretched my arm over my head. "Where is the briefing being held?"

"In the Mission Support Group conference room."

"Good." The briefing was being held in our building. That way they were on my turf. "I'll be there."

5

HOWARD

"What the..." I let the rest of the sentence fall from my lips as I swerved my Navigator into an empty spot and dropped it into Park. I practically yanked the keys from the ignition as I jumped out the SUV.

"Airman Winslow," I bellowed, placing the hat on my head and stormed in his direction.

The young, lanky teenager startled and so did the other two boys walking beside him toward the front entrance of the 176th Maintenance Group building. Seconds ago, all three were shooting the shit in the parking lot pop locking or doing whatever young folks called it these days.

"Where's your cover?" I shouted. Winslow quickly reached inside his pocket. I walked purposely over to the three and by the time I was close enough to snatch him up by his collar, the hat was on top of his head.

"Lock it up."

Immediately, all three drew their backs into a tightly rigid stance. I didn't stop walking until my chest was close, towering over him. "Why wasn't your cover on?"

"I'm sorry, Chief. I-I forgot," he stuttered.

"You forgot? *You forgot?*" Instinctively, I leaned closer, but caught myself. "You just got out of basic training and technical school so there's no way you could have *forgot.*" My eyes shifted over to the others. "And what's your excuse? You couldn't see he was missing his cover?"

Airman Payne's response was ridiculous. "Chief, I was about to tell him."

"I-I didn't notice," Airman First Class Campbell was stupid enough to say.

"That's because the three of you are too busy break dancing to notice." I was yelling and they were shaking in their boots. I didn't care. These new Airmen were soft and lazy. Servicemen are supposed to be trained and mission ready, so I didn't have time to be holding hands and wiping their little asses.

"Did you report to medical at 0700 as instructed?"

"Yes, sir. We all did," Winslow replied.

"Then where should you be?"

Payne stared straight ahead and didn't dare look at me as he said, "Nowhere, Chief. We're waiting to head to lunch."

"Go to lunch, then head over to CBRNE. Do you have your chem gear?" Chemical, Biological, Radiological, and Nuclear was mandatory protective measures' training that required wearing mock gear and a gas mask. Apparently these three were unprepared because they looked at one another dumbfounded.

"We didn't know, Chief," Campbell had the balls to say.

They were going to make me say something that would probably have them crying home to Mommy. "Go eat then get over to supply and get your chem gear. How are you supposed to have training if you don't have your equipment?"

They exchanged another dumbfounded look.

"Go get your gear from supply. If you don't know where it is over near the dock, then you better find someone who does. Training is at the Lincoln's building at thirteen hundred, and you better not be late."

"Y-Yes, Chief," Airman Campbell replied.

"Now, get out of here before I make you each drop and give me a hundred."

They nodded and slowly stepped away, as if I was the enemy. After training dozens of Airmen and serving eighteen years in the National Guard, I didn't have time for games. We had less than a month before Silver Hawk, a mission crisis response training event featuring readiness airborne forces from eight NATO nationals, and there was still work to be done.

I watched those three knuckleheads do an about face and haul ass out of there. Once I determined they were heading in the direction of the dining hall, I made my way into the building and acknowledged members of my team with a head nod.

"Chief."

I swung around to see Staff Sergeant Drake coming down the hall. He was one of my model NCOs. Uniform always cleaned and pressed, boots tightly laced.

"Master Sergeant James went to sick call."

Anthony James was the unit deployment manager. He had come in this morning complaining of a stomachache. "The deployment briefing is at fourteen hundred. Would you like me to send Technical Sergeant Garvin in his place?"

Pamela Garvin was seven months pregnant. Half the time the elevator in the Mission Support Group building was out of service.

I looked down at the Nike watch on my wrist then shook my head. "No, don't worry about it. I'll go."

6

MEEKS

"Day, what's on your mind?"

I stared across the table at my sister and shrugged. "Nothing new." There wasn't much enthusiasm in that response, and Layla knew it. Big sisters always do.

"What's going on with you? I thought you were excited about moving to a new area. Meeting new people."

"I was...I mean I still am." I drew a sigh and pushed my salad away. "I guess I just miss my old unit."

"Well, this isn't your first rodeo. You've PCS'd before."

"I know but relocating has never felt like this." I was whining but I didn't care. "I guess it's because I really loved being a part of the 131st Bomb Wing. We had this comradery that I just don't feel here."

"I understand what you're saying. I felt the same way when I left Italy and had to come back to the states. I think I cried for an entire month." My sister had served six years before she decided she'd rather be a military spouse, but Faison ended up being medically discharged.

I released a sigh of relief. "Okay, so you're telling me that what I am feeling is normal?"

"Of course, it is. Before you know it, you're going to start meeting people and making friends, and Virginia is going to feel like home to you."

"I hope so."

We were sitting out on the patio at Panera Bread, which is one of my favorite restaurants. I was able to come and get my comfort food when nothing else felt right. But today, even the salad didn't taste all that great.

I gazed over at my sister and smiled. Layla was a cutie. She got all the qualities I got, and then some. I had to watch my weight to stay slim, but Layla could eat whatever the hell she wanted and didn't gain a pound. Unlike me, she was a petite five-four and wore a size four. She had a big ass and a small waist and D-cups just like me. She got the hazel eyes, small nose, and caramel completion from Mama. In those areas, I took after our father. The first thing Layla did when she was discharged from the military was shave her hair low and colored it platinum blonde. The look was so amazing, she still wore it that way.

"Faze and I are planning to go to the Funny Bone next Saturday. You want to come? We have four tickets," I heard her say.

"Four?"

"Last time we were there, Faze put a business card in the bowl for the weekly drawing. Whatever card they draw gets four tickets to an upcoming show. The money they make is really about the food and the drink, not the tickets." She studied my eyes. "C'mon, it will be fun. They have Eddie Griffin as the headliner."

"Eddie?" My eyes immediately lit up. "I love me some Eddie."

"Good. Then we'll pick you up at six. If we get there early enough, we might even have a chance to stop by the Cheesecake Factory and grab a slice of red velvet cheesecake." Now she really had my attention considering that was my favorite dessert, and my sister knew it.

"I'll go. It can't be any worse than sitting around my

townhouse feeling sorry for myself."

"Thanks a lot, Day."

I laughed. "I'm sorry, I didn't mean it like that." I laughed some more, and it felt so good. "Who would have ever thought my life would have gotten so pathetic that the only excitement I have is hanging out with my sister and her husband."

"Ha-ha. Very funny. Matter of fact you couldn't go wrong by hanging out with us more often."

I frowned at that idea and changed the subject. "How's Maya?"

"She's feeling better. She's back to summer camp and being bossy."

"That's my girl." My niece was athletic, dominant, and very opinionated. She was a miniature replica of myself and the closest thing I probably would ever get to a child of my own at this rate.

I spotted my sister studying me over the rim of her mug of Chai tea.

"What?" I asked.

"Have you heard anything from Dame?"

I gave a rude snort. "No, and I don't care if I ever do."

"So, that explains the sour mood."

"Not sorry. Maybe bitter," I admitted. "He did break my heart."

"You said yourself he was honest with you from the beginning. Until the ink was dry on the divorce papers, you knew the risk."

"Yes; I just never thought he'd take her back." I was pouting, but so what?

Layla was trying not to take sides but was doing a poor job at it. "He felt obligated to his family and wanted to give his marriage another try. You can't fault the man for that."

"I know. That's the only reason why I don't hate him."

I could tell by the far-off look in her eyes, Layla was thinking about the one time she caught her husband cheating on her. Somehow, she'd found it in her heart to forgive him and fight for their marriage. Not me. Once is all a man gets, and if he messes up, too bad, so sad.

Okay, so maybe I do have issues when it came to trust.

"I think you've wasting enough time being the victim. Like Mama," she added with a rude snort.

"I do not—"

"Hear me out," Layla interrupted. "Dame's back at home with his family. He's gotten on with his life. It's time that you do the same."

As much as I hated to admit it, my sister was right. I needed to stop living in the past by constantly whining about a broken heart and begin creating a new life.

ΘΘΘ

I made it back to my office and headed straight to the conference room. The deployment briefing had already begun. A Tricare representative was at the podium, talking to the room full of Airmen about their medical and dental insurance benefits. They wouldn't apply for the exercise because a service member needed to be on active duty orders for more than thirty days to qualify, but this was the only availability we could find on the representative's schedule to brief since she supports the entire region. Our justification was that most of the members participating in Silver Hawk were being mobilized in January to UAE.

I stood at the back of the room along with a few other senior NCOs. Bailey was up front facilitating the briefing. It was my job to make sure all the presenters arrived on time and all the deployers were in attendance for the briefings. A sign-up sheet was going around the conference room. Later, Bailey would check the list against the roster to make sure everyone had been present. All absentees were going to receive a call to their supervisor from me. Even though this was an exercise, the wing expected members to handle it like a real-world event, which meant we needed one hundred percent cooperation.

I listened as finance gave their spiel on pay and entitlements. Members needed to remember to certify their orders in the system, upon their return from Silver Hawk, if they wanted to get paid. My eyes traveled around the room assessing the crowd and landed on the door just as it opened. In stepped a man that made my mouth water.

He was wearing ABUs, so I knew he was a chief by the rank on his sleeve. Despite holding one of the highest enlisted ranks in the air force, he was someone who made you pay attention. Hell, he could have been a slick sleeve, without a chevron, and you still would have noticed him. The man had rich mahogany skin that was smooth and too perfect to be wasted on a man and, yet, it was justifiable for him. His hair was cropped close and faded lightly while still managing to meet dress and appearance regulations. His nose was strong, jaw squared, and his cheekbones chiseled. His lips looked so sensually delicious I caught myself licking mine just thinking how good they'd feel pressed against my own mouth, on my breasts, and between my parted thighs. He was tall with broad shoulders and filled out his uniform in the most amazing way. In fact, not once had I ever been so turned on by the sight of a man in his ABUs. The sleeves were rolled, exposing tattoos covering the entire lower half of both arms. I wasn't sure what the pattern was, but I had a strong urge to run my fingers along a maze that circumference the area. He stood to the right beside Captain Spade from the Intelligence Squadron, who was going to give the Operation Security briefing. Something the captain said caused Mr. Yummy to grin, and I felt a pinch at the pit of my stomach at the sight of his dimples and sparkling white teeth. I blinked and realized I had been gaping at him. Damn, he had no business being that fine. I had to turn my head away to stop from staring at him.

Remember, Dayana. He's military. You're no longer interested in military men.

Then tell that to my nipples because they were tingling and beading with arousal.

I cleared my throat and focused my attention on Bailey, who had moved to the podium again. She went on to explain how important it was that all the electronic mobility folders were signed off by the end of the week. My eyes swept the rear of the room where maintenance was sitting; several were talking and not paying attention.

Oh, hell no.

I was taking the mobility folder issue straight to the Chief and, if he wasn't cooperative, I would speak to my commander and have her reach out to the Maintenance Group commander.

After the Intel briefing, the group was given some additional instructions from the logistics officer and then dismissed. I moved quickly up to the front and over to Bailey.

"Sergeant Bailey."

She swung around and smiled, chestnut-painted lips parting. "Yes, ma'am?"

"Here are your sign-in rosters. Now, which one is the maintenance chief?" I asked as I handed the lists to her.

She looked around the room then pointed toward the door. "There he is."

I followed the direction of her eyes and my heart thumped when I landed on Mr. Yummy. Damn.

I gave her a sidelong glance. "I'll go talk to him."

Her shoulders sagged with relief. "Thank you again, ma'am."

I saw him step out the door into the hall. I moved quickly in that direction and, when I turned the corner, I spotted him.

"Excuse me, Chief. May I speak with you a moment?"

He turned around and looked me over, and I nearly gasped as I took in the sheer size of him up close. He had impossible broad shoulders and a wide chest. He was taller than I had realized. Six-four maybe. But it was enough that I had to tilt my head to look him in the face. Our eyes met and held for several electrifying moments before I recognized a predatory grin on his lips. Oh, he was sexy; there was no doubt about that. He had me tingling once more, but I didn't want him to even think for a moment that anything about me was weak.

"Hello, I'm Keim Howard. I don't think we've met," he said in a deep, velvety voice laced with a mid-western twang as he held out his hand. As soon as our hands touched, I felt light-headed and struggled to breath. I snatched my hand away and the spinning stopped.

"We haven't met. I'm Dayana Meeks. I've been with the FSS for four months now."

"No wonder I haven't seen you. Welcome to the wing." His eyes took a slow trail down the length of my body causing it to tingle, before returning to my eyes. "Did you take Superintendent Larson's position?"

I nodded. "Yep, that was me."

"When he got the position at National Guard Bureau,

quite a lot of people applied for his job. And you were the lucky one. Congrats. Active guard reserve positions are hard to come by."

"I've been in the program for twelve years. Hoping to make this my final stop until retirement."

"Well, with that determination I'm sure a beautiful woman like yourself will make it to chief," he said huskily, and I found his smoldering gaze fixed on my mouth.

My breasts throbbed and yet I scowled as I replied, "What
does beauty have to do with it?" I shot him a look.

"Sorry I didn't mean to offend," he said as he tried to clean up his words. "I'm just giving accolades. Beauty and brains take you a long way. It's that total package, and you appear to have both."

I pointed a finger at him. "My beauty had very little to do with my success. It's called hard work and determination. Not to mention I have a Bachelor's in Business Administration from the University of Delaware."

"Congratulations. Were you living in Dover?" He'd changed the subject. Good move.

"I was attached to the Dover Air National Guard for about four years before I left and went back to Whiteman."

He was watching me with interest. "Sounds like you enjoy PCSing. Why didn't you just go active duty?"

"Because I like being in control and the active guard and reserve program allows me the control and flexibility that regular active duty Air Force does not." How the hell did we get on this subject? I cleared my throat. "Speaking of control, I need your assistance in getting the electronic mobility folders signed for your unit."

"My UDM has been working on them."

"Well, I need him to do more than just work on them." I didn't mean to sound like I was telling him what to do but... Chief also looked surprised considering the way his brow lifted.

I pushed my shoulders back and regained my military bearing. "What I'm trying to say, Chief Howard, is that we still have a big piece that we need done. Sergeant Bailey can't do her job until the members and the UDM have done their jobs."

He smiled with a confidence I didn't share. "I'm sure my UDM is working it, but I'll check and see where he's at."

"I need you to do more than check." It took effort to maintain a steely front, but I refused to be intimidated by his charm. "You have sixty members participating in the exercise and less than half have done what they are supposed to do."

"Half? Are you sure about that?"

"Absolutely. I saw the report," I countered without hesitation. "Now, if you need my office to request that the wing grant us UDM access, then we can just do *your* job for you. But I don't think you want that because it wouldn't look good for your stats. Besides, I don't want my Airman being responsible for your unit's discrepancies."

"What discrepancies?"

"The discrepancies we'll have if your UDM doesn't do his job. The fact that you have Airmen who haven't even initiated eQIP worksheets for their security clearance reinvestigation is enough reason to cause some heads to roll." I could tell by the muscle ticking at his temple that he'd had no idea.

Howard cleared his throat. "I'll need to verify that information."

"No need. I already have; however, if you'd like to go downstairs to my office and log onto a computer, I'll be more than happy to show you." I managed a wan smile for the handsome man.

"There's no need," he said dismissively. "I'll make sure to get with my UDM and find out what's going on."

"Excellent."

"What kind of suspense are we working with?" He pulled out his phone, and I assumed he was looking at his calendar.

"The deadline for electronic folders was scheduled for completion by COB yesterday, and that was the second suspense. But now that we are within days of arranging travel, we need all the folders completed, or a status report as to why they aren't, before COB Friday, *if* that's not asking too much, Chief." Oh, I was being a bossy bitch and knew it, but I was too far gone to stop now.

"I'll see what I can do. How about I call you on Friday and give you a status update?"

"An email will be better. That way I can have a paper trail for documentation. In fact, when I get back to the office, how about I send you an email recapping our discussion?"

He nodded. "You do that."

"Thank you, Chief Howard. You have a good rest of your day." I nodded, showing him the respect that he'd earned. With that, I turned and headed down the hall toward the other side of the building, eager to escape the attraction simmering between us.

Been there. Done that.

No more relationships with men in uniform.

I'd rather poke my eye out than be that woman again.

7

HOWARD

I think I just met my wife.

My dick was so hard it strained against the fly of my ABU pants. The entire time she was giving me attitude, I had the strong urge to snatch her into my arms and shut her up with my tongue. I was certain she tasted just as good as she looked.

Damn.

I watched the sway of her hips as she moved down the hall. Her curvy body made that uniform look good. I felt like a lost puppy wanting to follow her back to her office and allow her to bark at me some more. Anyone else, I would have pulled rank and immediately reminded them of their military bearing. But Senior Master Sergeant Dayana Meeks was feisty. The molasses brown beauty had enough fire to keep a brotha on his toes. I liked it. I liked it a lot. In fact, she was compelling. Unlike anyone I've met in a long time. The moment I looked at her, I felt like that beautiful creature had cast her spell on me. Damn. She was the total package with exotic features; smooth, even skin; high cheekbones; sultry lips; and dark brown hair that she wore up in a twist, baring her neck and a pair of diamond studs that pierced her earlobes. But what caught and held me hostage were her eyes. They were the color of a shiny new penny and almond shaped, almost as if she had some Asian blood in her family heritage. And her eyelashes were naturally thick. Not those fake things I see so many women wearing these days. Nope. Hers were wispy and real.

Damn.

When I reached the door, I plopped the hat on my head and made the five-minute walk across the lot to the Maintenance Group building. I walked through the door and down the sterile, beige hallway to the last office where I found Technical Sergeant Clyde Washington on his cell phone laughing. I could tell it was personal by the smirk on his lips. The moment he spotted me coming through the office his eyes grew big.

"I'll call you back." He ended the call and sprung from his seat like a jack-in-the-box. "Hello, Chief. Can I help you?"

"Yes. Aren't you an alternative UDM?"

"Uh, yeah, I guess so."

I stepped close into his personal space. "Garvin and James are both out so what do you mean, *I guess so*?"

"I mean, yes, Chief. Yes, I'm the alternate UDM."

"Good. I need a list of every mobility folder that isn't ready for signature and then I need to know why the hell not."

"Chief when—"

I raised a hand, cutting him off. "I need it before the end of the day, which means you won't be leaving until it's done." I exited and made my way back to my office. The thought of seeing that sexy feline was burning hot and heavy in the forefront of my mind. It was crazy, but part of me hoped the mobility folders were all screwed up. That would give me a reason to head back over to the Mission Support Group. Not that I needed an excuse. I could always just drop by for a visit.

The idea made me smile.

My cell phone buzzed. I glanced down at the screen, cursed under my breath, and sent the call to voicemail.

After meeting Giselle at the All-Ranks Club last week, I called her that Saturday and invited her out to lunch. She was a nice woman. Both beautiful and intelligent but I just didn't feel a connection. But even with that said, I am a man and when a woman offers herself after a long spell of nothing, a brotha will take what's given to him. On the drive back to her house, Giselle had leaned over, unzipped my pants, and was giving me a blow job that had me weaving on the road. Before I had even made it to her house, it was over. Like I said, it had been a while. Unfortunately, by the time I had pulled onto her driveway, she was ready for me to return the favor.

"C'mon in so we can finish where we left off."

I was so embarrassed by my reaction to her warm lips around my dick that I could barely look at her. She, on the other hand, was smiling triumphantly. One of my exes had once told me that nothing makes a woman feel prouder than being able to make a dude nut by simply using their mouth. Giselle had skills.

"Nah, I better be going. How about I give you a call in the morning?"

She looked disappointed but said, "You make sure you do that." She leaned over and tried to kiss me on the mouth, but I diverted my lips to her cheek.

"I'll call you."

I never did. And by Sunday evening she was calling and inviting me over. Damn right, I went because at this point, I had something to prove. I hadn't even been there an hour, sipping wine on her couch when she was doing a striptease. We didn't even make it to her bedroom. Instead we were down on the rug getting it in. She tried to get me to go down on her, but I couldn't, something just held me back. It wasn't something I did for every woman. You had to be special. And although she was nice, Giselle was missing something that I was looking for.

I put in a performance, enough to have her crying out my name. Exhausted, I dozed off. She invited me to stay but, before midnight, I was back at home in my bed. She'd dropped by the unit and we'd talked on the phone, but that spark I was looking for still wasn't there. In fact, I'd forgot what that energy felt like until I spotted Meeks at the deployment briefing.

Now *that's* a woman I wanted to see again…soon.

8

MEEKS

I pulled into the townhouse community where I was renting a three-bedroom unit and sighed with exhaustion. It had been another long day with back-to-back meetings and deadlines. On the way home, I grabbed a strawberry pecan salad from Wendy's; only I was so tired, I wouldn't eat but a few bites. Instead, I was ready for a hot bath and bed.

I stepped onto the Spanish-tiled foyer and walked past a small living room and a recently updated kitchen with black appliances and granite countertops. I made my way to the family room where I flopped down onto a gray couch and reached for the remote. *Family Feud* was on. Reaching down, I unlaced my boots, slipped my feet out, then shrugged out of my ABU top and laid it across a matching blue armchair. I would be wearing it again in the morning before I dropped it back at the cleaners and picked up my other set. I lifted my feet onto the ottoman then leaned back. I needed a bottle of water but was too lazy to get up and grab one from the refrigerator.

There was a black family from Georgia on the game show. One of the brothers was asked to name a place never to go to pick up women. He answered, a strip club. He looked so much like my ex-boyfriend Dame the smile slipped from my face. Damn.

I hated that I was still so affected by a man to whom I hadn't meant much of anything.

We met at the 131st Wing Christmas Party. He was still with his wife at the time, so we were just friends. But then that changed. The more we saw each other and interacted, the harder it was to resist. We'd started off in an emotional relationship, not a sexual one. He talked. I listened. But once we made love, I was in heaven. Dame had a way of taking his time and torturing me with his slow sweet love I never got enough of. He was handsome and his sex game was so on point. I couldn't believe how lucky I was. Most importantly, he was mine. Days, nights, and eventually even the weekends. I was so in love. We talked about the future and marriage. Dame was going to be my husband and the father of our children.

All he had to do was file for divorce.

Only it never happened. His wife started calling about the kids and he was always over to the house to see them because they needed him almost every damn day. And even back then I knew. I knew it was just a matter of time before he was going to say those words that was going to destroy the future I had planned for us.

"Day, they need me."

I flicked away warm tears and cried, "I need you."

I remember sobbing and making a fool of myself. I know I was unreasonable. Dame tried to get me to understand that he had to go back and fight to make his marriage work for the sake of his children. But I didn't want to understand. I was hurt and in love and feeling so damn selfish.

"What about me? What about me?" I remember screaming. After he moved back home, I would call him into the night while he was lying in the bed with his wife, still screaming, "Don't you love me?" Dame begged me to understand, but I didn't want to let go.

It was Captain Julia Janus who'd pulled me into her office and told me to get my shit together. She had no idea about the affair. Because that's what it was and if anyone found out I would have been given an Article-15 or lost a stripe from my sleeve. What she meant was I was fucking up. I was forgetting to process promotion packages and messing up reassignments. Coming into work with my uniform less than perfect and a bad wig on my head because I had no desire to scrape up my hair in a neat bun. What she meant was my military career was in jeopardy, and I better get it together.

That flipped the switch.

I stopped calling Dame. When I saw him at a senior leadership meeting, I nodded and moved to the other side of the room to take a seat. And eventually I got myself together. Made sure my hair and make-up were always on point. Stayed late at work to make sure I had crossed my Ts. And as the months passed, it got easier. I even dated a few times, but no one was remotely close to what I'd had with Dame.

When I flew to Virginia to celebrate my niece's birthday with Layla and Faison, I decided I needed a change. So, I started watching the assignments until I found the perfect position. Force Support Squadron Superintendent at Weyland Air Force Base, Virginia.

And the rest is history.

Since the move, I've dated only twice, and those fiascos put the brakes on my desire to meet anyone else.

I finally rose, grabbed my salad and a bottle of water, and moved back to the couch to eat my dinner. While I chewed on a slice of strawberry, my thoughts shifted back to Keim Howard. If he wasn't in the military, I would have been all over him. I remembered every detail, from the close-cropped dark hair on his head to the large boots on his feet. After I ate, I leaned back on the couch, eyes closed, and my thoughts went wild.

After the deployment briefing, Howard follows me back to my office. I shut the door, he drags me into the circle of his arms and lowers his head. Oh damn. The kiss is demanding and has my insides sizzling. He arouses me on so many levels, I'm practically delirious. His tongue slides inside, parting my lips, and explores. I whimper with need while his fingers quickly unfasten the buttons of my shirt and pants. My fingers are trembling as I work his buttons. By the time he lifts me into his powerful arms and carries me over to my desk, I'm only wearing my bra and panties. In my opinion, I am still way overdressed.

He sets me down near the edge and, when he leans back, an expression of male satisfaction simmers in his dark eyes. "I've been wanting to do this from the moment I saw you," he murmurs huskily, ripping my panties with a quickness that makes me gasp.

"It's the middle of the day."

"So?" Amusement slashes his handsome face as he looks down at my body and groans. "You are absolutely beautiful. It would be such a waste to only make love to you in the dark." With that he unhooks my bra and tosses it away. Totally in control, he lowers his head, taking one of my hardened nipples into his mouth and caresses it. Shocked by the pleasure zipping through my body, I arch towards him. Howard has mad skills.

"I love the way you tremble when I touch you," he groans, and with strong hands he lifts my legs up around his waist. At this angle, I feel the thickness of his cock pressing against my wet heat causing a burning between my thighs. Howard raises me up off the desk and positions me to take him inside.

"Howard!" My cry of shock turns to a sigh of ecstasy as he enters in a smooth thrust, his body stretching and dominating me. He is completely in control.

Just the way I like it.

"You're mine," he murmurs against my lips. His thrusts are fiercely possessive. "You belong to me."

Flushed and gasping for air, I sprung upright on the couch. The room was dark, and *Sex and the City* was playing on the television. Carrie Bradshaw just had an orgasm that left her breathing just as heavily as I had been. I took several deep breaths until my heart began to slow. However, my nipples remained hard and my body on fire. I was still turned on by my dream.

Chief Master Sergeant Keim Howard.

"No, no, no. Not *him*."

He was military and not at all what I was looking for. I just needed sex. That's all the dream had been about and only because it had been too long. So long that I turned off the television and moved up to my bedroom. I had something in my top nightstand drawer that usually did the treat. However, as I stepped inside my room, I had a sinking feeling this was a time self-gratification was going to be unable to satisfy what my body was craving.

9

HOWARD

"We need to reschedule AMS for CATM training. See if there are any slots available in September." Combat Arms Training and Maintenance or rather, weapons qualifying, is a required training for Air Force personnel in the use of small arms. Back in the spring, the air maintenance squadron was scheduled at Camp Shaw but, due to significant rain, the grounds had been too soft for training. And now that the weather was dry, units throughout the state were trying to get on the training schedule.

"I'll make it happen, Chief," SSgt David Arnold said with the confidence I wanted to hear. He's in charge of training.

"Thanks for taking care of the problem. Please let me know once you have those dates." The wing was up my ass because our training numbers weren't looking good. I had direct orders to get us back in the green as soon as possible. I was scheduled to load statistics for the maintenance group into a classified system after lunch. Since the system was used to transmit classified information, the only machines accessible were in a secure area behind my UDM's office—which was currently inoperable—and over in the Installation Deployment Readiness Cell. I would have to call SSgt Bailey and get on her schedule if I wanted access.

Arnold disappeared down the hall and before I could put my military identification card in the CAC reader to access my laptop, there was a rap at my door. I looked up to see Washington standing at my door.

"Chief, you wanted to see me."

I signaled for him to come in. "How are you doing on those deployment folders?"

"We still have several members who need to report to medical, a few that require self-aid and buddy care, and I found out two members have expired security clearances."

I reacted like this was the first time I'd heard about this. "How the hell is that?" There was a pause as he contemplated his answer. "Spill it, Washington."

I could tell he didn't want to respond. "You'd have to talk to Martin."

Technical Sergeant Amelia Martin was the security manager.

Dammit. It was a good thing this was just an exercise or there would be hell to pay. No wonder Meeks was so upset. Unlike some of the other branches of service, in the Air Force, members had to be able to get and maintain a security clearance. They were reinvestigated every ten years. Someone had dropped the ball.

"Tell Martin I need to see her," I said firmly.

"Will do, Chief," he replied with an obedient nod.

As soon as he left my office to deliver the news, I drew in a heavy breath. My UDM had the flu and was going to be out for at least the rest of the week. Garvin's pregnancy was causing concern with swollen ankles, and Washington had never been properly trained. *The show must go on.* We still needed to get our unit ready to go. There was no way the maintenance group was going to have discrepancies. Not on my watch.

I looked down at the list of participants scheduled to participate. I was going to have to swap-out the two members with security clearance issues. Fortunately, I had several new Airmen—including those knuckleheads who I'd caught pop-locking in the parking lot—who could gain a lot from the experience. Any one of them would be happy to go to Anderson Air Force Base, Guam for twenty-seven days to participate in the exercise. Thank goodness the trio were currently on seasonal days, which meant they were already on active duty and available to knock out all the requirements on the checklist in a few days. The issue was the traditional members who only reported to the unit one weekend a month. Everything that was on the checklist would have to be completed over the two days before Meeks' team would sign off approval on the deployment folders.

Just thinking about the feisty woman caused a grin to curl my lips. I wanted to see her again. She'd been on my mind the last few days and I couldn't help but wonder what her story was, considering she was a mid-western girl who'd decided to settle on the east coast. I asked around and other than she was professional and easy to work with, no one seemed to know much about her. And that was a good thing because I wanted to be the first to get to know her.

10

MEEKS

On the way home from work, I headed over to the Base Exchange to raid the sales rack. I wanted something new to wear to the comedy club on Saturday. Despite my initial disinterest, I was looking forward to having something to do over the weekend and you can never go wrong with laughter.

"Hey, Meeks."

I lifted my eyes to see Master Sergeant Blue Rein, the senior non-commissioned officer in charge of military finance, standing in front of a display of Michael Kors' jeans. She had already changed out of her ABUs and was wearing a long, pink sundress that showcased her curves. White flip-flops were on her feet.

"Rein." I smiled. "How was your week?"

"The same as it always is after a Unit Training Assembly weekend. Crazy. Pay issues. Folks forgetting to certify their orders."

I smiled at the beauty because I could feel her pain. "It's just as crazy in the FSS."

Rein lifted her shoulders in a dismissive shrug. "But it's all good, girl."

Once a month, the entire unit—all twelve hundred plus Air National Guard members—was in attendance for training over a two-day weekend.

I took a moment to admire how cute Rein was with a slim nose, high cheekbones, and the arched eyebrows. She was of mixed race. Not sure but something Hispanic was my best guess. Her hair was long, thick, and wavy and pulled back in a ponytail high on top of her head. I noticed the tattoo of a cross on her forearm before my eyes landed on an orange Michael Kors' blouse. "Ooh!" I held it up then sent her a sidelong glance. "Whadda you think of this?"

She nodded in approval. "I like that color. There's some jeans over there that I think would look good with that." Carrying the blouse, I followed her. While we browsed the racks, she and I chatted. Our arms were heavy with clothes by the time we headed toward the dressing room.

"With these hips I have to try on everything just to be sure."

Rein chuckled. "Me too."

The jeans and blouse were perfect. I walked out the dressing room strutting like a peacock. The blouse had a scooped neckline that showcased my perky twins. The skinny jeans were snug on my ass. Rein thought I looked good, so I carried the outfit to the register.

After we paid for our purchases, she and I went over to a Thai food trailer outside the Base Exchange. I ordered spicy Pad Thai noodles and she ordered drunken chicken.

"What made you decide to come to this unit?" Rein asked. We were seated on the bench while we waited for our orders.

I couldn't help but smile. "I was at Whiteman Air Force Base. Been in Missouri most of my career and I was ready for a change. My sister and her family live here."

"Whiteman? You were at Knob Noster?" She scrunched up her nose.

"I know, right?" I laughed and crossed my legs. "There was nothing at all to do around there unless you drove into Kansas City, and honestly that's not saying much. Especially for nightlife."

"What do you think of the area so far?"

"In comparison?" I shrugged. "So far I like it. I'm near my sister and close to the beach."

"Girl, I'm talking about a social life," Rein said all pushy, which made me laugh.

"I haven't had much yet, but I'm going to the Funny Bone Comedy Club on Saturday."

"Oh, you'll like it. Who's the headliner?"

I told her and she started smiling. "Oh yeah, Eddie Griffin is hilarious." I nodded in agreement. "We need to go out one weekend. I'll take you to a few nice happy hour spots," she added.

I pursed my lips to say, "I'm not a club person."

Rein lifted her slender shoulders. "No problem. Do you like jazz?"

"I love jazz."

She looked pleased. "Then I have the perfect place to take you. They even have a female saxophone player. Let me find out the next time they are performing."

"Ooh, I'm sold."

By the time our food was ready, I could already tell this was the start of a new friendship.

11

HOWARD

I stopped by the Base Exchange to grab another headset for my iPhone. During unit fitness training this morning it had stopped working, which pissed me off royally. Nothing worse than jogging and listening to the sound of your own breathing. I needed Travis Scott and the Migos rapping in my ear, schooling me all kind of bullshit while keeping me hyped and motivated. Friday, I planned to take the young Airmen out along the flight-line and show them age was nothing but a number when I smoked them in a two-mile run.

I parked my SUV, put the hat on my head, and moved across the parking lot. I saluted two lieutenant colonels before I made it into the building.

As I made my way past Starbuck's, heading in the direction of the Base Exchange, my eyes strayed over toward the food court where they landed on the woman who'd dominated my thoughts for the last few days.

Dayana Meeks.

I stumbled and had to catch myself. Luckily, no one was around to see me. I slowed and walked around a kiosk, pretending I was interested in shopping for a purse for my mother while I stared. My pulse had accelerated at once. Meeks was a beauty with an earth-shattering smile on her lips that was begging to be kissed. I got hard just looking at her mouth. Then there was that magnetic pull I was feeling, urging me to go over and speak to her. But this wasn't the place and neither the time. Too many eyes and ears. And especially since she was sitting and eating with Rein, who would be a pain in my ass if she even suspected I was interested in Meeks. She and I were close, like brother and sister, knowing each other for most of my career at Weyland Air Force Base. Often, Rein gave relationship advice that I'd preferred not to receive, especially since most of the time it was after some female went running to her, crying of a broken heart. Rein also used to date my boy, Hooks. Now, I'll admit the way he'd played her was dirty and so foul that after she ended their brief relationship, Rein had bad mouthed him so bad, good women shy away from him. Since then I decided to be private about my relationships and made it my mission not to share my business or the women I was interested in until I was ready for the world to know. And I wanted to know everything there was to know about Dayana Meeks. I hoped like hell she didn't have a man at home waiting for her. Just the thought made my fists clench. No way, not when I wanted to get to know her and potentially make her mine.

Feeling like a stalker, I had to force myself to stop staring, a feat requiring the strength of a higher power. I hurried into the BX and headed straight for the electronics section. Apple products were on two shelves, so finding what I wanted was super easy. I grabbed one of those Sudoku puzzle thingamajigs that my daughter loved so much and then made my way to the front. Shit. The line at each register was way too long. I was hoping to catch another glimpse of the beauty and maybe even have a few moments to chat with her. That's if Rein had left.

By the time I made my way toward the food court, both

women were gone. I cussed under my breath for failing to seize the opportunity, but there would be plenty more opportunities, even if I had to create one.

As soon as I reached the vehicle, my cell phone rang. I started the engine and the Bluetooth connected.

"Hello?"

"Daddy?"

A smile curled my lips. "Yes, princess?"

"What are you doing?" Ava asked.

"Talking to you."

"You are so corny." We shared a laugh. My teenage daughter always knew how to brighten my evening. "Are you still at work?"

"No," I began as I headed toward the main gate. "I decided to get off on time for once."

"Good. You work too hard. You need to meet someone nice. Mommy's happy so I want you to also be happy."

My ex-wife was married to a physician who practiced family medicine. Ava liked Daddy Joe. When they'd first announced their engagement, jealousy brewed hot and heavy. I didn't want another man spending more time with my daughter than I could, but over the years, I realized I was being ridiculous. I knew I couldn't be the only man in Ava's life forever. I just never considered that person would be another man she called Daddy.

"I'm sure I'll meet someone when the time is right," I replied although my thoughts were once again on Meeks. Could she be my Ms. Right?

Come on, Howard, get yourself together. You don't even know the woman. She could be crazy like some of the others.

"Daddy, I need a new pair of sneakers," Ava announced as I drove through the gate and headed off the base.

"I just bought you a pair."

She giggled. "No, those were Converse. I can't jog in them."

"When did you start jogging?"

"Yesterday. Allison and I are planning to meet every day at the track until school starts and get in shape. We've decided to try out for cheerleading."

"Cheerleading?" I didn't like the image flashing in front of my face of my daughter in skimpy outfits shaking her behind in front of a bunch of horny teenage boys. I knew because I used to be one of them, and I knew what I had been trying to do when I was their age...every chance I could. "Sweetheart, you sure you want to be a cheerleader?"

"Yes, Daddy, more than anything. Tryouts are going to be the first week of school. I want to be ready," she pointed out.

I counted from ten backwards. I knew the day would eventually come that my daughter would be interested in activities that didn't involve me. I just hadn't expected that to happen so soon.

"Sure, sweetheart. I'll take you to get some new sneakers this weekend."

"Thanks, Daddy. You're the best," she said in her soft daddy-girl voice. I couldn't ask for a smarter or sweeter daughter. And that is the reason why I was going to die broke because Ava had her daddy's heart. The best part though was that she was willing to share me with someone else. All I had to do was find that special woman. Something told me I might already have.

12

MEEKS

I placed my car keys and cell phone in the bin outside the room, typed in the four-digit passcode on the keypad on the door, and entered. Bailey was sitting at the round table in the center of the small room. The pleased look on her face meant she had been waiting for me.

"Hey, I hope you had lunch?" I asked.

She shook her head. "No, ma'am. I've been so busy trying to scrub the list before you got here that I didn't get a chance to eat."

"That's unacceptable. Let's go through the list and then I want you out the door." Especially since I'd just had a two-piece from Popeye's.

"Ma'am, we have customers coming over this afternoon. In fact, my calendar is full."

"So what? I'll watch the office while you're gone."

"But—"

I held up a hand, silencing her. "That's a direct order."

She smiled. "Yes, ma'am."

I walked over and put my hat and purse on the table in the corner that I used when I was in the building. The room was small. Four desks along the wall and a cubicle that belonged to Bailey since she was full-time. Naturally, she needed to feel at home. She also had a small fridge and a microwave. At the center was a conference table that was used mostly for small groups of deployers. Along the back far wall was the safe where we kept secure classified documents, and then there were the two classified computers. No windows. No electronic devices. Customers came in throughout the day and, being that it was drawing near the end of the month, units came more often to input statistical reporting for the wing.

"How are we looking for the exercise?" I asked.

"We are now at about seventy percent. There are still a few that I haven't reviewed, but it's better than our numbers last week." Baily pushed over a C-code list, which is a list of members assigned to participate in the exercises. She had check marks along the left margin for all the electronic folders she had already signed off. I looked at the ones she had not. *Maintenance.*

"You speak to their UDM today?" I found my pulse racing at the thought of Chief Howard.

"Their UDM is out with the flu and the alternate UDM is pregnant, but the next in line, Washington, has been in contact. He's working on getting his people taken care of."

"Good." My eyes scanned the list and there were still a few who hadn't been cleared by medical. "What's on the schedule for next UTA weekend? Is medical going to have everyone ready?"

"I spoke with Master Sergeant Carter and she has everyone schedule, but there are still a few with issues she's trying to get cleared medically."

"We are running out of time for swap outs." Having to find replacements at the last moment and trying to get them cleared was even harder to accomplish.

Bailey nodded gloomily. "That's what I told her." She drew a sigh. "Ma'am, do I have permission to speak freely?"

"Proceed."

"The problem with this wing is that we don't take these

exercises serious. Especially Ops and Maintenance. The pilots think they can do whatever they want to do, and maintenance personnel feel that since they have their fingers on the pulse and nothing happens without them, they can take their sweet time."

I wanted to give her a high-five because she was right on point, but that would be inappropriate. Instead, I nodded and said, "Well, you and I are going to have to start working on change management. Because I want our numbers to look good." Every year, a grade card was sent down from National Guard Bureau and the wing had to provide a justification for every discrepancy and the low score. It was an embarrassment to the wing commander and that trickled down to the units. Major Michaels and I would have to answer to my group commander. I was the new girl, and I did not want that kind of pressure. Not if I could help it.

I bit my lower lip before saying, "I think you and I need to meet every few days and see where we are with the progress."

"Yes, ma'am."

I rose from the chair.

"I'm expecting a classified email regarding one of our taskings for the new FY. I'm going to fill in the names security forces provided while you go ahead and get some lunch."

"Yes, ma'am. Both machines are already up. Updates pushed through the system this morning."

"Good deal. Now go and enjoy your lunch and I don't want to see you back here before fourteen-hundred."

"Yes, ma'am."

I could see the sparkle in her eyes at being allowed an extended lunch. She worked hard and I believed in rewarding my people.

Bailey grabbed her hat and purse and headed out the room. When she shut the door, the sound echoed. The room was like a tomb with secure doors on both sides. Logistics Planning was on the other side of the wall. They took care of equipment and travel, while the IPR office focused on making sure our members were ready for the mission. Together, the two sections were called the Installation Deployment Readiness Cell. We were going to get everything done even if I had to do some hand holding.

I reached inside the safe and removed my SIPR token, which is used in the CAC reader to access classified documents. I logged onto the system and, while I waited for it to authenticate my access, I walked over to the refrigerator and smiled when I discovered a Mountain Dew. I popped the tab and took a seat at the computer. While I drank, I sifted through the emails. Taskings were already coming down from Bureau. We had a business year ahead of us.

I was responding to an email when I heard a knock at the door. I rose and walked across the room. When I looked through the peephole, my stomach rolled.

Chief Howard.

I took a deep breath trying to prepare myself. I rushed over to Bailey's mirror beside her desk and glanced at my appearance, making sure everything was in place. After a five second assessment, I decided it would have to do. There was a second knock just as I opened the door. I saw the way his eyes lit up in surprise. His gaze was upon me, reaching for me like a man's arms in the morning.

"Yes?"

"I have an appointment to use the machine."

"Okay," I said, hoping he hadn't detected the shakiness in my voice. "Make sure to put your phone and any other electronic devices in the bin."

"Already did."

I looked down to see a cellphone and Fitbit in the box along with my phone. Nodding, I opened the door wide so he could enter. As he brushed past, I smelled masculinity.

"Please sign in on the clipboard."

He nodded and put his notebook down while he signed.

"I'm surprised to see you over here," he said glancing over at me.

"Why is that? Bailey reports to me."

"Maybe so, but I've never seen you over here before."

I wanted to say, *Get used to seeing a lot of me because I'm going to be in your ass until your unit is green and ready to go.* Instead, I shrugged and said, "I try to come over when I can to help. We're busy. Especially with this exercise coming up."

He nodded. "I did speak with my UDM and he's working to get everything done. Like I said, I'll have updates for you before COB on Friday."

"I appreciate that." I pointed to the machine I wasn't using. "You can use that one."

With a nod, Howard walked toward the desk, and I couldn't help but admire the air of confidence that he presented. Damn, he was just too fine. He removed the card from his pocket and straddled the chair.

The phone rang, startling me out of my ridiculous thoughts. I went back to work, answering questions for a member who was getting ready to deploy and was glad for the distraction. I hoped Howard would be done by the time I finished the call. But he was still there. I was starting to wish I hadn't given Bailey orders not to return before two o'clock. There was still forty minutes left.

"So how do you like being in this area?" I heard him say.

My back was to him, but I could feel the heat of his gaze. I didn't dare turn around. Not yet. "It's okay. I'm trying to learn my way around the area. It's a big difference from Knob Noster."

That brought a hearty laugh from him. "There isn't a damn thing in Warrensburg."

I swirled around in my chair. "You been there?"

"Whiteman?" he nodded. "My Mom's from Sedalia."

My brow arched. "I wouldn't tell anyone that."

Howard chuckled heartily. "I know. Small town. I still have family there and try to get home whenever I can."

"Well, I'm from Kansas City."

He looked away from the computer, brow lifted, and said, "Now I wouldn't tell anyone *that*. At least we have an excuse for being country. Kansas City on the other hand is just slow."

Kansas City, Missouri residents didn't want to be associated with Kansas City, Kansas folks and vice versa. I had to laugh at that because, as far as I was concerned, they were all the same. I suddenly realized I was the only one laughing. Howard was staring.

"You have such a beautiful smile."

I had a pretty good idea I was blushing at this moment. "Thank you," I replied tightly, pretending to be unmoved by his compliment.

"Are you married?" he asked.

The question caught me off guard. I held up my hand. "No rings."

"That means nothing these days."

He was right about that.

This conversation was getting way too personal.

Clearing my throat, I said, "How are you doing with your reporting?"

"I'm just about done."

I was relieved when he refocused his attention on the screen in front of him and not on me. I logged into the MILPDS—military personnel data system—and began running a mobilization report. Anything to shift my focus away from Howard. Only that was almost impossible to do. Just his presence in the small space was enough to have my entire body on high alert.

I heard someone outside the door followed by the sound of the passcode being entered on the keypad. I breathed a sigh of relief when Bailey pushed the door open and stepped inside. She was early and I was glad.

"I know you told me to take my time, but I forgot my textbook so I could get some reading done while I ate." She was pursuing a degree in communications. "I figured I'd bring my lunch back and sit here and read for the next half hour. That's if you don't mind."

"No worries." I rose from the chair. "As soon as Chief Howard leaves, I'll be out of your way."

"Ma'am feel free to go back to the office. I can study while Chief Howard finishes his reporting."

"Excellent." I quickly grabbed my purse, anxious to escape.

"Actually, I'm done," Howard said and rose. "I'll walk down with you." There was that predatory look again.

All I could do was nod as I followed him out the room and shut the door behind us. He removed our things from the bin and held my phone out to me.

"Thank you." I tried to walk off, but he fell into step beside me.

"Where are you headed?"

"Back to the office. Why? You need something?" I sure

hope not.

"I was thinking I'd come by and we go through the electronic mobility folders together."

Together? I was trying to get away from him. I headed for the stairs and glanced down at my phone. "Actually..." *Think, Dayana, think!* "I have a meeting in about thirty minutes. That gives me just enough time to run to the shoppette and grab a diet soda."

"Diet?" Howard stopped at the bottom of the stairs, cocked his head, and crossed his arms over his chest, causing his impressive biceps to bulge and strain against the sleeves of his ABU shirt. I quivered at the sight and found myself wondering what it would feel like to have them wrapped around me. "You know that stuff isn't good for you, right?"

"I like the way it tastes," I replied.

"Taste, huh?" There was that sexy grin again.

Was he flirting with me?

"Chief Howard?"

We both turned to see Rein standing at the end of the hall.

"Can you come see me before you leave?" she asked.

That was the excuse I needed to get away. "You better go see what she wants." I reached inside my pocket for my hat.

"I'll be in touch," he told me.

I turned and stepped out the door. I waited until I was almost to my car before I allowed myself to breathe. Goodness. I'm a grown woman but I handled that like I was an inexperienced teenager instead of someone who'd been dealing with boys since I was sixteen and had my first date.

Taste, huh?

Goodness, he was really flirting with me, and I was a stuttering fool. My mind had drawn a blank. What in the world would have happened if Rein hadn't shown up when she had? I swallowed and acknowledged that I probably would have invited him back to the office with me. As I drove away, my mind began to spin erotic images of where that time together would have led me.

Down a path I had no intention of going.

13

HOWARD

Talk about bad timing. Damn.

I watched Meeks walk out the building and out of sight.

"You see something out there you like?"

I turned and narrowed my eyes at Rein. "Is there something you need?"

"From the look of things, I should be asking you if there is something you want and need," she teased.

This was why I preferred that she was not in my business. Now I was never going to hear the end of it.

"What do you want, *Master Sergeant*?" I hated to pull rank, but I was pissed by her interruption.

Rein frowned at the reference. "Chief, I have a couple of pay issues I need to discuss with you." She signaled me to follow her down the hall to her office. I looked out in the direction that Meeks departed and saw a small white Mercedes pulling out the lot. I smirked. It was just the type of car I'd expected her to drive.

I turned and made my way into Rein's office. She was sitting behind a large desk. The space had makeshift walls, so it didn't provide any real privacy.

"What pay issues are we talking about?" I asked impatiently and straddled the chair across from her.

"Airmen Larkins and Pace. Their orders were curtailed after they had already been paid for the additional day."

"So, they each have to pay it back." It wasn't a question because I already knew the process.

She nodded and I cussed under my breath because the debt also included a reimbursement of the taxes as well.

"Here's a copy of the debt letters that will go out in the mail on Friday." She slid their paperwork across the table. "They can either bring in a check for the total due, otherwise the overpayment will be deducted from their next check."

I gave her a hard stare. "You know I can't stand this process. We overpay our members and then they have to give the government back more than they actually received because they also have to return the money that you sent to the IRS."

She shook her head. "I don't make the rules."

"You know what I mean." I drew a hard breath. "I will tell them." Since I was the chief, I was responsible for my entire unit, which included any personal or professional issues.

"Thank you."

"I better go." I got up from the chair, but she held out a hand.

"Hold up, bruh." And then just like that her expression changed from professional to nosy. I groaned under my breath because I knew she was about to get all in my business, and yet I sat my butt back down on the seat.

Rein arched one perfectly sculpted eyebrow to say, "So how you been?"

"Really? You want to know how I've been?"

"Okay, okay." She held up a hand. "What I'm really trying to find out is if you're seeing anyone."

"Why? You want to go out with me?"

"Ewww, no." She scrunched up her lips like something didn't smell so good. "I'm just asking because I saw you talking to Meeks."

"And?"

"And she's new to the area and very single."

That was what I wanted to hear, but I tried to keep how the revelation affected me from my face. "And what does that have to do with me?"

"Don't even try it. I know you're interested. I saw the way you were looking at her."

A chuckle escaped my lips. "You think you know me."

"Oh, I know you, bruh." She was challenging me. "You like her, don't you?"

I cleared my throat. "You're reaching," I warned.

"I know but I just wanted to say, good choice. She is really a nice woman and I think she would be good for you."

I tried to talk but once again she stopped me.

"But she's not one for games, so if you're trying to step to her with those old Mack daddy raps, you're not going to get her attention."

I had enough with her meddling, so I stood back up. "I know how to talk to women."

"But do you know how to talk to *that* woman? Because if not, you're going to strike out."

"I'll make sure to take that into consideration." I winked and headed toward the door.

"Go get her," she called out after me.

A smirked curled my lips as I mumbled under my breath. "I plan on it."

14

MEEKS

It was going to be one of those days. I could already feel it. I had commander's call at 0600 and two other meetings scheduled with her later this afternoon. I don't know what's going on with Major Michaels, but I wished she would lay off and just let me do my job.

I finished doing some position moves in the system and decided I needed to get out my chair and stretch before I let a crook in my neck set in. I got up and was headed to the microwave to warm my coffee when I spotted Chief Howard coming through the door. Damn. That was just too much sexy. Trouble was, I'd been unable to forget him. The last few nights, I'd been plagued with dreams of him. It was just too much.

"Hey, just the person I wanted to see."

I smiled and kept on walking over to the microwave and stuck my mug inside. "What can I do for you, Chief?"

"I thought I'd come by and make sure Washington got all our folders ready for you."

Lifting my chin, I replied, "You'll have to check with Bailey to make sure."

"I promised I would give you a status update, not her."

"Okay...true. What did your UDM say? He should know if there is anything missing."

Howard had that skeptical look on his face. I groaned inwardly. This was the problem with our units, they expected the FSS to have all the answers.

"Just give me a minute and I'll log on and see what I can find out."

He was standing so close and all that masculinity was surrounding me. Goodness, how did the females in his unit stand it?

The microwave dinged and I reached for my mug. I spun on my heels and made my way back to my office and away from Howard except he followed.

I walked around my desk and took a seat. "Let me log onto the system and see what we're looking like." I pulled the CAC card out my pocket and logged onto the computer. He lowered on the chair across from my desk and his amazing scent found its way to my nose.

"I see you've personalized your space."

"I figured if I'm going to spend much of my life in this office I might as well make it feel like home for me."

"I like it. Larson never bothered."

"Thank you," I said like I didn't really care, when I really did.

I logged onto the Air Force Portal and waited uncomfortably as the computer was spinning. *Goodness, this was taking way too long.*

"I got time," he said, and I realized I'd said those words aloud. I looked up and something blazed in his eyes for a second. I swallowed and quickly looked down at my screen. Dammit, it was still thinking.

"What have you been doing for fun since you moved here?"

"Fun? What's that?"

"Oh, okay. I see you have jokes." He chuckled softly.

I grinned and met his gaze. "I'm serious. I spend so much time here. Who has time for fun?"

"You've got to find time for yourself." Howard leaned back on the chair and slid a tongue across his beautiful lips. "For example, I always leave for lunch to make sure I break up my day."

"I bring my lunch." I tilted my head toward the small refrigerator in the corner.

"Oh no. Don't do it to yourself."

"I have to." I pointed to the screen. "I'm trying to log on, but the portal has been up and down all day. With connectivity that half works, this is how I waste most of my day."

"So how about we go have lunch, and you can check with Bailey when we get back?"

"Lunch?"

"Yes, lunch." He rose. "C'mon. I'm buying."

"I really don't have time."

"Then make time." He winked. "C'mon. I feel like barbecue. Have you been to County Grill and Smokehouse?"

My stomached growled just before I replied, "No."

"You don't know what you're missing. Their warm potato salad will make you want to slap your mama."

Warm potato salad. Goodness, it sounded too good to say no.

"Okay."

He moved toward the door. I removed my ID from the computer then reached for my purse in the bottom drawer of my desk. I followed him out my office. I noticed Staff Sergeant Hayes eyeing us with interest. She was our personnel systems manager responsible for producing all personnel reports for the wing.

"Hayes, I'm going to lunch. Text me if Major Michaels comes looking for me."

"Yes, ma'am." There was a curious smile on her lips. She was going to be asking questions later that I was going to deny.

With my hat on my head, I followed Howard out the building.

"You can ride with me," he said, and it was clear he wasn't waiting for my answer because he had already moved over to a black Lincoln Navigator and was opening the door for me. I couldn't believe I was getting in a vehicle with him, but I reminded myself that there was nothing wrong with having lunch with a coworker. I did it all the time at my last two units. This was no different.

Except none of them were as fine as Howard.

I climbed in and leaned back comfortably on the seat. By the time he'd moved around, I had fastened my seatbelt. When he started the engine, the sounds of soft R&B filled the vehicle. I appreciated the distraction.

Howard put his hat on the seat behind him and ran a hand over his cropped hair while I stared at his profile from the corner of my eyes. Goodness, he was yummy. This was going to be more difficult that I'd thought. Neither of us spoke until he drove off the base.

"I haven't used this gate before," I commented.

"This is the fastest route."

"I see," I said, nodding.

"It's also a way to bypass all the traffic at five o'clock."

"I never leave before six so..." I shrugged. He already knew the rest.

"Yeah, I feel you." Howard chuckled. I felt the rumble all the way at the center of my stomach. "Most nights the sun is about to rise when I'm ready to head out."

It took me a moment to realize what he said and then I was laughing. "I guess I do the same since by the time I make it home I'm ready to fall out and the sun is up by the time I wake
up again."

"That is because we're responsible for so much." He

took his eyes away from the road long enough to say, "And if you're as passionate about your job as I am, you don't know how to let go or say, enough."

His response caused me to smirk and say, "So true."

"Except for the weekends. I turn that place off and focus on me and mines."

I was curious what "me and mines" meant, but I reminded myself I wasn't interested in getting to know him better, so the answer really didn't matter.

Howard turned off onto an outer road, and I saw the red, white, and blue sign ahead for *County Grill & Smokehouse*. The windows of the SUV were raised and yet the aroma of smoked meat was coming through the vents.

"You smell that?" he asked with a pleasing smile.

I took a long, deep breath. "Oh yeah. Smoke and charcoal."

"That's what I'm talking about." His voice boomed. "My boys have the nerve to invite me over for barbecue cooked on a gas grill. That's not barbecue."

"So true. There's nothing like smoke and charcoal."

He reached over and I gave him a fist bump. "We're going to get along just fine," he said with a wink.

I cleared my throat and realized for a second there I had let my guard down.

Howard parked the car and opened my door before I could get my seatbelt off. I stepped out and rubbed all against him. Between the two cars, we were standing way too close. As soon as my hand brushed his, I gasped and looked up and our eyes locked for a fraction. A knowing smile curled the corner of his mouth. I stepped away as if I'd been burned and followed him inside the restaurant. The smell inside was much more intense and my stomach began to growl. We were escorted to a large, wooden table covered with brown paper. Crayons were there for drawing. Within minutes we placed our order, and a plate of warm corn muffins was brought to the table.

I took a bite and moaned. "Oh, they're good."

Howard's eyebrows raised as if to say, *I told you so.*

I grinned from across the table. "And very addictive." I took another bite while I looked around. "This place is really..."

"Country?"

I laughed. "Exactly." I reached for another muffin before saying, "Thanks for bringing me here. You're right. It's good to get away from the office sometimes. I need to do it more often. When I first started, I would run home, kick up my feet, watch *Steve Harvey,* and eat a sandwich, then go back in."

"You need to get back in that habit," he managed between bites. "I bought a house forty minutes away, so I don't have the luxury of running home for lunch."

"You're a homeowner?" I was sure the surprise was all over my face.

"Why the surprise?" he probed.

I shrugged and wished I wasn't quite so transparent. "You just don't seem the type."

"And what type is that?"

"Settled," I replied without hesitation.

Howard tossed his head back with laughter, killing the tension.

Our food arrived, and that was the perfect interruption. I stared hungrily at a half of slab of Memphis dry rubbed ribs, barbecue baked beans, and warm sour cream potato salad. I draped a napkin across my lap then reached for a rib bone. The meat was practically falling off the bone as I brought it to my mouth and took a bite. "Oh, this is good," I moaned. I also took a taste of potato salad and another rumble of approval escaped my lips.

Howard winked. "I told you it was good enough to slap your mama."

"I don't know about the slap your mama part, but it *is* delicious." I tore my eyes from his face and focused on my plate again. I wasn't even ashamed to lick the sauce from my fingers.

"Are your parents still around?" he asked.

Nodding, I wiped my mouth with the napkin before saying, "Yes, my mother is in Kansas City. My father is…around." I didn't want to talk about him and was grateful Howard caught the hint.

He pointed a forkful of baked beans my way as he spoke. "My mom lives in Delaware. My old man passed away two years ago."

"I'm so sorry to hear that."

Howard shrugged. "He was a workaholic. Never found time to enjoy life and collapsed on the job."

I took a sip of iced tea before saying, "Is that why you make time for fun?"

"Yes, that's why I take the time to enjoy life. Life is too short to sweat the small stuff. When I leave work, I turn that place off and don't turn it on again until zero six hundred."

"So, you don't answer your cell phone?" I asked between bites. I saw the work phone identical to mine on his hip.

"Only if it's an emergency. My Airmen know it better be important and not to bother me with the dumb shit."

"Sounds like you have it all under control."

"Nah," Howard began, raising his hand in protest. "I've just been doing this a long time, and I have a lot of Airmen that I am responsible for."

"And I see you take your job serious."

"Absolutely, because you know there is always someone waiting for you to mess up."

"What do you mean?"

He laughed. "Don't act brand new. You know the deal. It took forever for me to make chief. I waited for others to retire. One chief was sixty before he left and, even then, I didn't think they were going to give it to me. I'd been sitting in a senior slot for four years."

"Wow. I've been a senior now for a little over a year."

"Congratulations. Do you plan on sticking around to make chief someday?"

"Absolutely," I replied confidently.

"And with that determination, I'm sure you'll get it. Your chief has been around for a minute."

"Yes, he returned to Weyland so he could be close to home. By the time I'm eligible for chief, he should be ready to retire."

Howard nodded. "You came on the scene at the right time."

"I think so."

"What about your personal life?"

Wow. I can't believe the way he just slid that question in. "What about it?"

"Well, it sounds like you got your professional life together, but what are you doing about your personal life?"

Leaning in a little closer, I said, "Why are you worried about my personal life?"

"Probably because I want to get to know you better." There was that grin. "Is that possible?"

I exhaled an audible sigh. "I don't mix business with pleasure." I was such a liar. I used to date my chief.

"There is a first time for everything." He was licking his lips again.

Oh, he was cocky, and it was such a turn on. Only I was not going to let him know that. "I find time when I need to find time."

"Good. Then how about we go out this weekend?"

"Nope. I have plans."

"Change them." Okay, he was a little on the arrogant side.

"I'm spending time with family." I shook my head and started to say more but Howard raised a hand and stopped me.

"I can't argue that. I have a daughter who is my rock."

"Really?" So, she was the *me and mines*. It irritated me at how good the revelation made me feel. "How old is she?"

He scowled. "Ava is sixteen going on twenty-five."

"Aren't most of them? My niece is a handful and she's only four."

"Do you have any children of your own?"

I frowned. "Nope. Never been in a relationship long enough to have any, and I refused to be a single parent. It's just too hard."

"That I understand." He was staring at me. "I'm still waiting to hear what you like to do for fun."

"I'm simple. My sanctuary is being able to spend quiet time at home watching television."

"Don't tell me… HGTV?"

"How'd you guess?" I said with a laugh. "I'm really good with a hammer. I can also install tile and change light fixtures."

"A woman after my heart. Where have you been all my life?" he teased and then winked.

The rest of the lunch, the conversation focused on a property he'd flipped with a friend and I couldn't have been happier.

15

HOWARD

Having lunch with Meeks confirmed what I already knew. I wanted her now just like I'd wanted her the moment I laid eyes on her. Hell, maybe even more. Every time I got within so many feet of that woman, I had a battle with my libido.

By the time I'd dropped Meeks off at the front door of her building, she was smiling. That was a good sign. Even though she still refused to let me take her out after hours.

"Nope, I already told you. I don't date military men, but I appreciate you taking me to lunch." She leaned down inside the window of my vehicle so I could see the depth of her gorgeous eyes when she said, "Oh yeah, and don't forget I need those folders ready no later than tomorrow." She was all business once again and, despite it, I felt the power of my imagination kick through me.

I watched Meek turn on the heels of her boots and sashayed her sexy ass back into the building. I pulled off laughing and more determined than ever. I had a plan. She just didn't know it, but she was about to find out.

I made my way back to work. When I stepped out my vehicle, I found Chief Master Sergeant River Reid coming across the parking lot.

"Just the person I need to see," he said with a grin.

"What's going on?" I asked.

We both saluted a lieutenant as he passed and then were interrupted by a master sergeant. While Reid stopped to answer the female senior NCO's questions, I made my way into the building and down the hall. I stopped and stuck my head in the office on the corner. Senior Airman Jenner sprung up from her chair.

"Yes, Chief?"

"Where's Washington?" I asked and gestured for her to return to her seat.

"He's at lunch, sir."

"Tell him I need an update on those mobility folders before he leaves today."

"Yes, Chief. I will tell him as soon as he returns."

I grinned. "Thank you, Airman Jenner. By the way, you've been doing a great job with scheduling medical appointments."

She beamed. "Thank you, Chief."

I moved to my office and over to the small refrigerator and removed a bottle of water. As soon as I took my seat, Reid appeared at my door.

"What's going on?"

"Just dropping by. I've been trying to catch up with Rice for the last week to get on the vice wing commander's calendar. I think she's been avoiding my calls." Master Sergeant Robyn Rice was the XO—executive officer's—assistant.

"Probably heard the rumors about you."

"Then it's all good news," he replied and straddled the chair.

"What's on your mind?" I asked because Reid never dropped by.

Reid looked at me long and hard as if he was looking for the proper words to say. Expressing himself was something he had no problem doing so whatever it was,

he was wrestling with. "I've been thinking long and hard about
something."

"And what's that? Spit it out." I lifted the water bottle and took a long swig.

"I'm thinking about pushing the button." The expression on his face was dark and intense.

"You're serious."

He nodded. "I think it's time."

I leaned back on the chair and breathed. "Wow."

Reid released a sigh and dragged a hand down the length of his face. "I've been doing this for twenty years. I'm tired. I'm ready to retire and start working on my next life."

"And what is that?"

"Probably go ahead and start a security firm. I've been looking around at spaces to lease," he said, not quite meeting my eyes.

I drew a long whistle. "Damn. You *are* serious."

He nodded. "Yep. I have one more deployment coming up but after that, I'm out." We've toured together. Afghanistan and Iraq. Neither of us spoke a word about our experiences but Reid's quiet intensity told me he'd seen and done more things than he'd ever forget.

"Good for you." I reached across the desk and gave him a fist bump. "I don't know what I would do if I wasn't wearing this uniform every day."

"You'd start spending more time with your family."

I met his hard stare. "By the time I retire my daughter will be finishing college." I took another swallow. Like myself, Reid was single. "Maybe now you can make time for a relationship."

Usually he scowled at that idea, but today he had this solemn look on his face. I sat up in my chair and tried to read his expression.

"Maybe. If I find the right woman," he said calmly.

I gave a rude snort. "Bruh, you really need to get out of my office because I can't believe what I'm hearing."

He rose and walked over to my refrigerator and grabbed my last water. "People change," he replied between sips. "I'm ready to be a part of that change." He turned to me. "What about you? You ready to put that player card away and meet someone with some substance."

His comment caused me to grin. "Actually, I think I've already met her." Before I could elaborate there was a knock at my door. I looked over to see Washington standing in my doorway.

"Enter."

He stepped in and stood with his arms behind his ramrod-straight back. "Chief, I'm here to report that all of the deployment folders have been signed and, other than pending medical appointment, the rest are now ready for Bailey to review."

"Good job, Washington." I couldn't wait to call and share the good news with Meeks.

16

MEEKS

By Saturday, I was hyped and looking forward to an evening out. Layla was right, I was too damn cute to be spending my life at home binge-watching television series.

I got up and headed to the salon in a strip mall near my house, hoping if I was early enough, I just might be able to get in without an appointment. I was in luck. Carol had a no-show.

"I don't know what the hell is wrong with young folks today." She'd been ranting since I'd arrived. "You can't be making an appointment for a Saturday and think just because you partied too hard the night before and 'feeling lazy' you can cancel. That chick got me confused with one of her homegirls." Carol's head was rolling on her neck as fast as that curling iron twirling in her hand. "She better recognize. I am a professional and time is money."

"I know that's right," I chimed in.

"Just wait until she tries to bring her narrow ass up in here next week. I'm going to tell her she owes me a thirty-five-dollar no-show fee."

"Preach, sis," Bunny cackled from over in the next booth. Her nails were so long they were like claws. I'm not sure how she managed to braid hair, but the sistah could hook up some heads.

"You got a hot date?"

It took a moment before I realized Carol was talking to me. I gazed up at her reflection in the mirror, her gray contact-tinted eyes looking my way and said, "Why you say that?"

She gave a rude snort. "Because why else would someone be sitting out in the parking lot trying to get a haircut." That brought a round of laughter. Mine included.

"So, what's up?" she pressed.

I caught myself blushing when I replied, "I have a date with my sister and her husband. They invited me to tag along with them to the Funny Bone."

"Oh damn. I can't remember the last time I went there. Bunny, do you remember? I think that was when we went on that double-date."

The short, round woman tossed a hand in the air like she was swatting flies. "Chile, that was when I was dating Rickey and you hooked up with that Navy dude with halitosis."

Carol sucked in air as if the stench of his breath had just hit her. "Ugh. That was the most miserable night. We went to see Tommy Davidson. Now you know his little skinny ass is funny as hell. Tim was laughing so hard the smell of his funky breath was like a black cloud hovering over our table. Our food, even the drinks, were polluted."

The entire shop was laughing now.

"As soon as he took me home, I jumped in the shower trying to get that smell off."

"Maybe he just needed a breath mint," I teased.

"Uh-uh." Carol pointed a rat-tooth comb at me. "A bottle of extra strength Scope couldn't help that dude. That was our third date and the smell got worse not better."

She spun my chair around and reached for the flat iron

again.

"You'll probably see a few cuties roll into the Funny Bone with their boys before heading to the club, but mostly it's couple's tonight."

I frowned up at her. "So, in other words, I'm going to feel like a third wheel."

"Yep, probably so." She combed out another lock of my hair before she spoke again. "Who's the headliner?"

"Eddie Griffin."

"Oh snap. He's funny as shit," Bunny said. A couple others agreed.

Carol tossed her hand dismissively. "Chile, you will be so entertained, you'll forget all about not having a date."

That made me feel a little better. Sort of.

After I left the shop with my natural hair flat-ironed and parted off to the side, so it bounced around my shoulders with every step, I decided to get my eyebrows and toes done as well. Might as well do some full-fledged pampering. And about time, too. I believed in self-care every opportunity I got. That's what happens when you're single and have no kids; you can spoil yourself.

By six o'clock I was dressed and waiting for Layla and Faison to arrive. We needed to be at the comedy club by seven for the eight o'clock show. Standing in front of my mirror, I struck a pose and liked everything I saw. I wore the jeans and orange shirt I'd found at the BX and looked fucking amazing. I had also found a pair of blue jean-dyed wedge sandals that showed off my perfect French-tipped toenails. I reached for my eyeliner and applied it to my eyes, then brushed rose-colored blusher across my cheeks. Yes, I looked good. The outfit highlighted all my assets.

I went into the kitchen and scanned the refrigerator shelves. We were going to the Cheesecake Factory—which was my favorite—after the show, so I made myself a ham and cheese sandwich to tide me over. Since I wasn't driving, I sat on the couch sipping a glass of wine until I received a text from Layla that they were pulling up. I put the glass in the sink, grabbed a cute little gold pouch that I wore low on my waist, and headed out. I was surprised to see my niece, Maya, in the backseat.

"We're dropping her off at Kaitlyn's on the way."

Maya smiled at the mention of her best friend. "Auntie Day, you look pretty."

"Thank you, ladybug." I climbed in then leaned over and kissed her cheek. She was so beautiful with big brown eyes and long hair bundled into two loose braids. I gave her another kiss and a squeeze from her favorite aunt. I love that little girl.

My eyes switched to the front. "Hey, Faze."

My brother-in-law scratched at his salt and pepper goatee as he caught my reflection in the review mirror and said, "What's up, Lil' Sis." I love Faison like a brother so imagine how pissed and hurt I was when he messed around on my sister after only two years of marriage. Layla had fallen apart and moved in with me. Crying and so depressed, she had lost her job as a retail manager. I was all about telling my sister to divorce him and get on with her life. But she—unlike me—believed in forgiveness and second chances. Since then, Faison has made a 180-degree turn and caters to my sister. They now had Maya and he spent every day showing them both how much he loves his family. Over time, I had allowed myself to forgive him for treating my sister that way, but I would never forget what he had put her—and me—through.

"You are rocking that outfit," my sister said, looking at me over her shoulder.

"Thank you. I needed an excuse to dress it up a bit."

"You never need an excuse to look good. I even forgot

you had that much hair on your head," she said, her eyes traveling over me with approval.

"Aunt Day, your hair is long." Maya was stroking my hair like she was petting her cat.

I gave her beautiful brown cheek a loving pat.

"It's my treat to myself."

Layla drew a sigh. "That what I need... A 'me' day. We really should plan a spa day. I hear there is one in Virginia Beach."

"You know I'm game. Just let me know when and where."

"Babe go ahead and book it. It will be my treat." Faison brought my sister's hand to his lips and kissed it. Sometimes I think he tries too hard to right his wrong, but who am I to judge, especially since he makes Layla happy.

"Aunt Day, I'm learning how to swim."

"You are? Maybe you can teach me," I added and leaned in close and gave her another hug and she squeezed me back. Maya is so warm and loving.

Maya and I chatted all the way to her friend's house, then I walked her inside with her sleeping bag and a cute little pink overnight bag that I'd bought her one afternoon during one of my auntie spoil sessions. After that we hopped onto I-64. Faze turned on some old school eighties music and the three of us rocked in our seats all the way to Virginia Beach. Since the move, I had only been to the beach twice, mostly shopping with Layla and another time because I was craving Macaroni Grill.

Faze parked on the second floor of the garage and we headed across the street. The Cheesecake Factory was right on the corner, and I could already taste the cream cheese from their red velvet cake on my tongue.

We walked inside the building. There was already a line of people outside the door chatting nonstop. Carol

was right. There were mostly couples, a few girlfriends hanging out, and I even saw some guys hanging out. One was checking me out, but he was too short for my taste. Layla and Faze started talking about going to Lowe's in the morning for their weekly home improvement project. I envied them being homeowners and having weekly routines. Maybe in the next year, I would
be ready to buy my first home.

I fished out my phone and scrolled through Facebook posts in my news feed while I moved up in the line with the rest of the patrons. I was reading a funny post that one of the girls from my unit back in Missouri had posted when I heard Faze say, "There he is now."

Curiously, I looked up from my phone and my heart did a Simone Biles, triple somersault when I saw someone familiar moving through the line.

Chief Keim Howard.

I froze at the sight of him maneuvering through the crowd headed toward us. He looked sexy out of uniform in a red polo shirt, the man on the horse right smack over a beautifully muscular chest. Dark jeans hung low on his waist and butter brown Timbs were on his feet. He walked with so much swag, other women stopped and stared at him as he passed.

"Whassup, Faze," he said, then reached over and gave him dap.

"What's up, Keim." Faze was grinning as he turned to his wife and said, "Baby, this is the dude I've been telling you about."

Layla and I exchanged looks before she walked over and extended her hand. "Hello." She was grinning that calculated smile I knew all too well as she turned to face me again. "And this is—"

"Dayana Meeks," Howard interrupted in that butter

smooth voice of his. "Hello again."

When his gaze suddenly locked with mine, I felt the floor beneath me sway. "Hey."

"You two know each other?" Layla asked as if she didn't already know.

He turned to her then his gaze returned to me. "We work together," Howard said.

My sister slapped me on the shoulder, almost knocking me over. "Such a small world, isn't it?"

I rolled my eyes at her.

"It's good to see you again, Meeks."

Same here. Only I wasn't about to say that.

We had moved up in the line, and it was our turn to be seated.

"How many?" the guy at the door asked and when I saw Faze hold up four fingers, I realized that this was indeed a hook up. As Faze and Layla turned their backs and went inside with their heads close, whispering, I vowed to kill them both.

"After you." Howard brought a hand to my waist and an electric charge shot through me that was so hot and intense I could have saved myself the sixty dollars I spent to straighten my hair.

I followed them down to a table on the floor to what appeared to be the VIP section. The table had a great view of the stage. I took the seat beside my sister. Howard moved to my other side. I noticed Faison and Layla were avoiding eye contact. Yep. Like I said, this was a setup.

Discreetly, I looked at Howard. I knew he was a big guy but out of uniform, the red Ralph Lauren polo strained against his massive chest. His arms rippled with tattoos and muscles that bulged.

"So, Howard…What do you do at the unit?" Layla asked. I found the question odd since she already knew him. Or at least I thought she did.

"I'm the Chief of the Maintenance Group."

"Really?" She looked impressed. Not that it took much to impress my sister.

Howard nodded. "Faze has told me a lot about you."

"How do the two of you know each other?" I asked because I knew my sister, and this felt like too much of a coincidence.

Faze shifted his gaze to mine. "Howard and I attended NCO academy together."

Howard chuckled. "Those were some wild days."

"Indeed, they were. So, imagine my surprise when I ran into him at the commissary a few months ago. I had no idea he was at Weyland Air Force Base," Faison said.

I cleared my throat and shifted my gaze on Howard. "How come you didn't tell me you knew Faze?"

Howard shrugged. "I didn't know he was your family."

I guess he could be telling the truth. "So, this isn't some kinda set up?" My finger was pointed at Layla and her husband.

Faison held up his hands, palms forward in surrender. "I told my boy we were going to the Funny Bone this weekend and my sister-in-law was new in town so come join us."

My sister was grinning. "Otherwise, Day, we'd have some random dude sitting at the table with us." She looked at Faison and the two grinned.

Layla thought she was slick. They both did.

"Why, what's wrong?" Howard had leaned in so close I could feel his sweet warm breath on my ear. "You got a problem with me spending the evening with you?"

With a shrug I tried to act like it was no big deal and hoped he didn't notice my hands were shaking. "No, not at all. Just surprised."

"So am I. But I am not at all disappointed." He was staring at me now. The same way he had at lunch on Thursday. "I asked you out and you said no," he reminded me. "But it looks like I'm getting that date after all."

My stomach did another one of those unbelievable flips. Dammit. Why did he have to be so sexy?

I caught Layla staring at us, her mouth hanging open. When she realized I was looking, she quickly dropped her eyes and reached for a menu. "Anybody hungry?"

The men ordered wings and a round of beers. And while they reminisced on the good old days, Layla and I exchanged looks until she finally rose from her chair and said, "Will you excuse us? I need to go before the show starts." She tugged my hand and practically yanked me up out the chair and through the crowd. As soon as we were far enough away, she squealed, "Shit, Day, Keim's sexy."

I kept walking and waited until we were inside the ladies' room before I turned around and said, "You think you're slick."

"What?" she shot back. "What did I do?" Layla was trying to act all innocent and shit.

"You set me up on a blind date."

A tell-all blush gave me my answer before Layla spoke.

"Girl, you'd have to be blind not to have noticed how fine that man is. He's in *your* unit. You already met him and didn't tell me," she added with a playful pout.

I groaned inwardly for the second time this evening. "Because there is nothing to tell. I work with gorgeous men all the time." Although I don't ever remember working with one that was that freaking yummy.

"Yes, but you didn't mention him," she argued softly. "And he asked you out on a date and you declined." A mysterious smile touched her lips.

I knew she had been ear hustling. "Because I do not want to mix work with my personal life."

She leaned against the sink counter, chuckling softly. "For someone who looks like that, I would make an exception."

The door swung open and two women walked inside. As soon as they passed, I rolled my eyes. "Enough about me. Didn't you come in here to use the bathroom?" With that I walked off and disappeared in a stall at the end.

17

HOWARD

Yes, indeed. The Lord does answer prayers.

"Yo, Faze, man..." I shook my head. "Thanks for inviting me. The moment I found out Dayana was your sister-in-law there was no way I was passing up this opportunity."

He grinned. "About time. I've been trying to hook y'all up since I ran into you on base."

"Well, I'm glad I finally took you up on your offer." He was right. He'd tried to hook us up once before, but I passed because I don't do blind dates. But when Rein told me who Meeks was related to, I practically broke my finger trying to dial Faison's phone number. The moment I asked him to hook me up with his sister-in-law, he'd invited me to come and hang out at the Funny Bone. I jumped at the opportunity.

"No disrespect, but Dayana is fine as hell. And you're telling me she's single?" I still couldn't believe my good fortune.

"Very single." Faze was nodding and looked pleased. "I was hoping the two of you would hit it off."

"We met at a deployment briefing and I even took her to lunch," I admitted.

He started laughing. "No shit?"

"Yeah and she blew off my offer to go out tonight." I

smirked.

"And look how that turned out?"

I tapped my Heineken bottle against his. "I appreciate the hook up."

"Hell yeah. That's what boys do. We look out for each other. Actually, you're doing me a favor. Layla's been hounding me to hook her sister up with one of my friends. Now maybe she'll get off my back."

We shared a laugh.

"She's as good as handled."

I looked up to see the women heading our way. Dayumm. When you wear a uniform Monday through Friday you often wonder what someone looks like in civilian clothes, and that cutie was breathtaking. When they say the clothes make the woman, in this case, the woman was making the clothes look good. Dayana had a pair of beautiful breasts that were on display with enough cleavage to make a man feel so uncomfortable in his jeans I had to shift to accommodate a serious hard-on. A pair of jeans hugged her round, curvy ass, and her hips swung as she strutted in those heels that had her legs looking long and simply delicious.

I caught Meek's eyes, and she gave a shy grin before she slid back onto the seat beside me. The soft smell of that sweet perfume of hers hit my nose and made me want to drag her close and run my tongue all along her neck.

The wings arrived just as the show began. With the lights dimmed, I focused on the stage and got caught up in the show. The comedian who opened the show was funny as shit. Meeks was laughing, and I saw the way her face lit up. I'm not going to lie...this woman was captivating.

By the time the comedian was closing, the audience was shaking with laughter.

"Bruh, how long have the two of you been dating?"

It took a moment before I realized he was talking to me. I looked over at Meeks. "This is our first date." I licked my lips. "But it won't be our last."

"Now, you see how he's looking at her? Like he wants to gnaw at her leg like them chicken bones in front of him. Matter of fact... Can you hold up your plate?" As soon as I did, he added. "You see that, he sucked the shit out of them bones!" The comedian started acting like he had a toothpick in his mouth. "And that's just an appetizer. I guarantee, this brotha is going to be having a full course meal of sucking the shit out of some pussy tonight."

The crowd roared with laughter, and I looked over at Dayana and winked letting her know it was all in fun. But inside, I have to say, I was already fantasizing about the thought of those sexy legs spread on the bed and my head buried between her thighs, feasting. Nothing wrong with a little foreplay.

Yes, there indeed was a God and He was showing me favor. Now that I had Meeks right where I wanted her, I planned on doing whatever it took to making this woman mine.

18

MEEKS

The show was funny as hell. I even forgot Howard was sitting beside me until the comedian started that joke about him sucking some bones. My bones. When he looked over at me with those big brown eyes, he had me so hot I was squirming on the seat. I couldn't stop thinking about those juicy lips of his traveling downtown. Shit.

That was one of the issues I'd had with Dame. He didn't believe in doing that. Said it was unsanitary. He didn't have a problem with receiving, but he damn sure wasn't giving. I had gotten to the point I stopped giving him head.

"My wife doesn't have a problem with it," he would say.

"Then you need to take her ass back," I'd flip back at him time and time again.

Now that I think about it, maybe that might be part of the reason why he decided he needed to go back home. *Why are you thinking about him?* This was my first night out in weeks and I wasn't about to waste it on a man who truly wasn't worth it. I brushed Dame aside and focused on my evening.

The show ended, and the lights were turned up. We all got up still grinning and laughing. Comedy shows were rated as one of the best first dates. Not that this was a date.

"Hey man, we're getting ready to head over to the Cheesecake Factory so these two can have a slice of red velvet cheesecake. You're welcomed to come join us."

Howard's eyes shifted to me. "That's if Dayana's inviting me."

He had put the spotlight on me.

I shrugged. "If you want to."

"Then how about you ask me to join you and see how I answer." His gaze locked on mine and my heartbeat quickened.

"Oh damn," I heard Layla mutter under her breath.

Howard was good. I had to give it to him. Cocky. Just the way I liked. "You want to come and have cheesecake with us?"

Howard grinned, licking his lips. "If it means I get to spend a few more minutes with you, then absolutely."

The line was corny, but I liked that about him. He knew what he liked, and I liked that it was me, despite my hang-up over dating military men. After a few moments, I forced my gaze away.

We all walked over to the Cheesecake Factory, and it couldn't have been a more perfect night. The humidity was mild. My hair appreciated that.

It was a Saturday night so of course it was crowded and a thirty-minute wait for a table. We talked. Howard stood so close to me I could feel all that masculine heat radiating my way, causing my body to warm in the most delicious ways. To put some distance between us I took my sister's hand and signaled her to follow me over near the bar where we ordered apple martinis. Theirs were the best I'd ever tasted.

"What do you think of Keim?" she asked over the noise of the crowd.

I tried to downplay what I was really feeling. "He is

nice."

"Nice?" Layla blurted out in her characteristic over-the-top fashion and then rolled her eyes heavenward. I started laughing because I couldn't even hold a straight face.

"Okay, he's better than nice."

She bumped her shoulder with mine. "Now *that's* what I wanted to hear."

Layla went on to talk about the comedian putting the focus on us as a couple and that the stars must be aligning and all that other crazy gibberish my sister likes to say. I allowed my gaze to rest on Howard. He ended whatever he was saying to Faison and looked over, and our gazes locked. Fuck. He nodded his head in a salute. I grinned, unsure what else to do. Only he didn't grin. Instead his eyes darkened with an intensity that made my pulse race.

Thank goodness, Faison waved the blinking buzzer in his hand, dragging away my attention and signaling for us to come back. Our table was ready. Carrying our drinks, we made our way through the crowd. Howard smiled and took his place beside me like we were a true couple, and as he led me to our table there was that hand at the small of my back that sent a lightning strike of sensation firing through me, lighting up every single nerve ending I had. Goodness.

My sister had her phone at her ear and was frowning by the time we took our seats.

"Everything okay, babe?" Faison asked.

"That was Clara. Maya is complaining that her stomach is hurting." There was worry in her eyes. "I hate to cut this evening short, but we're going to have to get our cheesecake to go."

"No apologies. Children come first," Howard said, and in that instant, I realized I wanted to get to know this man better.

My sister and Faison rose. So did I.

Faison looked from Howard and then to me. "I hate to ruin the evening for the two of you." Irritation showed in his face and voice.

I gave a dismissive wave. "No worries, I—"

Howard reached out and grabbed my hand. "Please stay. Have some cheesecake. My treat."

"Yes, stay, Day," Layla urged.

I stuttered and couldn't think fast enough. "But I-I—"

"I promise to get you home safely." His thumb was caressing my fingers.

Layla was giving that look that screamed, *Day, are you crazy? The dude is fine. You better sit your ass back down in that seat.*

They were all ganging up on me, including Faison. "Lil' sis, I wouldn't leave you here if I didn't think you were in good hands."

I pretended I was still considering staying although I had already made up my mind to stay. There wasn't anything at home to do but watch television. I had something better to look at in front of me. Besides, didn't I deserve one evening of fun?

"Okay," I muttered and then moved over to the opposite side of the booth where they had just vacated. "Text me and let me know Maya is okay."

"Will do." Layla was grinning as she and her husband waved and made their way over to the cheesecake counter. I wouldn't be surprised if that sneaky chick set the whole thing up and had asked Clara to call and pretend Maya was sick.

My eyes shifted over to Howard. "I guess it's just you and me."

"Is that a bad thing?" He was staring. His expression

was serious.

"No, it isn't," I said on a nervous laugh. "I'm just saying."

"Well, I'm saying I'm glad I have this time alone to get to know you better."

I folded my arms on the table. "What would you like to know?"

My response caused a warm smile to curl his lips. "For starters, I want to know why a beautiful woman like yourself is spending her evening hanging out with her sister and her
husband."

"I guess the same reason why you're hanging out with them."

Howard tossed his head back with a throaty chuckle that made me explode with laughter. "That's a good one," he said. "When Faze asked me to come join him, I almost passed. I'm so glad I didn't. You have no idea how surprised I was to discover my hook up was with you."

"Hook up, huh?"

He leaned back on the bench grinning. "Yeah, hook up. You turned me down and yet here we are anyway. You know it's fate, right?"

He sounded like my sister. "I considered it just a coincidence. We live in a small world."

The waiter came over, and I ordered the red velvet cheesecake and a cup of espresso. Howard ordered the turtle cheesecake and coffee.

I looked over at him, still watching me intensely. I was at a loss for words. "You ready for the upcoming exercise to be over with?"

He shook his head. "I have one rule tonight."

"What is that?"

He wagged his finger at me. "No talking about work.

Tonight, I'm stripping off the uniform and focusing on just you."

"A talker, huh?" I wasn't used to that.

"Hell yeah. How else will I know if you're crazy or not?"

"Crazy?" I was giggling and blushing at the same time. I noticed he was staring down at my mouth.

He grinned. "I love when you laugh."

"I was told my laugh is loud and goofy."

His eyes twinkled. "You're right. It *is* loud and goofy, but that's why I like it so much."

We were staring at each other like the rest of the world no longer existed.

"What is the earliest memory you have?"

"Seriously?" I croaked, surprised by his question.

He nodded. "I'm serious."

"Oh wow. Well, let's see. I remember being in a crib and waking up one morning to find a kitten curled up at my feet."

His brow rose. "You're serious?"

I nodded. "I told my mother that story one day and she started laughing. She couldn't believe I remembered that. I was barely two-years-old and yet I remember being in a room I shared with my mother."

"Damn. My earliest memory was when I was about four. I was on a merry-go-round. The only reason why I remembered was because I fell off and hit my big ass head."

"Oh no."

"Had to get stitches and everything," he confessed. "After that you couldn't get me to get on a merry-go-around. I was scared to death."

We were laughing and still talking about childhood

memories when our order arrived. We ended up sharing our cheesecakes. Any other man I would have had a fit, but with Howard I wanted to share everything. Even moments of my life growing up.

"Are you in a rush to head back to the house?" he asked after our dessert was long gone.

I shook my head. "No, why?"

"Because, if you don't mind and since we're already over on this side of the water, how about we take a stroll along the boardwalk?"

There were those damn somersaults again.

"Good thing I have a pair of flats in my pouch." Those little slippers that Dr. Scholl's created were life savers.

Howard took care of the bill and then took my hand and led me outside. We climbed into his SUV and made the short trip over to the ocean. Howard parked and we headed down toward the boardwalk. There was a lot of activity this time of the year—folks were out on skateboards, riding bikes, and there were several other walkers. With my slippers on, we made our way over to the walking path and fell into a slow stroll. The comforting warmth of Howard's hand made me feel so at ease, I found myself leaning into him. This evening felt too right, and that's what scared me. I was waiting for the shoe to drop and the red flags to emerge.

I caught him looking at me again. I could feel myself getting hotter and hotter. Blushing, I shifted my gaze off into the ocean.

"What are you smiling about?" he asked softly.

"Nothing."

"Nothing?"

It was dark except for a few streetlights. I was glad he couldn't see how affected I was by this whole situation. "Yes, nothing."

"I think you're lying."

Howard stopped walking and faced me. His broad shoulders and six-foot-four frame of unadulterated muscle was both sexy and overpowering.

"If you think I'm lying then you tell me what I'm smiling about."

"I think you're smiling and asking yourself, 'How did I get so lucky to meet a man like this?'"

"W-what?" I playfully punched him in the forearm and Howard erupted in a fit of laughter. I was laughing, too, until I felt his hard chest against my breasts. Then he was pulling me into his arms, and we were kissing. *Wow* was my very first thought because kissing was not at all what I wanted or expected. Especially not from him. It was like tasting a slice of forbidding fruit, delicious but so very wrong. He was everywhere. His heat, dark masculine scent, and all that smooth brown skin right in front of me. I tried to push away but, when the kiss deepened, I surrendered and parted my lips. That man had the kissing game mastered. His tongue slipped inside my mouth bold and controlled, forcing me to follow his strokes and let him lead, and I did willingly. His hard body molded against mine, waking up all my feminine parts that had been seriously neglected. He wound his hips. When I felt an erection pressed against my belly, I heard a moan that sounded like a desperate whimper. When I realized that sound had come from me, I jerked back from his touch.

"What's wrong?" Howard asked as if he didn't already know. His eyes said otherwise.

"We probably shouldn't."

"Why not?" Taking my hand, he drew me closer. "We're both grown. You're single, right?"

I nodded.

He shrugged. "Then I don't see a problem."

"The problem is..."

"What? What's the problem?" He was now holding both my hands, studying me. "Yes, I'm in the military. So are you. If anything, we understand what commitment means because we're both serving in the same branch. Integrity first…service before self…excellence in all that we do." He smiled with pride.

Oh, I had no doubt that he had integrity because Howard had no problem speaking his truth. The desire in his eyes promised he could service a woman's needs before satisfying his own. And the confidence in his smile guaranteed he was excellent at everything he did. The mere thought had all my girly parts tingling.

Reaching out, he cupped my chin, tilting my head so I had no choice but to look up into those beautiful dark eyes of his as he spoke.

"We're both adults. I want you. You know you want me."

I opened my mouth, but he cut me off.

"Don't even try and deny it. I heard it in your moan. I felt it in the way you were kissing me."

"*You* were kissing me."

He smirked. "*We* were kissing, and you liked it." He brushed his mouth over mine again and got no resistance from me. When he drew back, his gaze was dark and intense. "Tell me you didn't like it."

I swallowed and couldn't form the words to lie.

"C'mon, Day, tell me."

I loved the way he used my nickname.

"So why resist when we both know I could kiss you right now and you'll let me." Arrogance dripped in his voice but not in the eyes searching mine. Instead they held passion. Howard started leaning in slowly almost as if daring me to stop him. I could not. Instead I tilted my head and met his lips for another firecracker kiss.

Damn Howard, and damn Layla and Faison. In fact, I planned on kicking my sister's ass the next time I saw her for putting me in this predicament. She'd swear she had nothing to do with it, that it was all Faison, but I knew better. There were very few decisions my brother-in-law made without consulting his wife first.

Howard shifted, another subtle movement with his hips rubbing against mine. I groaned, unable to help myself, intense pleasure beginning to wrap itself around me. He deepened the kiss, caressing my mouth. His lips were addictive. The more I tasted, the more I wanted. I realized he was right. He could do whatever he wanted with me and I would let him. I broke free. Found myself breathing heavy. Howard grinned knowingly.

"I think it's time you took me home," I said and expected a tart comeback. Instead, Howard nodded.

"Sure. C'mon, let me get you home safely." He took my hand and we headed back.

Couples were everywhere, strolling and holding hands. We walked in silence and still had a forty-minute ride home ahead. Damn. I drew an inward breath and sighed. I had ruined the mood.

As we stepped off the boardwalk and passed a souvenir shop, Howard bumped into me. At first, I thought it an accident, but when his arm collided into my shoulder again, I knew it was on purpose. I glanced over at him, pretending to be focused on something straight ahead but the dimple at his cheek gave him up. It was my turn to deliberately bump into him. He bumped me back. We looked at each other grinning and then laughing. Damn, he was so sexy. Who could resist him?

Howard draped his arm across my shoulders and pulled me closer. "Can I treat you to an ice cream cone?"

he said with a silly smirk that made me giggle like a schoolgirl.

"I would like that very much."

We were licking ice cream all the way to his SUV. Howard popped the last of his cone into his mouth and started his vehicle. Before he pulled off, he swung around on the seat and faced me. The look on his face was so serious.

"What?" I was really feeling self-conscious.

Howard reached up and caressed my cheek, the contact causing shivers down my back. "I'm not going to apologize for what happened back there. I want you and I know goddamn well you want the same."

I didn't even respond or try to deny it. I bit into my ice cream cone instead.

"While you're contemplating if you want to get involved with another military man, let me share a bit of knowledge with you."

"What's that?"

"I'm good—correction—I'm a fucking beast. But you've got to be willing to find that out."

"Willing?" I needed to make sure I was hearing him correctly.

Howard nodded. "I don't take anything that isn't giving to me." His fingers traveled along my jaw in a gentle caress that caused another shiver. And then everything in me went still. His eyes had grown dark and so intense, looking at me with such raw emotion.

"What do you mean?" I whispered because I could barely speak.

"I've had the same training you've had. No means no. And I take that shit very seriously. If you want me then you need to let me know you want me. But please note that once you do, I'm coming at you with everything I've got." He leaned in and popped the last of my ice cream cone into his mouth. Probably a good thing because I was so turned on, I forgot I was holding it.

He didn't wait for a response before he put the vehicle in gear and headed toward the interstate back toward home.

The music was on, so I leaned back on the seat and closed my eyes as I thought about what Howard was offering me. I sighed inward. It was way too soon for me to even be entertaining the thought of dating, especially someone I worked with and, yet, I was seriously considering it. My mind began to replay my past relationships with military men, and it was always the same thing. Games, a broken heart, and bullshit.

I must have dozed off because when I felt the car stop, I opened my eyes. Peering out the window I noticed we were at a stoplight near the mall.

"Hey, sleepyhead. Unless you plan to go home with me, you need to tell me where you live."

Grinning, I lifted my arms over my head and stretched. "Sorry, I didn't mean to fall asleep."

"It's all good. That just tells me you feel relaxed around me." Howard winked just as the light turned green.

"Make a left at the next stoplight, take it past the movie theatre and turn left again."

"Got it." His eyes were on the road, but he was smiling. "I was thinking that we should have grabbed some extra slices of cheesecake."

"I know, right?" I laughed. "I was just thinking the same thing. I don't get across the water that often."

"I guess that means we'll have to go back…soon."

I smiled but refrained from responding. Making a decision when I was around Howard was just not a good idea. Around him, my body was in control instead of my brain.

I finished giving him directions and, once he pulled into the parking spot beside my car, he shifted the Navigator into Park and climbed out. Howard moved to the passenger-side door, opened it, and extended a hand to assist me. There went those backflips at the pit of my stomach again. Howard walked beside me to my covered porch. I waited until I had unlocked the door before I turned and looked at him.

"Thanks for bringing me home."

Howard responded with the barest hint of a nod. "It was my pleasure."

I stared up at him, watching the fire dancing around in his eyes that I was certain mirrored my own. I stood, waiting while he stood looking down at me with his fingers interlocked behind his back.

My heart accelerated. I didn't know what else to say. "Thank you, again." Okay, that was stupid.

"Ask me, Dayana," he whispered.

I searched his eyes and asked, "What?"

His gaze was intense. "Ask me to kiss you."

"I—"

"Just say it and I'll give you everything you're wanting," he assured me.

He was just so cocky I couldn't even get the words to form.

Howard flashed a satisfied grin. "How about I help you?" He stepped forward, placing his hands on both side of the door frame, blocking me in. "Day?"

"Yes?"

He touched my mouth, tracing my lips. "You want me to taste you again, don't you?"

I started breathing heavily.

"Either nod your head yes or tell me no."

Before I realized what I was doing, my head moved up and down like a bobble-head doll. Leaning closer, Howard brushed a warm kiss over my lips.

"You want my tongue inside your mouth, exploring and tasting."

It wasn't a question, but I still nodded in a gesture just as desperate as the first one.

"This time I want to hear you say yes." His words were a whisper, almost begging me to say aloud what he wanted to hear. So that he would be able to distinguish between the two; no means no, but yes means hell yeah.

I sighed and shook my head. "Yes, Keim. Please kiss me."

His eyes searched mine. "Now, that's more like it," he whispered against my lips, and then he pulled me into his arms. Bending, he kissed me. His warm lips, the strokes of his tongue, it could have gone on forever and it still wouldn't have been long enough. I could have kissed him all night, but I knew I needed time and distance in order to think clearly.

Reluctantly, I ended the kiss and drew back from the comfort of his arms. I looked up into his eyes, desire burned in their depths so intense it was frightening. I drew a deep, ragged breath and blinked several times before turning away.

"Thanks again," I said.

"Sweet dream, Dayana." Howard stepped aside so I could turn around and open the door. I hurried inside the house before I changed my mind and did something ridiculous like invite him to stay. Once inside, I closed the door and, with my back to the frame, I slid down onto the floor.

There would be nothing sweet about my dreams tonight and that's if I got any sleep at all. Keim Howard made a woman want to beg him to be her baby daddy. Hell, I was seconds away from opening the door and asking him to come inside and show me how it's done. After all he *was* from the Show Me State.

Take a deep breath and calm down.

Yes, that was a good idea. I needed to slow my roll because I was doing it again, allowing my emotions to get in the way.

By the time I had poured myself a glass of wine, my brain was back in control. I shook my head and withdrew a long breath of frustration. There was no way I was going to be swept up in that emotional bullshit again. Searching for love in all the wrong place. It was way too fast and too soon. Nope. I wasn't going to be that girl again. I had come too far to travel down that gopher hole again.

I took another sip from the glass and leaned back on the couch and my thoughts shifted as I reminded myself of the heartache and pain and how far I had come.

It had taken months of meditation and self-reflection to realize I'd wasted enough years searching for someone to fill the hole in my heart left there by my father's years of hurting and disappointing me with false promises and then the men who had all come into my life doing the same, including Dame. All of them left me scarred, feeling sad and empty. But no more. I spent months with a therapist who taught me how to love myself and to believe I was worthy. Sometimes I'd forget and had to remind myself. When I couldn't, Layla was always there to let me know I was smart and beautiful, and I deserved to be loved. I no longer needed a man to make me feel whole. Instead, I wanted someone to complement me. Not save me. I wasn't a little girl waiting for her father to show up on scheduled visits and crying for hours when he did not. And then there was my mother who would stand in the corner, laughing at me as she said, "Girl, you stupid. Ain't no man ever going to love you like me." Nope. I wasn't that lost little girl looking for love and acceptance anymore. This time I wanted more, and I wasn't rushing or settling for anything less.

I opened my eyes, swirled the red liquid around in the glass while I reminisced over the evening. Howard had been a perfect gentleman. There was something about him that was different, almost genuine. He made me want to—

Uh-uh. Don't say.

Yep, I was doing it again. Hoping this time would be different. Only to be hurt and disappointed. I tilted the glass, finished its contents and went upstairs to get ready for bed.

Only time will tell.

19

MEEKS

I was having the best sleep ever when I heard my cell phone ringing. Blindly, I reached over onto the nightstand, grabbed the phone, and silenced the call. I needed to get back to my dream. Unfortunately, whoever was calling didn't care because the phone started ringing again.

Ugh…

I pushed Talk and brought it to my ear. "Hello?"

"Are you awake?" It was my sister.

I groaned, "I am now."

"Oh good," Layla replied, sounding chippers like she had been awake for hours. Unfortunately, she didn't catch the hint that I wanted to go back to my dreams. "I'm just checking to make sure you made it home safely last night."

Yeah right. "Yes, I'm home safe and sound. Now, can I go back to sleep?"

There was a brief pause before she got to the reason for her call. "Is he still there?"

I decided to play dumb. "Is who there?"

"Keim."

Uh-huh. Just as I thought. That wasn't concern I heard in her voice, that was nosy curiosity.

I rolled onto my back. "No, what made you think he

would be here?"

"Well, because..." Layla paused as if she was searching for the right words. I knew better.

"Because you think your sister is a slut." I knew what she was thinking.

"Being a slut has nothing to do with it. That man is gorgeous."

That I couldn't argue. "And because he's gorgeous I need to spread my legs?"

It was her turn to groan impatiently. "No, I'm not saying that. I'm just saying he's gorgeous. The two of you were having such a good time," my sister continued without pausing. "And he *did* take you home."

"He did and then I said goodnight."

I heard her mumble something under her breath. "I hope you didn't blow the man off."

"No, I didn't blow him off. I also didn't *blow* him."

Layla laughed at that one.

"I don't want to rush."

She squealed with excitement. "Does that mean you like him?"

I had to smile at that. Like was an understatement. I liked him a lot. "Yes, I like him."

"Thank goodness. I was so sure you were going to be pissed when you found out we were matchmaking."

This time was an exception, but I knew better than to tell Layla that.

"Please tell me you're going to see him again." She was practically begging.

"I don't know," I replied, stretching my arms over my head.

"What do you mean? He's sexy *and* he's single."

I took a breath to dispel some of the tension in my chest

before saying, "Yes, he is both of those things. He's also military."

"That didn't stop you before."

I rolled onto my side. "Thanks for the reminder, and it's for that reason I don't want to go out with him again. Dating someone you work with is too messy."

"That's because Dame was married. Married men are always messy. Too much drama," she argued.

"Yes, but I have to work with Chief Howard. If it doesn't work out, I still have to work with him."

"His name is Keim," she pointed out as if I didn't already know. "If you stop thinking of him by his rank and instead as a perfect match, the relationship might work out. Just think of all those heated nights." Layla drew a sigh like a smitten teenager. "Day, at least tell me if the man can kiss."

Her words brought memories of last night and a smile to my lips. "Yes, he can kiss but that's—" I had to drag the phone away from my ear at the sound of her earth-shattering scream.

"I knew it. With those lips I knew that man could kiss."

"Really, sis?" I laughed. "Excuse me, but aren't you married?"

"What? I can't live my life vicariously through you?"

I chuckled. "You are hilarious."

"No, I'm just being honest. Keim and Faze have been good friends for a while, and he has nothing but good things to say about him."

"Why hadn't he mentioned him before?"

She laughed. "Would you have listened if he had?"

I chuckled because she did have a point. "He has a daughter."

"So what? She doesn't live with him," Layla was quick to point out especially since I never said I wouldn't date a man with children.

"Maybe not, but..." I began. I'll admit I was looking for excuses. "...but I'm sure she spends a lot of time with her dad." I wasn't sure how I'd feel about sharing again.

"Faze says Keim's a really good father."

Well, at least that was a plus. I couldn't deal with a deadbeat father after growing up with one of my own.

"Faze says he has a great relationship with her mother who's happily married to a doctor so at least you don't have to deal with that angry black woman bullshit."

Thank the Lord for small blessings.

"Day, if you let that man get away, I am going to kick your ass," Layla warned.

"I'm not going to let him get away. If it's meant to be it will be," I managed around a yawn.

"But you have to do something to help the situation. It's not going to just happen on its own," Layla reminded.

I groaned. "I know. I know."

"So, can I plan a barbecue and invite him over?"

"No. No more matchmaking. Let me handle this."

Layla was mumbling again.

"Can you at least let the man know you like him?"

I tossed the covers back over my head. "Trust me, he knows."

Now she was screaming, "Details!"

I giggled. "You know I don't kiss and tell, but I'm sure we'll be going out again. I just need to make sure I keep things in perspective." His good looks and charm were somewhat of a liability.

I heard a rude snort. "What does that mean?"

"It means that I need to make sure I don't cross the line. Dame and I were messy. Almost everyone knew our business, and I almost lost a stripe because of that. I can't let that happen again, especially if I'm ever going to make chief."

She blew a heavy sigh in my ear. "He's single, you're single, and you're overthinking things again. Give the man a chance."

"I'll think about it. Now can I go back to sleep?"

"No. Since you're wake, how about going to Costco with me?"

I groaned. I'd moved to the area to be close to family, but now I remembered why I enjoyed being so far away. "Give me an hour."

"Wonderful. I'll even treat lunch," she offered.

"Oh, hell no. You're taking me out for breakfast. I want waffles."

"You're on."

It was after two, when I made it back home with several bags in my hands. Damn my sister for the temptations. After Costco we ended up at Marshall's where I always found an excuse to buy something. I drew a sigh. Oh well, we only live once.

Kicking off my sandals, I slowly made my way up to my room where I put my bags away and then slipped into a pair of cotton shorts and a matching peach t-shirt. Fall was right around the corner and then it would be back to leggings and sweatshirts. Padding down the hall, I descended the stairs and went into the living room to watch a movie I'd recorded from TV One. I was sipping a glass of iced tea when my cell phone chimed with a text message.

Hey. What are you doing?

I had no idea who it was from. I typed, **Who is this?** It wasn't long before my phone chimed again. I looked down and saw Howard's name and felt my stomach do a somersault. My damn sister. I made myself wait until the commercial break before I texted him back. I didn't want him to think I was anxious.

I'm watching television.

He sure wasn't playing games because he messaged right back.

What're you watching?

I quickly typed out a message. **Chick flick.** And instead of Howard messaging me back, my phone rang.

Deep breaths. You got this.

"Hey."

"Hello, beautiful." Howard's voice sounded lazy, a deep rumble I felt echo down the length of my spine. "You said a chick flick. What does that mean?"

I sighed, leaning back on the couch and crossing my legs. "It means that it's some crazy psycho female movie where the guy cheats on her and she decides payback is in order."

"And do you agree?" His tone demanded honesty.

"Nope. All that drama isn't necessary. I would just leave."

There was a pause. "I hear something in your voice. Bad memories from a past relationship?"

I wanted to lie but figured he would know I wasn't telling the truth.

"Something like that, but who hasn't experienced drama in their life? I'm sure you've dated some crazy chicks in your day."

"Yes, I've dated cray-cray. Tires slashed, breaking into my house."

"Oh damn." I laughed.

"But I've been drama free for a few years now."

"Yep, me too."

"Good. Then we should get along just fine."

I couldn't help it. His words brought a smile to my lips.

"What're you wearing?" he asked.

There go those somersaults again. "A t-shirt and shorts."

"Shorts, huh? I bet you have some pretty legs."

"They're okay." They were better than okay, but I wasn't going to say.

"I'll be the judge of that," he said like he'd read my mind. "Put some shoes on. I'm coming over to pick you up."

"What?" I sputtered. "Where are you taking me?"

"You'll see." There was a pause. "See you in a few."

20

HOWARD

The moment Meeks said she was wearing shorts, there was no way I was not going to see her in them. A man can only handle so much, and my imagination wasn't prepared at all for how good she looked up close and personal. I pulled in front of her townhouse, and Meeks came out wearing shorts that were a respectful length, but they were no less sexy.

Damn…

She had gorgeous legs. They were tone and shapely in all the ways that made me glad I was a man so that I could appreciate the qualities of a beautiful black woman.

"Are you going to tell me where we're going?" she asked as she moved over to the driver's side door to stare down at me.

My eyes drifted over her face slowly, taking in every detail before traveling down to admire her delectable cleavage. "Nope, now get inside."

Meeks leaned inside the window. "What if I don't want to go?"

Leaning forward, I kissed her chin and then couldn't resist nibbling it. "Cutie, if you didn't want to go you wouldn't have locked your front door behind you."

The smirk on her lips said she was impressed. She should be. It took a lot of years to understand women, and

I rarely second guessed the decisions I made.

As she sauntered around my SUV, my eyes clung to every delicious curve that swayed with a melody that was hypnotizing. I had to give it to her. Meeks had one of the fiercest bodies I've seen. She took my breath away. As soon as she was seated, I looked over at her golden-brown thighs.

Lawd have mercy.

Meeks strapped her seatbelt then turned toward me with a raised eyebrow and a mischievous grin. "Okay, let's go."

I chuckled as I pulled away from the townhouse community.

"How's your day been?" I asked because women loved when I showed an interest.

"Good. Relaxing. How about you, Keim?"

I liked the sound of my name coming from her lips.

"I went and took my daughter to lunch. Of course, she wanted to go to the Cheesecake Factory."

" A girl after my own heart."

"Yep, and she was texting on her phone the entire time."

I liked the way Meeks shrugged a slender shoulder before saying, "She's a teenager. That's what girls her age do…text their friends and talk about boys. Just wait until she has a boyfriend."

"She mentioned some little boy that she wants me to meet but I'm not ready for all that. I told her when she turns twenty-one, we'll talk about it."

Meeks chuckled and met my gaze. "Didn't you like girls when you were sixteen?"

"Hell yeah. I came out the womb loving women."

She gave that playful eye roll that did crazy things to my inside. "So, if you came out of the womb loving women, how can you expect your daughter to hold off until she's twenty-one?" Before I could comment, she added with an insightful smirk, "I don't know if you realize but there is this thing called hormones."

I looked at her like she was speaking Chinese. "Yeah, well, she needs to turn hers off for five years."

Meeks turned in the seat, tipping her head to the side as she laughed and said, "You know it doesn't work that way. It sounds like the two of you have a great relationship, especially if she can come to you and tell you she likes a boy."

"Yes, I'd like to say my daughter and I have a great relationship."

"Good. You don't want to ruin that," she said, sitting back on the seat. "When the hormones are in control, there is nothing you can do about that. I started sneaking around and lying to my mother about where I was and who I was with so I could see some light-skinned boy I thought I was in love with."

"And what happened?" I asked even though I had an idea of where this story was going.

"I gave him my virginity and two days later he was dating someone else."

My fingers tightened around the steering wheel. "See, that's the stuff I be talking to her about. I don't want her going through that bullshit."

She shook her head again. "You can't stop it. We all gotta bump our heads and learn from our mistakes. You just need to have your arms open and ready to comfort her when she does."

I thought about what she said as I pulled off the highway at the Oyster Point exit and, within minutes, pulled into the parking garage. What Meeks said was true; unfortunately, I wasn't ready yet to hear it.

"The City Center? What is this place?" she asked, eyes twinkling.

I glanced over at her and grinned. "Shopping, dining, movie theater, you name it."

She looked impressed. I don't know why but I wanted to do everything in my power to keep that sparkle in her eyes.

I parked and walked around and helped her from the SUV. Meeks climbed out and I shut the door and immediately moved beside her and lead the way with a hand at the small of her back. "I figured we could come down here and take an evening stroll. And if you're hungry, there are quite a few places to eat with nice views of the fountain."

"I'm impressed."

"That's what I wanted to hear."

We walked through a metal archway, and when I heard the intake of breath, I knew I had made the right choice. In front of us was a five-acre fountain that was surrounded by restaurants and shops. The City Center district had been the happening spot in the last few years with prime real estate and high-end luxury apartments.

"This is beautiful," Meeks said. She was so childlike and genuine. Was it any wonder I was falling under her spell with every passing second?

"I hoped you would like it." I took her hand and we stepped down and took a seat near the gazebo. I couldn't help but watch the rhythmically sway of her delectable ass.

I had to swallow and take several deep breaths to control an erection. Fuck. It took a moment before I was able to say, "They have events over there near the stage. I come down here sometimes just to listen to the fountain and clear my head."

Lowering her lashes, she murmured, "What in the world would you need to clear your head about? Our jobs are easy."

"I see you have jokes." I liked that she possessed a sense of humor. Meeks laughed, a low, sexy sound that caused a quiver to roll through my body and land right smack at my groin. Fuck.

I still had her hand in mine. We stared at the water. It was a long moment before either of us spoke again.

"What do you think about Virginia so far? You think you're here to stay?"

She met my eyes and nodded. "I like it here. If professionally things work out the way I hope they do, I plan on putting down roots. Maybe buying a house in another year."

I was hoping she'd say that. "I love the area. I've left and came back. Nothing compares to it for me."

Her eyes twinkled. Meeks was sitting so close I could count her eyelashes.

"I'm starting to see why my sister and Faze came back here after he retired from active duty. The area has a lot of the things to do and it's close enough to make a quick weekend trip up to D.C."

"Yep, and with Virginia Beach less than an hour away this is considered one of the hottest vacation spots." I studied her before saying, "I'm about to get personal."

The corner of her mouth twitched.

"Tell me about your last relationship."

21

MEEKS

"Why you ask?" I was curious to know the answer.

"I believe in being a student of the woman I'm trying to get to know." There was an unmistakable twinkle in his eye.

I hesitated, debating whether to tell him about my last on-the-job relationship, but when he looked at me with those dark intense eyes it was hard to resist.

Howard nodded. "I want to learn everything I can about you. That's how I determine if I want to know more."

"A student, huh?"

He nodded and stretched his legs out in front of him. "You're the first woman I've met who's caught my attention in a long time."

I stuttered at his words. "I-I've never had anyone tell me that before."

"Next time you'll get to be the student." He licked his lips. "I can think of quite a few things I can teach you." He was ridiculously handsome and distracting. My insides got all warm.

Howard gestured with a sweep of his hand. "C'mon, cutie pie. Get to talking."

I dragged my left leg up against my chest, rested my chin on my knee, and said, "He was military and married." I expected to see a judgmental look but there was none, so I continued. "They were separated." I was trying to justify my actions. "I put my heart on my sleeve, but his family needed him and eventually he went back home because he owed it to them to try and make it work."

Howard shook his head. "No, he went back home because he wanted to go home. He owed it to himself."

I sighed. Howard was right. I often wondered if Dame had loved me more would he have chosen me over his family.

His eyes were studying me. "May I ask what made him leave in the first place?"

"While he was deployed his wife had an affair with his First Sergeant."

"Oh damn. How'd that turn out?"

"The First Sergeant got demoted and received an Article 15. Dame waited until he caught him off base, after hours, and beat his ass." I shrugged. "It was never reported."

"With every decision there are consequences."

So true, which was why I didn't want to date someone in my unit again. The consequences would be great. "Anyway, he finally found it in his heart to forgive for the sake of the children and went back home."

"Sounds like despite his wife creeping, he loved her."

I shook my head, dismissing the word, love, and yet he was right again.

"How was that for you?" Howard asked and looked completely interested in hearing about my life.

"It was hard at first, but I respected his decision," I grumbled. "I wanted all of him. Not part of him and I knew that I would've had to share him with his family."

"I don't believe in sharing," he muttered, and I felt a thrill of pleasure heating between my thighs.

"Me, either, so I eventually applied for this job and you

know the rest. Okay, so enough about me. What's your story?"

"The last serious relationship I had was with my ex-wife and the same situation. She messed around and I left, but I never went back."

"Did you ever think that maybe you made a mistake?"

"Yes, not long after I moved out, but I was too hurt to forgive or forget." He gave a strangled laugh. "Since then I've dated lots of women but—"

I cocked a brow at him. "Lots?"

He laughed again. "Yes, I've had my fair share." His eyes fell to my mouth. "But no one who's made me want to be a student of her life...until now." The way he was staring at me was so hot and intense that it had all my girlie parts heating up.

Oh boy. I really was in trouble.

22

HOWARD

We stopped talking and sat watching the fountain when I caught her looking at me.

"What?"

Meeks shook her head. "Nothing."

"Don't lie." I swung around on the step and dragged her closer until her legs were straddling mine. "What's on your mind?"

"Just thinking that maybe I like you," she admitted and blushed.

Now she had a brotha smiling. "Is that so?"

"Yes, I would say so."

"I like you too, Dayana." I didn't even wait to find out if it was okay. I kissed her. I figured we already kissed last night so why did I need permission since she literately let me know it was okay. And now that she was feeling a brotha, I had every intention of taking claim of her mouth every chance I could. Dayana moaned and then parted her lips, granting me access, and I explored and took and made sure she knew who was in charge. I gave deep strokes, slow and controlled, and she followed my lead. I learned early that women don't mind being submissive to a man who is confident and has his shit together.

I eased back, but it wasn't easy. I wanted to take things slow and be a gentleman, allow Meeks a chance to get to know me. I knew enough about her already to know I liked everything sitting in front of me. She was smart, beautiful, and competitive. Just the way I liked a woman.

"You hungry?"

She shrugged. "Maybe a little."

I rose, held out my hand, and brought her gently to her feet. "C'mon. Let me introduce you to The Cove."

23

MEEKS

Okay this had to be a dream or something because everything I'd been looking for in a man, Howard possessed—looks, charm, intelligence, and confidence. And he was cocky. Oh, hell yeah and I liked that. It took years of being large and in charge with the Maintenance Group to know he was no pushover, and I liked that in him.

We walked around the fountain and headed over to a restaurant on the other side. This was beyond romantic. And that is rare in the men I dated. The Cove was a sports bar with an outdoor patio that boasted views of the fountain. There was also a large fire pit that was certain to warm up chilly nights. Inside, we were greeted with a long bar and lots of big screen televisions mounted on the walls around the restaurant. There were also two stone fireplaces and lots of intimate tables and chairs. The hostess ushered us to a booth near the windows. Howard took the seat so that his back was to the wall. That protective instinct was such a turn on. Instead of leaning back on the bench in a comfortable stance, he leaned forward with his hands on the table and gazed over at me. I watched his eyes searching my face. He was so damn observant.

"What do you think?"

"I like this," I said as my eyes swept around the room again.

A smile touched his lips. "They have live bands on Fridays. We'll have to come back."

He was already planning our next date. I couldn't help but grin. I didn't want to get ahead of myself, but I was too impressed not to be. The waitress came over and brought menus and two glasses of water. As soon as she left, I reviewed the selections. "What do you recommend?"

"The Baja fish tacos are good. And I love their fried pickles."

"Ooh, I love fried pickles," I cooed.

"And they also make the best fried potato chips."

I'd heard enough. "I'm sold."

He winked and signaled for the waitress. We also ordered iced teas.

Howard relaxed a little on the seat and was back to staring at me. Self-consciously, my eyes wandered over to the different televisions. Sports Center was on.

"Are you going to stare at me the entire time?" Our eyes locked.

"I might," he murmured.

I crossed my legs and willed the throbbing to slow down.

"I like what I see." He took a sip of his iced water, watching me over the rim. "Enough that I want to really get to know you. If you'll allow that."

See what I said about being cocky. I didn't want to come across as being too eager, so I shrugged and shifted my gaze momentarily to the TV behind his head. "Isn't that what we're doing now…getting to know each other?"

His dark, gaze heated my blood. "Yeah, I guess you could say that."

I briefly dragged my gaze away. "Please stop. You're

embarrassing me."

He smiled and changed the subject. "You like sports?" He nodded toward the screen.

I looked up and then shrugged. "It's a seasonal thing for me. I like football and basketball and depending on my mood, I can get into hockey and baseball."

He groaned and looked faintly amused. "Not baseball."

I shrugged. "It's really not that bad once you start to understand the game."

Shifting his gaze up at the sport's highlights, he scowled. "It's too damn slow. I need action."

I just bet you do. "You play ball?" I asked. It was my turn to study him.

Howard looked away from the television and nodded. "I shoot hoops whenever I get a chance."

"So, do I," I said and instantly saw the surprise in his eyes.

"You shoot hoops?" When I nodded, Howard's mouth curved ruefully. I had his full attention. "Are you any good?"

I took a sip from my glass before saying, "I guess you'll have to play me and find out."

"You're on." I saw the challenge gleaming in his eyes. "This I can't wait to see."

I laughed, enjoying our camaraderie. "I guess we'll see." Reaching across the table, I gave him a fist bump. The waitress returned with a bowl of chips and our iced teas. While we dipped them in homemade dressing and munched, the conversation shifted to the NBA. We debated stats and argued about who was the greatest NBA player of all time. I should have known he was going to be a Curry fan. LeBron had my heart and soul.

Just as Howard promised, the food was delicious and

more than enough to fill our bellies. We continued talking and ended up trying the mango beer and ordering another basket of chips. I don't think either of us was ready for the date to end yet. Instead, we walked around the City Center. Howard hooked his arm around my shoulders and pulled me close. When we reached the movie theatre and saw a movie, we both were hyped about starting in ten minutes, Howard bought tickets and we went in and got great reclining seats. I rested my cheek on his chest while he got caught up in the movie. Like I said, we didn't want the date to end. By the time the movie was over, it was after nine and the sun had gone down, but the City Center was lit up like Bourbon Street. Howard took my hand, linking our fingers, and led me back to his SUV. On the drive to my townhouse, I placed my hand on his lap and barely spoke a word. There was no need. I was caught up in the moment and I could tell he was, too.

Howard pulled in the visitor spot in front of my townhouse, got out, and opened the door for me. He was such a gentleman. Holding my hand, he guided me to my front porch and, before I could get my key out, Howard drew me into his arms and brought his lips down over mine. Our lips met abruptly and, like striking a match to presoaked charcoal, an inferno ignited between us.

Howard groaned. The sound was deep and rough and added fuel to the flame. I rested my palms on his broad shoulders and held on to him to steady myself. He parted my lips, deepening the kiss, and I allowed his tongue to slide inside, and mine danced against his. Want and need ricocheted through me and landed right smack between my thighs, leaving me throbbing and aching. His fingers slipped up and down my body, teasing and squeezing gently. My head was spinning, and all I could think about was having this man sinking deep inside me, stroking and teasing me. At this moment there were no military ranks, no core values, nothing but sweet pleasure, and him and me, flexing my hips, pressing my body firmly against his erection. I knew what he wanted as we kissed and sucked at each other's lips. I knew damn well what his body was asking. It was the same thing my body was yearning for. And that's where the problem existed. When I was around him, I couldn't think straight. But I had learned from my past mistakes. This time, I needed to think with my head rather than let my body lead the way.

I drew back and there was a harsh groan. He lowered his hands from the undersides of my breasts to grip my hips and pulled my body back alongside his. We both stood there, breathing heavily, and stared.

He was the first to speak. "Thanks for hanging out with me again."

"Thanks for asking. The City Center is dope." My voice was husky, almost unrecognizable.

We went back to staring and then there was silence. Shifting his position slightly, he tightened his hold. An erection was still there pressed against me. My body ached to feel it. My hands itched to squeeze it. My lips yearned to taste it. And a traitorous whimper escaped my lips.

"Day, I think you need to get inside." His warning was more of a rough growl reverberating from somewhere deep. His eyes were dark, intense, and predatory.

I licked my lips and forced myself to step back away from his grasp. I fumbled in my purse for the keys, got them in my hand, and tried to open the door but, instead, dropped them. My hands were shaking.

"Let me get that for you." Howard reached down for the key ring. As he lowered, his hand traveled down my bare leg and as he rose his fingers traveled upward along the front of my thigh. His hand wasn't where I wanted to feel him but close enough to bring a rush of desire so intense, I jerked away.

Howard put the key in the lock for me and pushed the door open. Leaning forward, he allowed his lips to brush my neck and then my cheek before reaching my ear. My eyes fluttered shut with a sigh.

"Day, I need you to get inside, *now*." There was no mistaking the strain for control on that last word.

Nodding, I stepped away from the warm comfort of his large body and into the house. When I was far enough away to breathe, I turned and forced a painful smile.

"Thanks again," I said then pushed the door shut and turned the lock before I could change my mind. I stood still, waiting, and heard him on the other side breathing. Several moments passed before I heard Howard walk away, followed by the sound of his engine when he finally pulled away.

24

HOWARD

I woke up to loud knocking at my door. Damn. And there I was dreaming about making love to Meeks all night, then waking up in the morning and loving her some more.

After I dropped her off, I had spent the rest of the evening, fighting a serious hard-on. No easy feat. It had been a long time since I'd gone unsatisfied. When I wanted sex, I was able to get it. Yesterday hadn't been the case. And the thought, although painful for my loins, gave me reason to grin.

My life would never be the same.

There was that knocking again. Whoever was at the door was persistent and determined to wake me up. Reaching over, I grabbed my cell phone and glanced down at the screen.

"Damn." I had forgotten to set my alarm and overslept. It was already after six.

Saved by the bell. Or in this case, the doorbell.

I guess I should be thankful that someone had disturbed my dream; otherwise, I'd be still asleep. I slipped on running shorts and stumbled to my front door. I turned the lock and swung it open.

Damn it.

"Good morning."

I frowned with puzzlement to find Giselle standing on my porch. The smile on her face and the eyes that traveled up and down my body signified she liked what she saw. I guess so since I was standing there in shorts and hadn't bothered to put on a t-shirt, so my chest was bare.

"I thought I'd be a good neighbor and bring over breakfast." It was then that I noticed the bag she was waving in her hand and the cup holder.

"Giselle, I—"

She brushed passed me before I had a chance to stop her.

"I brought coffee and soufflés," she explained as she sauntered toward my kitchen as if she owned the place. My eyes slid over her. She was wearing a purple paisley printed dress that molded her slender frame like a second skin. On her feet were the "come-fuck-me" shoes she'd worn the night I'd met her. She tossed a look over her shoulder to ensure I was looking at her shapely ass. I'd be blind not to be. Pleased, Giselle smiled and turned her head, sending her straight ebony mane whipping loose across her shoulders. By the time I made it into the kitchen, she had napkins on the table and soufflés at two place settings.

"Come, have a seat." Giselle pointed to the seat closest to the window and lowered on the chair on the opposite side.

I collapsed in the chair.

"I got you a dark roast with two sugars just the way you like it."

I reached for the Styrofoam mug and took a sip. "You remembered."

"I don't forget much. Especially when it's someone I'm interested in getting to know better," she purred.

I wasn't sure how to respond so I took another sip

instead.

"I thought you were going to call me?" Her expression was sheepish.

Damn, this was why I hated dating civilians. Too needy. Of no fault of her own, I started dating her the week before I met the woman, I intended to move heaven and earth to claim as my own. I busied myself by opening the small box that
contained the soufflé. "I've been preoccupied."

Giselle brought the cup to her lips and her sultry hazel eyes were fixed on me as she said, "Too occupied to call me after tasting a sample of what I have to offer."

She slipped the plastic fork into her mouth and licked it seductively. Thoughts of her down on her knees swallowing me deep came rushing back. She was good. *Really* good. But I needed more than someone to pass the time. Now that I'd met Dayana, I knew what that more was.

I nodded. "I like you, but I'm looking for more than sex."

"Me too, so what's the problem?" Giselle asked waving dismissively. "Remember you're the one who told me you weren't looking for a relationship." She pointed a finger as she reminded me.

"I'm not or at least I wasn't until... all that changed. Look. You are a beautiful woman, but I've met someone."

Her eyes widened with surprise or maybe disappointment. "And what does that mean for you and me?"

Why was she making this so hard? "It means there is no us. I'm sorry."

"I'm not good enough for you." It wasn't a question. "You didn't even give us a chance." She was pouting.

"It wasn't intentional," I said, trying to let her down

easy. I didn't know what else there was to say. I discovered I no longer wanted the night clubs, hanging out with my boys, meeting random chicks, and having brief relationships. I honest to God wanted more.

"Keim, you're making a terrible mistake," Giselle said as though it was the worse decision she could ever imagine. "When you realize it, please come and see me. I'm sure I can be all the woman you need."

I doubted it, but I wasn't going to say that to her. Instead I ate the soufflé, allowing silence to stretch between us. Tension crackled as the meaning of what I said hit her fully. Her eyes met mine, momentarily startled by the realization that I wasn't interested in her. I was probably the first man to ever turn her down.

Giselle tilted her head to the side, eyes narrowed, glittering with poorly suppressed rage. She shrugged and tried to save some pride. "Well, it's your loss, not mine."

I frowned. Maybe so, but I wasn't about to admit that. "I'm going to go and take a shower. Thank you so much for breakfast. I'll reimburse you for your time and trouble." I stood and look down, my eyes clashing with hers.

She smiled and brought the Styrofoam coffee cup to her lips. "Since I paid for it, can I at least finish my breakfast before I leave?"

As much as I wanted to tell her to get the hell out, I figured it was the least I could do considering she'd saved me from being inexcusably late to work. "Of course. Take your time. Just make sure to lock the front door on your way out," I said without looking back at her. I carried the coffee to my room, walked into the ensuite, and started the water. I decided to lock the bathroom door behind me just in case Giselle had ideas and decided to join me. I shook my head. There was no point in wasting her time when I already had my mind made up.

I wanted Meeks and that feeling was not going away.

I stripped out of my shorts and climbed inside the shower. Hot water beat down on my body as the dream replayed in my mind of Meeks in my bed, withering around on the sheets beneath me. I dipped my head under the spray of water and smiled. We had something remarkable that wasn't going away. The good thing was that she was finally starting to realize that as well. I lathered then wrapped my fingers around my cock, stroking all the way to the head and back again. My hand was nice and soapy, so my fingers slid back and forth in a rhythm that had me fantasizing about how snug Meeks had felt surrounding me. For a moment I forgot the sex had only been a dream because the arousal and the desire were real and had me hard as a brick.

Fuck.

I needed to see her. She was more than just beautiful to look at, she had a big heart. Excitement built in my gut and I couldn't wait to meet her for lunch. I might even suggest going back to her townhouse for a kiss since public display of affection in uniform was frowned upon. I sighed and caught myself chuckling. I didn't want Meeks to think putting my lips on her was all I was after. I would have to make sure to show her how important she had become every chance I got.

Grinning, I stepped out the shower and reached for a thick bath towel. I wrapped it around me, opened the door, and walked into my bedroom.

What the –

Giselle was lying on her side in my bed, giving me a view of her naked breasts.

"Keim," she purred with feline seduction.

"What are you doing in my bed?" I croaked at her daring act.

"You invited me to take a shower." Her eyes were sparkling with anticipation.

"No, I didn't."

She chuckled with amusement, and shifted, letting the 800-count sheet slide away from covering her private gem. "Of course, you did. Why else would you have mentioned it?"

I swallowed hard, looking every bit like a horny man, especially when my dick sprung to life beneath the towel. I didn't even respond because I could see where she might have gotten that impression. It had been stupid of me for not getting rid of her before I had disappeared to take a shower.

"When I found the door locked..." she paused with a shrug of her slender shoulders. "I figured you wanted me waiting out here instead."

"Look, Giselle, I'm sorry that I gave you the impression I wanted you waiting in my bed, but I didn't, and I don't, so please get dressed."

"I'd rather you come over here and make love to me," she said softly, a smile glazing her lips. Slowly, she brought her hand down to stroke the dark curls at the apex between her thighs.

Giselle was a beautiful woman, so naturally my body responded just the way she wanted. Back in the day I would have been all over her despite having another female in my life. But now that I've met Meeks, I wasn't about to fuck that up.

Giselle slid off the bed. Her hair was brushing against her breasts, and my dick got harder just that fast. She came close to me, breasts bouncing, hips swaying. "You know you want me," she said with a confident smirk, setting off my temper even more.

"Whether or not I want you is irrelevant," I told her, trying not to make eye contact with anything below her shoulders. "I already told you I'm involved with someone else."

"Who? Meeks?"

How the hell…

Giselle gave a feminine shrug. "While you were in the shower, your phone rang."

"So now you're answering my phone." I sighed and moved mechanically across the room to the nightstand and picked it up.

"No, but I saw her name and figured since you'd saved her number, she must be someone you're seeing." She planted a hand to her small waist. "Especially when I realized you saved her contact information as *Meeks Wifey Potential*." There was no mistaking the bitterness in her voice.

I didn't deny her claim. "She's special to me."

Giselle's expression flickered with annoyance. "And what about me? I could be special if you'd given us a chance."

I frowned. "Trust me, if I wanted a relationship with you, I would have already claimed you as mine."

She stepped toward me, closing the short distance I tried to impose on her. I attempted to hold her rigidly at arm's length. Caught off guard, I stepped back, but her hand had already yanked the bath towel from around my waist.

When Giselle looked down at my erection her eyes flickered with excitement. "Your mouth says one thing, but your body is telling a completely different story." Her soft laughter irritated me.

"I'm human, not dead," I said to distract myself.

"You're a gorgeous woman. I doubt very few men resist you."

"Actually, none have."

"Well, I guess that makes me the first." I stepped away and moved over to my dresser. I opened the top drawer and removed a pair of boxer briefs and slipped them on before turning to face her.

"Nice view," she murmured. There was wicked pleasure in her eyes.

I growled an obscenity. "Giselle, I'm trying to be a gentleman, but you need to leave."

She started toward me. "I never asked you to be a gentleman. Hell, in fact, I like it a little rough from time to time."

I dragged a frustrated hand down the length of my face. "I asked you to leave. If I have to ask you again, I'm going to call the police, and have you removed." I've seen it before, being caught alone with a woman at the wrong time and she's crying wolf. Hell no. My career and my future were just too important for that.

Giselle stopped walking and laughed. "You can't be serious. You're going to give up all of this?" she said with a sweep of her hand.

"Yes, because what I've found is worth it." I pointed toward the bathroom. "Now, please, get dressed and get out."

"You'll regret this," she muttered angrily. Saying nothing, I watched as she snatched up her clothes and stormed toward the bathroom. The door slammed behind her.

This time I kept my eye on her until she was in her car and pulling down the driveway.

25

MEEKS

I was on my way to work when I gave Howard a call, but it went to voicemail. A moment of insecurity rolled down my spine, but I pushed it away and composed a quick text message. "Hey you... Just wanted to say good morning and I'm thinking about you." I hit Send before I could change my mind.

As I drove toward the Air Force Base, it felt strange putting my thoughts out there like that, but I knew I needed to get over that feeling and just be me. I'd met a man who wasn't trying to change me, and I liked that. Howard made me feel comfortable and alive, and I needed to go with the flow, not try to rush into anything or make it more than it was. A part of me felt ready to open up a little more and let go of some of the resistance. I couldn't believe I was tempted by what he was suggesting.

Knocking boots with a man in uniform again.

I smiled wickedly at the thought. Howard made me crave things I'd never imagined. It felt good and, despite my initial apprehensions, I wanted this feeling to last. When I was around him, I could barely breathe. To hell with my stupid rules and everything else. Last night I had lost myself completely, and I would like to blame it on being lonely and horny, but I knew it was him. I wanted to dive in and focus on my own pleasures with a man that made me feel like a woman. Howard had caressed and kissed me in ways no other man had, and I wanted more.

Layla had already called this morning.

"Day, I can hear all that happiness in your voice."

I drew in a breath and, I kid you not, I exhaled. It did feel good to know I had something that truly felt genuine. No baby mama drama or checking his phone all night. Nope. When we were together, it was all about him and me.

I made it into the office. Our unit assemble weekend was ahead, so on Saturday all the participating members would be onsite for two days. It would be busy, and I probably wouldn't get to see Howard much the next few days, but he was going to be just as busy getting his unit ready for the upcoming exercise.

When I walked in, Senior Master Sergeant Simone Carlson from the Logistics Readiness Squadron was standing in front of the copier. She worked in the Installation Deployment Readiness Cell in the office next door to Sergeant Bailey.

"Good morning," she said, tossing a strand of blonde hair from her face.

"Carlson, good morning. What time's the ATSO rodeo?" The rodeo provided Airmen with in-depth instruction on warfare survival and operational skills ranging from ordnance training to self-aid. The goal was to process the entire wing through the training each month for the next six months so that we were mission ready and fit to fight.

"It begins at thirteen hundred on Saturday and all day on Sunday."

"Do we have anyone from the FSS on the list?"

Her green eyes sparkled as she nodded. "Anyone scheduled to deploy in the next six months is scheduled to attend this weekend. I sent an email to the distro with the list of names this morning. I will also be briefing to the commanders at Wing Staff meeting this morning."

"I'll take a look at the email and get the word out," I said and began walking backwards toward my office.

"I'd appreciate it." She waved and a three-carat diamond ring glittered. "I'll see you later."

Back in my office, I finalized the unit training schedule for the upcoming weekend. It was productive. I made calls. My team and I prepared reports and team assignments. Most of the morning had passed before Howard texted me a thinking-about-you text that made me smile. He also mentioned that he had several suspensions, so he wouldn't be able to pick me up so we could spend lunch together. I had already expected as much and had brought a salad. I was then so wrapped up in my day I barely had time to think.

I went to Wing Staff and briefed on the upcoming exercise. I reported to Lieutenant Colonel Tennison, the maintenance commander, that his unit was now in the green for deployment folders and added that Chief Howard and the UDM had done everything to get his people ready. It took everything I had to maintain my military bearing when I mentioned Howard's name.

By the time I returned to the office, everyone had already left for lunch. A beautiful, slender woman was standing in the lobby. She looked lost.

"Hi, may I help you?" I stepped over to assist her.

Her thick, dark lashes lifted to reveal hazel-colored eyes. "Hi, can I get my CAC card unlocked here?" she asked in a raspy voice.

Smiling, I shook my head. "I'm sorry, we don't do that here anymore. You have to go to the DEERS office." They were the issuers of common access cards and military IDs.

She scowled. "Do you have any idea how long those lines are in the afternoon? Half the day will be over by the time I get done."

My brow rose. "Yes, I know, but this office stopped doing them last fiscal year. It was too expensive, so contractors handle it now."

"That's too bad." She waved a pink manicured hand. "I was supposed to have lunch with my boyfriend today and I was hoping I had time to do both."

"I'm sorry. Do you know where building 113 is?"

The woman's lips twisted into a scowl as she nodded. "Yes, I know. Thanks for your help." She was already reaching for her phone as I was walking toward my office, but when I overheard her phone call, I stopped in my tracks.

"Keim, baby. I'm going to have to see you later. I need to go get my CAC unlocked. How about I drop by your office with lunch after I'm done?"

I clutched my neck as if I were wearing pearls. She was giggling as she walked out of the room. Once I was over the initial shock, I turned and stared in the directions she had disappeared before going into my office. What were the chances that there were two men named Keim? I told myself not to get upset but next thing I knew I was picking up the phone and calling Howard. When I didn't get an answer, I felt even more suspicious.

Quit it. The man told you he had a lot of work to do today.

Then why did that bitch say otherwise? I was supposed to be working on position moves and yet all I could think about was Howard making love to her, pressing his warm, sensual mouth against her skinny ass lips.

Who the hell was she?

I looked up to see Rein coming to my door and forced

myself to put my trust issues aside while I focused on her. "What's happening, chica?" I said. I know that sounded fake, but I couldn't help it.

"Hello. I thought I'd make my rounds before the busy weekend. Just as a reminder, we'll need to process payroll early on Monday."

"No problem." I forced myself to act normal. No point in wasting time dwelling on something I couldn't control. I wasted enough years being disappointed by first my father and lastly, Dame. "How you been?"

She was all grins. "I met someone on this dating site called Plenty of Singles."

"Dating site? Girl, bye," I said with a rude snort. "Been there. Done that. Nothing but a bunch of cheating ass husbands looking for their next hook up." After the last fool stood me up, I'd had enough.

"Not this time. Matthew is fine and so sweet. I've been to his apartment. No wife living there. One better, he's never been married and doesn't have any children."

"That's good. I'm so happy for you." Those men were rare.

She smiled wickedly at my response. "Girl, I wore that dress and worked it."

We both started laughing so loud I pressed my index finger to my lips to signal we needed to be quiet.

Rein sobered and leaned in, practically speaking in a whisper. "I also came by because I heard a rumor that you're dating Chief Howard."

Wow. Word sure did travel fast. Despite that I was the topic of discussion I knew I was blushing. "Yeah...it's something like that," I whispered back.

"Alright now. He is a good guy. I've known him for quite a few years," she said with a knowing grin.

My brow rose with curiosity. I hoped it wasn't too

obvious. "Really? He says he's single, but I don't know... You know how men are."

Rein immediately shook her head. "Not Howard. He's as good as they get. He doesn't play games. Always straight up
with women. And he doesn't make promises he can't keep."

"You sound like you know from experience," I said with a tone urging her to continue.

"I know because he's dated friends of mine. He's a good guy." She shrugged. "Women get caught up, but he's waiting for the right one."

"Does he date anyone now on base?" I couldn't just bring myself to ask her.

Rein regarded me thoughtful before saying, "Not that I know of. I don't think he would have let anyone know he was interested in you if he was seeing anyone else. It just isn't his style."

It made me feel good to hear her say that. "I like him. He's funny, and really down to earth."

"That he is. What you see is what you get. That's what everyone loves about him."

I nodded. He was popular... and he was single. I would love to be the woman who was responsible for changing his status.

Since when? I thought you weren't interested in a relationship with a man in uniform.

I pushed that annoying reminder from my thoughts and noticed Rein's expression grow serious. Leaning in close, she said softly, "My advice is to take it slow and watch the signs. If you can get your claws into Howard, then you are a lucky woman. But I've seen many who have tried and failed, so just be true to yourself."

In the short time, I've known Rein, we had become

friends. She was right. Howard hadn't made me any promises. In fact, I was the one who had been resistant to something deeper because of my hang ups with men in uniform. Just because I have issues with trust, the last thing I wanted was to come across like a jealous woman. Nevertheless, Mama didn't raise no fool. I wasn't crazy. That chick had been on the phone with Keim. *My Keim*. I would wait and watch the signs. The truth would eventually reveal itself.

Fool me once, shame on you.

Fool me twice, shame on me.

My days of playing boo-boo the fool was over. I was no longer willing to play games in a relationship. Eventually I wanted a husband and children, and I would never find that wasting time with men who could never offer me more than a good time. But I had a good feeling about Howard even after the woman coming into the office wanting to unlock her common access card. But maybe I was jumping ahead and once again moving too fast. Therefore, I needed to take Rein's advice and take things slow.

After she left, I went back to work. Probably went through three pots of coffee. I finally finished a dozen duty status moves and updated the discharge spreadsheet that the commander requested for 0800. The rest of my staff had gone home, and I decided to stay and get a head start on tomorrow. Anything was better than going home with nothing to do but think about Howard.

I raised my arms over my head and stretched. When my eyes shift to the clock, my body stiffened. *Shit*. It was after six and we had a commander's call in the morning. I had enough work to keep me busy the rest of the night, but I had a full day tomorrow so I might as well go home and get some rest. I began straightening my space when my cell phone rang. I reached for it.

"Hello?"

"Hey, babe," he greeted, the husky tone of his voice flowed heat into my ear.

"Busy day?" I asked. Part of me was so excited to hear from him. The other half was feeling insecure.

"Very busy, trying to get everyone scheduled for that damn ATSO, but I'm getting ready to leave now."

"Me, too," I replied softly.

There was a pause. "How about I come take you home? We can leave your car here and I can bring you back in the morning."

"Okay." I couldn't pass up an offer like that and felt a shiver of anticipation at seeing him again.

"I'll be their shortly, Day."

I loved the way Howard said my name.

I gathered my things and rushed to the restroom for a quick assessment. Worry lines were around my mouth and eyes, but otherwise I looked good.

I was locking the side exit when he pulled into the parking lot. As soon as I saw his smiling face, my nipples grew hard with memories. He was so damn gorgeous.

By the time I made it to the car, Howard already had the door open.

He reached down for my backpack and then leaned forward, pressing his lips to mine. It felt so right. I climbed inside the vehicle and he shut the door before he moved his large frame around the car to his seat. He walked with so much swag I couldn't take my eyes off him.

As soon as Howard put the vehicle in gear, he reached over and placed my hand on top of his knees. I arched a brow. He shrugged.

"I like when you touch me. Especially after a long day."

I licked my lips and there was a long sigh at the end of his sentence. I knew exactly how he felt because I felt it too.

"Sorry, I couldn't have lunch with you today. My afternoon has been brutal."

At the mention of lunch, I remembered my encounter this afternoon. "Did anyone bring you something to eat?" I asked and then waited.

26

HOWARD

I almost drove through a red light at her question. Quickly, I pressed down hard on the brake and my tires squealed at the intersection just as a red truck sped past in a blur. Even though her seatbelt was strapped, I instinctively drew a protective arm straight out in front of Meeks just as she jerked forward.

"My bad. Sorry about that." I studied her intensely, making sure she was all right.

She looked at me with a hand pressed against her chest. "You okay?" she asked, breathing heavy.

"Here I am worried about you, and you're worried about me." I couldn't resist a grin. "I'm sorry. I didn't realize the light had changed."

Meeks shrugged. "It's all good. No one's hurt. Your vehicle is still intact."

I grinned. "Yes, it is." I heard a horn blow. I looked up and the light was green. I pressed on the gas and started driving again. "I believe the problem I'm having with driving is with you."

"Me?" she said innocently. "Why me?"

"It's not often that I have a beautiful woman riding beside me." I winked and noticed she was blushing. "I'm starving. And the answer to your question…no, I never got around to having lunch. So, I'm starve. You want to stop and get something quick like Chick Fil-A?"

I noticed the puzzled look before her eyes brightened and her lips curled upward to say, "That sounds wonderful."

I headed toward the area of the city where I lived, which was within minutes to the City Center. The restaurants were nicer, and it offered more shopping. Most importantly, I wanted to show her my house. Although a part of me wondered if Giselle would pop up again.

After the shower incident, she showed up at my office with lunch. She waltzed in there like she was the president of the Key Spouse program, like she belonged. As soon as I saw her sauntering my way with all my young Airmen staring at her like she was a movie star, I got up from my chair and closed the door behind her.

"Giselle, what are you doing here?"

She made her way over to where I was standing. "I brought a peace offering." She held up the bag of food and gave me a knowing smile. "I figured a foot-long roast beef and Swiss was a good way to start."

"Thank you." I took the bag from her proffered hand. "Now I would appreciate it if you'd respect my wishes and not come by here again."

"I'm sorry you feel that way." Her eyes studied me. "I hope Senior Master Sergeant Dayana Meeks realizes how lucky she is."

I shook my head. "I don't know what you think you know, but my—"

"She's not even that cute." Giselle had the nerve to laugh.

I held the bag out to her. "Here. Please, take your food and leave. If you come back, I'm going to report you for harassment. I think I heard you already had one complaint from a Lieutenant Miles."

Her expression dropped. "That was a misunderstanding,"
Her voice wasn't anywhere near as confident as before.

"Really? And what's this…another misunderstanding?" I put the bag in her hand, walked over, and pulled my door open. "You have a nice day."

Giselle tilted her chin upward in a stiff and primp manner, but I already knew better. As she walked towards the door, she stopped abruptly, turned toward me, then dropped the bag of food in the trash before she rolled her eyes and departed.

I felt sorry for the man who ended up with her.

I pushed Giselle from my mind and focused on the amazing woman beside me. We sat in a booth in the corner of the restaurant, talking and laughing until we were yawning, and our eyes were droopy. Neither of us, however, wanted to cut our time together short. It was something I hadn't done in a long time, so I knew it was a good sign. Because I didn't care what time it was or that I would be paying for the shit in the morning when it was time to report at 0600 for commander's call.

"I think we need to get out of here so they can lock up." Meeks was looking out the corner of her eyes. Two of the staff were mopping the floors and changing the trash.

"You up for a ride?" I asked, then slurped down the last swallow of my chocolate milkshake.

She didn't even hesitate. "Sure, where to?"

"I'd like to show you how I live."

I watched her expression. If there was any hesitation, I would pull the plug on the idea and wait. That meant it was too soon. Instead her eyes lit up with a smile.

"I would love to see where you live. But don't be upset if I fall asleep on you when you get me over there," she added with a wink I felt warm my loins.

"No problem. My bed is big enough for the two of us."

On the drive over, I tried to contain the excitement. I was bringing Meeks to see my place. Damn, just think if Rein hadn't told me Meeks was related to Faison. I would have missed out on this golden opportunity sitting beside me.

"I still find it hard to believe you're a homeowner," she said.

I tore my eyes away from the road to glance over at her. "I've always wanted a home, even when I was a teenager."

"Really?"

I nodded. "Yep, my parents taught me why pay someone else's mortgage when you can pay your own."

"Smart parents."

"The first several years of my career I was moving around and deploying too much to think about buying a house. But after the divorce and I moved back to the east coast, I knew I needed a stable home for my daughter."

She was staring at me. "You really are a good father."

"I try to be, but Ava is getting older. So far, being a father has been easy, but I know all that is about to change now that she's in high school."

"I have confidence that you will handle it just fine." Meeks reached over and squeezed my thigh affectionately. It was a small gesture, but it had a huge effect on my libido.

At the corner, I made a right turn and passed Christopher Newport University. "My realtor took me out seeing houses for four weeks before I finally found a place that felt like me."

"How long have you owned your house?"

"For about three years now. It's still a work in progress, but I feel I have thirty years to get it together."

She laughed. "Yes, you do."

I turned into the subdivision and immediately felt a sense of pride. I had moved into an established neighborhood with lush yards and mature trees. Houses were custom built with federal roofs, large porches, and some with all brick frames. "Most of my neighbors had been here for decades, raised their kids, and now enjoying their grandchildren. The good thing is they welcomed a brotha with open arms and casseroles."

Meeks laughed as she stared out her window. "Very nice."

"Yeah, I got pretty lucky to move in this neighborhood. They rarely have a house on the market, and when they do there's a contract on it by the end of the week."

"Really?"

"My house went on the market on a Sunday. My realtor called and I met her out here at 0800. We had a contract on it before noon." I followed the road around and pulled onto my driveway in front of a three-car garage, then killed the engine.

"This is pretty," Meeks said, and by the time I climbed out and made it around to open her door, she was already out the vehicle and walking up the sidewalk toward the house.

"Well, what are you waiting for? Open the door so I can see."

Laughing, I moved up to the door and turned the lock. "After you, beautiful."

27

MEEKS

I'm an HGTV House Hunter's junky, so imagine my excitement about seeing Howard's house. There was absolutely nothing cookie cutter about the neighborhood. His house was on a huge lot with wonderful curb appeal and a wide porch. The door opened to a living room with vaulted ceilings, followed by a gourmet kitchen with granite counters, stainless steel appliances, and beautiful wood cabinets. Not that builder grade material. What made me gasp was the adjoining screened-in porch with high ceilings that added a dramatic feel to the room. My eyes shifted to a wooden swing hanging from a chain bolted to the covered porch.

I walked over and took a seat. "I always wanted one of these. I had fantasies as a girl growing up, going out after dark, and swinging while the rest of the world was asleep." There was a soft breeze, so the evening couldn't have been any better if I'd planned it myself. "My grandparents used to have one of these on their porch."

"So did mine." Howard stood in the doorway arms folded, staring at me with amusement dancing in his eyes.

I lifted my feet from the floor, allowing the swing to sway back and forth. "Southern porches are made for swings, rocking chairs, and sweet tea."

"Would you like a glass?"

"Absolutely," I replied with a laugh.

Howard chuckled and moved inside. While he was gone, I gazed out into the large, privacy-fenced backyard. There was an outdoor kitchen with a huge barbecue grill, a gazebo, and an in-ground swimming pool. The space was surrounded by lounge furniture and had been designed for outdoor entertainment.

"It's probably not how grandma used to make it," Howard said as he stepped out onto the porch. "But it will definitely satisfy a sweet tooth." He handed me one of two tall glasses, then took the seat beside me.

I took a sip and was surprised. "Mmm, this is good. Did you make this?"

"If pouring a glass of Bojangles's sweet tea into a glass counts, then yes, I made it." He gave me a playful look and we both exploded with laughter.

He stretched his long legs out in front of him and used them to rock the swing. We both sipped and stared out into the floodlight-lit yard.

"You have the perfect backyard for entertaining guests."

"Yep, that's what all my boys say, which is why I'm hosting a promotion party for Chief Gage Taylor."

"He just made chief?"

He shook his head. "No, he just made command chief."

"Wow. That's huge."

He nodded and I could see the pride in his eyes. "Yes, it is, which is why I am hosting a party Labor Day weekend." He clasped his free hand with mine. "I would love for you to come."

"I would like that very much." I took another sip, then there was a long pause before I sighed and said, "I could stay right here forever."

Howard looked over, smiling with perfect white teeth and a sexy smirk on his lips that sent a tingle through my body. "Forever, huh?" he nodded knowingly. "You know we can make that happen." He laughed and I laughed. It felt good, then we grew quiet and went back to sipping and staring out into the yard.

"Every time I get a moment to sit out here, I clear my head of the daily bullshit, reflect, and thank God for everything He has given me," he said with a sweep of his hand. "Once I retire, this is what I see, sitting out my back porch, watching the sunset, sipping iced tea with my wife."

His words caused my head to turn, and the desire in his eyes caused that tingle to zip through my body and settle between my thighs. Howard was studying my face as he nodded. "Yep, the future gets more promising with each passing day." There was so much meaning behind his words. That and the intensity in his eyes was so overwhelming I looked away, but I could still feel his gaze zeroing in on me. It took everything I had not to look back.

I leaned my head on his comfortable shoulder. Howard draped an arm across the back of the swing. We rocked back and forth while finishing our iced tea. The silence between us didn't last.

"I remember when I was ten, I would sleep out on the back porch," he said.

"Where was this?"

"Gulfport, Mississippi. It used to be so hot, and back then there were only window air condition units." Howard laughed. "My grandmother couldn't afford to have that thing running all day, so in the evening when it was cooler, we would open windows and turn on the fans." His arm shifted, drawing me closer to him. "To me, it was still too hot, so I would come out onto the porch with my pillow and blanket and sleep on the swing."

"That's sounds like a lullaby sleep."

"It would have been if the porch had been screened in. Those mosquitos would tear my ass up."

We laughed until we grew silent again. Howard brought my hand to his. His warm, soft lips brushing against my nipples was enough to make my girly parts yearn for the same attention.

"I can tell I'm not the only one who isn't in a rush to start the UTA weekend. How about we curl up together in my big chair and watch a movie?"

"Sure but, like I said, I won't promise how long I can keep my eyes open."

"Neither can I, but I'll get to hold you in my arms while we sleep," he said and winked. "I'll make sure you get home in the morning with plenty of time to change."

"Okay."

He rose and scooped me up in his arms effortlessly and carried me into the house. We left our empty glasses on the counter and moved into the living room where he lowered me to my feet. "Go ahead and make yourself at home."

Howard removed his ABU jacket, and I admired the outline of his chiseled torso nestled beneath the bland military-issued brown t-shirt. There was absolutely nothing boring about what I was looking at; instead, it was long rock-hard muscles and large arms that were so dark they looked dipped in chocolate. I took a seat beside him on the couch and unlaced my boots. He toed his off and carried both pairs over near the front door. Loosely laced, and ready for an immediately call to duty. I also removed my top. He had taken a seat on an oversized recliner and had reached for the remote control.

"Have you seen *Acrimony*?" he asked.

"No, but I heard it's good."

"I guess we're about to find out." He said and pointed

the remote at the large screen television, pressed a button, then looked over and caught me staring. "C'mere, beautiful."

I bit my lower lip and walked over. The moment I was close enough, Howard dragged me down on the chair across his lap and reclined the chair, lifting his feet off the floor. His hot skin next to mine. He pulled me closer to him so that I was lying on my side. I leaned my head on his chest and relaxed as we watched the movie. I was such a fan of Taraji P. Henson, but no matter how much I tried to fight it, I dozed off. I felt him tighten his hold on me and I nestled closer.

"Day, baby, let's go get in the bed," I heard him say. I wasn't sure if I was dreaming or not, but it was Howard's voice.

"Okay," I moaned and then felt myself being lifted and carried again. I wrapped my arms around his middle and he leaned in and planted kisses to my forehead and cheek. Within minutes I felt myself being lowered onto the bed. I drifted back to sleep with Howard's strong arms wrapped around me.

During the high point of a delicious dream, I had to pee. That was the only reason why I left the comfort of his arms. I slid out from beside Howard and padded in the direction that I thought the bathroom would be. I yawned and raised my arm, sniffing my armpit. Goodness, that smell was real. I noticed that a set of fresh towels had been laid out on top of the sink and a brand-new toothbrush. My heart fluttered. That man was so full of surprises.

I decided to take a shower. I pulled off the rest of my uniform, hopped under the spray of the hot water, and drew a sigh. It felt amazing, but as the water beat down against my breasts, they grew hard and aroused with thoughts of Howard. I was crazy over everything about him except the questions I had about him and that woman. But he wasn't with her tonight. He was with me. I was done trying to resist him. I responded to him in every way and there was no denying that no matter how much I tried.

The water had grown cold. I climbed out and wrapped in the towel. I had no plans of putting my musty t-shirt back on. I was sure Howard had a clean one I could wear as a night dress. I gathered my clothes and turned off the light before I stepped out the room so I wouldn't disturb him. I padded barefoot across the room and over to a chair where I saw a pile of clothes. I reached for a t-shirt and brought it to my nose.

"Ewww..." It smelled worse than mine.

"Looking for something?"

Startled, I dropped the shirt and pressed a palm to my chest. "I thought you were sleep."

"I was until I realized I was lying in bed alone."

I noticed his eyes weren't on my face. I had lost my grip on the bath towel. It was now at my waist. My breasts were exposed. I stood still, barely breathing, my blood boiling by the desire in his eyes. I couldn't stop staring at him; his gaze scorched with need as his eyes focused on my nipples. Then he lifted his hand and crooked his finger, signaling for me to move closer. I swallowed hard and walked slowly over to the bed.

"You have incredible breasts." He slid across the bed until his feet were on the floor. I stood between his legs, and his lips were leveled with my beating heart. But it wasn't my heart he was interested in. For endless moments he didn't move. He just stared at my breasts with hunger blazing in his eyes as if waiting for permission or protest. When he received neither, he leaned forward and took one nipple between his lips. I inhaled as heat shot through me. I forgot about my rules or resisting; if anything, I was wondering what had taken him so long. I arched towards him, instinctively seeking more. His tongue rolled my nipple then sucked it deep into his mouth.

"Fuck."

He tugged and pulled, using his teeth and the flat of his tongue to stroke and ignite a fire. I cried out again, but this time nothing came out. Once again, he was showing me better than he could tell me. When Howard finally lifted his head, my breathing was unsteady. I followed his gaze on my nipple, now shiny and wet from the sensation of his mouth. Then he lifted his eyes to mine.

"Yes or no?" His voice was deep, almost husky. I nodded my head, unable to speak, my body a mass of sensation. With a satisfied smile that was purely male, Howard lifted me up in his arms and onto the bed. He rolled me on to my back, our bodies touching, then lowered his head to my other nipple which underwent the same treatment while his fingers focused on the other. I writhed and arched overcome by the pleasure he was creating inside me.

He continued his relentless assault on my breasts, his free hand sliding up my back and teasing. I'm not sure when the towel had fallen away, but I was lying there naked as the day I was born. I quivered and my flesh heated. Howard slid down on the bed, kissing a path along my body until he reached the most intimate part of me. I had been wet since the moment I'd stepped out the shower.

"Keim…" I tensed with surprise as I felt his mouth touching me with no barrier. I tried to push him away, but he gave a soft laugh and held my thighs apart as he swept over me with his tongue. I shuddered.

"I want to taste every inch of you, baby. Every single

inch."

"Please..." I cried, which turned into a gasp when Howard used his tongue to caress my clit. Desire bubbled through my veins and settled at my center. I was sensitive down there and thought I'd explode.

"Fuck, you taste good." He pushed my legs further apart.

He used his lips to suck and his teeth to nibble until I was writhing and moaning. So damn good. I never felt so close to anyone as I did Howard at this moment. He teased me to the point of coming, then drew back. I cried out with frustration.

Howard laughed softly and whispered, "Patience, baby. I want to be inside you when you come." He lifted his head and slid up the bed and covered me with his powerful warm body. I gazed at him, dazed, unable to look away.

"No more rules about not dating men in uniform or a man you work with," he said softly, his dark eyes burning into mine as he used his fingers where his mouth had been. "I am both of those things. I'm also a man who wants to explore every part of your mind and body until I know you intimately."

Frantically, I dragged the t-shirt over his head. He had a fascinating tattoo of a serpent that wrapped around his broad chest with spirals and circles on his upper arm and over his shoulder. There were also Greek letters on his left arm, halfway between his shoulder and his elbow. I reached for the buttons at the fly of his pants and released them. He rose and wasted no time pushing them down over his hips followed by his boxers until they were both on the floor and he was just as naked as me. He was gorgeous. All that dark skin right in front of me. I ached and was desperate to have him there, where I craved to feel him. I searched his eyes and the message was clear.

He was going to fuck me in ways I'd never imagined.

Howard moved back onto the bed, parted my thighs, and moved to lie between them.

"Yes," I muttered. "You said the ball's in my court, so I'm telling you yes."

His expression spoke volumes as he whispered, "There's no need. Your body already gave your secret away."

He brought his lips down on mine, kissing me passionately. A moan slipped from my lips and he slid his tongue inside, exploring and increasing my sexual arousal for him. My head was spinning with desire. Howard was right. My body was totally outside my own control. I shivered underneath him as I felt him take my hand and guide me towards him, encouraging me to touch him. I let my fingers wander, caressing him. He was so fucking hard. I wanted it inside of me. I clamped my fingers over his dick and stroked him in short, quick bursts, registering his size and power. His moans encouraged me to please him. With my thumb, I swirled the precum that I felt at the tip. I could tell by his reaction he liked it. I continued, traveling lower to his balls where I squeezed gently and then massaged. I teased him to the point of almost exploding in my hand. I barely had time to mentally prepare myself that he and *this* were mine for the evening before he reached for a condom and spread my legs, positioning me under him. I gazed up at him, my breath coming in shallow pants as he stared, and then I waited for the feeling I craved so desperately. Sexual tension had built to such a feverous level I didn't expect him to pause, but he did, lifting a hand and stroking my face with long, strong fingers.

"I'll try and take it slow but I'm not making any promises. You arouse the shit outta me," he groaned huskily. "I thought you were sexy and beautiful in your uniform, but now that I have you lying in my bed, naked, you are so freaking lovely I can't wait another moment to be inside of you."

Neither could I. I grounded my hips, begging him to take me.

I didn't want slow. I just wanted him. And I didn't care if I got hurt in the end. All that mattered was now.

He raised my hips and sunk inside, stretching me beyond my expectation. I sucked in air, shocked, and dug my fingernails into the flesh at his back. Howard paused. "Fuck, you feel good," he hissed then moved slow and steady, and I felt myself relax. His dark eyes hot with passion, he slid an arm underneath my hips, drawing me off the bed, and then plunged forward, thrusting deep inside me. I couldn't breathe, all rational thinking…gone. I was on edge, so ready, so willing. Howard was in charge. Poking. Stroking. Building a rhythm until he created a sensation so intense, I cried out his name. I grabbed his ass, whimpering, rocking, and meeting his strokes in a desperate attempt to ease the need he'd created within me. Howard's lovemaking was powerful and possessive. My legs were shaking. My body was in a state of fevered ecstasy.

Make me come, I wanted to shout.

"Is it good to you?"

"Yes, it's so good," I gasped, clutching his buttocks. I whimpered, begging for release. And just as I tumbled over the edge towards what I imagined was insanity, he nudged my clit with his thumb. I exploded in a climax so intense I screamed in disbelief. There was no way this was real. I had to be dreaming. Savoring the moment, my hands wandered, nails raking across the muscles dominating his back while he continued to drill into me, probing. Every cell in my body sizzled as I took flight in my mind until I felt the strong thrusts of his completion.

Held securely in his arms, I melted into the bed and closed my eyes, wrapped in the incredible feeling of his powerful body on top of mine. I never wanted the moment to end. Howard shifted his weight and looked down at me, a strange expression in his dark eyes. I lay still, my eyes locked with his, totally shocked by the longing that had erupted inside me.

What was he thinking?

Afraid to speak in case I ruined the incredible moment between us, I remained silent, the only sound was my shallow breathing while I waited for him to make the next move.

And move he did.

Muttering a soft curse, he lowered his mouth to mine again, and I ceased worrying about what was on his mind. I focused on what he was doing to me. Teasing me. Torturing me. Probing inside until I was crying out his name and exploded.

The following morning was the same.

I woke to find him beside me. He sat up on his elbows, looking down at me. There was no ignoring the heat sizzling beneath my skin.

"What's this between us? Sex?" As soon as the words left my mouth, I wanted to smack myself.

Howard brought my hand to his mouth, kissed it, and desire swept over me like an electric shock. "This is more than sex, but don't define it. Not yet. Let's allow us to evolve to the point you're forced to make a decision."

"A decision about what?" I braced myself for what he was about to say.

"That you're going to be mine."

"Yours?"

He nodded slowly. "Heart, body, and soul. I already know the answer. I'm just waiting for you to figure it out." His words were sensual, wrapping around my body.

I smiled then laughed. It was a happy laugh. These had been the best few weeks of my life, but he was right. I wasn't ready to define what we had just yet. So many times, in the past I had rushed into relationships thinking I had finally found the one to only be disappointed. Not too long ago I was putting a guy out of my house because I had been too blind to see he was married. Nope. I wasn't doing that anymore. This time I wanted more.

Howard kissed me, dragging me from my thoughts, then rose and moved toward the ensuite. I watched his well-defined muscles in motion and asked myself how I could have been so lucky. I brought the pillow to my chest, hugging it close. Life in Virginia was truly looking up for me.

I heard a cell phone vibrate. I looked over at the nightstand, bit my lower lip, then glanced back at the door. Slowly, I leaned across the bed and lifted the phone. The name Giselle flashed on the screen. I felt my heart sink. I had just coached myself into believing I had gotten it right.

You have. Quit making something out of nothing. Giselle could be anyone.

I nodded and put the phone down. Yep, Giselle could be anyone.

I heard the water running then Howard said, "Day, come take a shower with me." It was not a question. He moved to stand in the doorway. His broad shoulders tapered down to a slim waist in all his naked glory. His beautiful penis was hard and swinging toward me. I pushed my uncertainty aside and practically broke my neck trying to get to him.

28

MEEKS

"About damn time." Layla hopped into the passenger side of my car and shut the door.

"Sorry, I overslept," I said as I pulled away from the curb.

"Overslept or overdicked?"

I gave her a saucy grin as I announced, "Both."

My sister was screaming and trying to stomp a hole through the floor of my car. "Oh shit. My sister is getting her some."

"*Some*? Sis, I'm getting a lot." There was something very sexy about waking up next to him. Hard and hot and smelling all male when I took a deep breath. "Yes, I am." Emotion swirled through me that was much more than just sexual fulfillment. I was so excited I was ready to tell whoever was around. "And it's good, too."

"Yass! My sister has a man." Layla gave me a two-finger snap.

"Well... I won't say all that but I'm enjoying it while it lasts."

"While it lasts? Really?" She rubbed her forehead. "Are we going there again?"

I'll admit, the sex for the last weeks had been so out of control, the fire raging between us couldn't be compared to anything I'd ever had before, including Dame. "I'm just keeping it real and not establishing expectations. That's how you set yourself up for disappointment."

Layla sighed. "I hope you're not straddling the fence with him."

I made a right turn at the corner before speaking. "No, not at all but I'm also not defining our relationship this early in the game. I get too caught up and then I'll have another married man trying to play me."

"Does Keim give you the impression he's married or trying to play you?"

I scoffed, shaking my head. "No, but they always seem perfect in the beginning and I just don't want to rush this time." I was downplaying my feelings because it really wasn't any of her business. I was crazy over Howard, but men had disappointed me so many times before because I rushed, so I needed to stay focused. I just couldn't go through that again.

"Don't mess this up because you're carrying old baggage and have trust issues," Layla said, her tone clipped.

"No, not that." I hesitated before saying, "But let me ask you a question. A few weeks ago, a woman dropped by my job and said she was dating Keim."

Layla jolted forward. "She told you that?"

"No, actually I overheard her on the phone talking to Keim. Well, at least a man named Keim. I just don't know for sure if it's my Keim."

"Did you ask him about it?"

I shook my head. "No, I didn't want to come off sounding jealous."

"Chile, please. What happened to trust but verify?"

I gave a rude snort. "I've been keeping my eyes on him." I pointed two fingers at my pupils to emphasize my point.

"Any other signs that might indicate he's cheating?"

I hesitated because I hated being that girl again. "There have been the phone calls. Even last night when he went to the bathroom, I looked at his phone and saw a text message from her." At least I think it was her. If so, her name is Giselle. *I need you.*

Layla tugged my arm. "But did you ask him about her?"

"No."

Her raisin-brown painted lips turned down in a frown. "Why the hell not?"

I shook my head. "Because he's not mine to ask."

Layla grew quiet, but I could see out the corner of my eyes that she was looking at me. I ignored her and pulled into the parking lot of Target. It was directly across from the Promenade Town Center and the best place to park other than the parking garage.

Layla got out and slammed the door. "Day, you better grab onto that man and hold him tight before that skank steals him away. I hope you showed him what he's got with you."

"Trust me. He knows that he has hit the Virginia Lottery with me, but I'm also letting him know that I'm not clinging or jealous or looking for a man to complete me."

"I trained you well." Grinning, she reached over and gave me a high-five and we laughed. We crossed the street and slipped inside Forever 21.

I decided it was time to change the subject. I was tired of my insecurities resurfacing every time that chick tried to contact Howard. He was different than all the others. I just needed to keep reminding myself. "I need something cute to wear to this barbecue."

"Me, too. There's going to be all kind of fine men there.

I can't look less than perfect."

"Watch it now. You're married," I reminded with a pointed stare.

"I'm married. Not dead. I know what single Airmen look like. And if it's anything like Howard, I know they are fine. Besides, I like for Faze to feel proud to have me on his arm, so I need to represent." Layla pointed to a rack of sundresses.

"Let's look over here for something cute."

"I was thinking ankle-length."

She frowned. "Hell no. Nothing long. As gorgeous as your legs are, I would be flaunting them every chance I got."

"Yeah, they are cute, aren't they?" I did plenty of lunges and squats to keep them looking this good.

We searched the racks until we found a burnt orange sundress—my favorite—with a racerback that was cotton and polyester. After a trip to the dressing room, I discovered it was perfect and clingy in all the right places.

After buying protein smoothies, we headed to Nine West where I discovered a pair of white wedge sandals that looked sexy on my feet. I planned to wear my gold ankle bracelet. Yep, I was going to have Howard's attention this afternoon.

ΘΘΘ

Around three, I pulled in front of Howard's house and found the driveway and most of the block already crowded with vehicles. I parked behind a red Volvo and climbed out the car. I dragged my dress down over my hips, then removed a pair of Steven Madden sunglasses from my eyes to use as a headband for my kinky, curly afro. I wanted Howard to see what a natural black sista looked like at her full potential.

Reaching into the backseat of my car, I removed the bags of potato chips I had picked up at the grocery store on the ride over. When I asked Howard what I could bring to the barbecue that didn't require cooking, he laughed and suggested chips. Too easy. I bought six of the latest Lay's flavors. I chirped the locks on my car, dropped the keys into a gold pouch across my waist, and sauntered toward the house where the smell of grilled pork floated in the air. I'd been at his house almost every other night since the first time we'd made love. Each time I told myself if Howard was seeing anyone else, would he really have me at his house so often?

Hearing music and laughter coming from the rear of the house, I followed the sounds into the yard where a crowd of guests were talking and laughing, standing and sitting in lounge chairs. Others were swimming in the pool. I spotted Howard over at the grill with several other gorgeous men. They were drinking beer and talking. Howard was flipping burgers. A man who can cook was a man after my heart. When he spotted me coming, his eyes lit up. Damn. He was so handsome. I couldn't hold back the pride that burned at my chest knowing he belonged to me. Well, at least for now since I refused to get ahead of myself.

"Whassup," he said with a shit-eating grin that caused my breath to hitch. I moved closer and Howard leaned in to wrap his free arm around my waist. Looking up, I tilted my head in time to see his gaze fall to my mouth. I caught my lower lip between my teeth just as he leaned forward and gave me one of his addictive kisses. Although brief, it was enough to curl my manicured toes. When he drew back, his gaze settled on mine. I saw the fire. He wanted me, and I wanted him. Damn, it was going to be a long afternoon.

Howard finally winked and said, "Sweetheart, let me introduce you to the crew." I shifted my focused to the assorted box of chocolates standing around the grill. From what he had told me one evening while TV binge watching, all five Senior NCOs were eligible bachelors.

"Dayana Meeks, this is my pack, Chiefs Tobias Cole, River Reid, Denver Tell, Cameron Watkins, and the high-yellow one is our new Command Chief, Gage Taylor."

"I'm also the most mature of the bunch." Taylor shook my hand. Yep, he was definitely bringing light skin back. Taylor had gray eyes and tattoo designs covering both of his large biceps. He also had Greek letters identical to Howard's on his left arm, halfway between his shoulder and his elbow. I was going to have to remember to ask him about it.

"Pleasure to meet all of you," I said as my eyes shift from one member of our wing to the next. I always heard wolves ran in packs, but this group of senior non-commission officers were a force to be reckoned with.

"Damn, bruh, you didn't tell us your woman was this fine," Cole said as he held out his hand. I took it blushing.

"That's because he was trying to keep her all to himself," Watkins chimed in.

"Watch it," Howard growled. There was no mistaking the possessiveness in his voice.

"Are you all with the 176th?" I asked because in my six months at the wing I had never seen them.

"Hell yeah. Nineteen years and counting." Reid, who was the tallest and cocoa-brown, paused and gave me a once over with an approving smile. "If I knew someone this fine was the new FSS superintendent, I would have dropped by the personnel office a long time ago."

"You aren't the only one." Watkins was the darkest and with the prettiest brown eyes. "Can I come by on Monday, so you can show me how many points I have towards retirement?" He gave me a gleaming white grin.

"Don't make me kick you out of my barbecue," Howard joked, although the look on his face said he was serious.

Taylor chuckled. "Meeks ignore these fools. One thing about this pack, we don't believe in sharing."

"That's after he's marked his territory," Reid added.

Howard looked over at me dark and intense, causing my body to get all fired up. "I always claim what's mine," Howard warned before he gave the group a long, hard stare.

Reid cocked a brow at him. "Relax, bruh. We already know the deal."

Howard trapped me in the heat of his direct gaze, I felt a tug of sizzling pleasure between my thighs. And despite my hesitation of making this thing between us official, I felt a shift in my chest like nothing I've ever felt before. Howard removed the burgers and lined the grill with seasoned ribs.

"Sweetheart, come with me while I take the meat inside."

Holding a pan of meat with one arm, he took my hand in his. I followed him through the crowd of guests toward the house. As we walked, Howard stopped and introduced me, saying, "This is my baby, Day." I felt so connected to him. Most of them were traditional guardsmen that reported to the base only once a month. But I saw quite a few familiar faces which was expected. Everything in an Airman's career started and stopped with the Force Support Squadron; therefore, at some point everyone would know me, and I would know them personally instead of as a position number on my manning document. Despite the warm reception, I also saw looks of surprise at seeing us together.

Let them look.

We made our way to the house. I stepped into the kitchen and closed the sliding glass doors behind us.

"You can put those chips on the counter near the buns."

I placed the bags onto a chocolate granite countertop and looked around. "You're going all out." There were large aluminum pans covering most of the counters.

"Absolutely. We got mac and cheese, green beans, and baked beans. In the refrigerator is coleslaw and potato salad and, now, your delicious chips."

I laughed. "You got jokes."

Howard gave a heartfelt laugh, then sobered. "This is a historic moment for the wing. Black chiefs on this base are rare, and six is unheard of. And now that Taylor has made command chief, you damn right we got a reason to celebrate." There was no denying the pride on his face.

"With his head always in those books I knew when Gage decided to get his Ph.D., he was headed towards big things. And it doesn't get any bigger than this for a senior non-commissioned officer at the wing level. But you already know that," he added with a wink.

"I agree. I'm so happy for him. I hope that can be me someday."

"We don't have any black female chiefs at the moment so when—not if—that moment comes, I plan to throw you one hell of a party."

"I like the sound of that." I liked it even more because he was talking about a future with me.

Howard rounded the island and drew me close in his arms. The heat of his warm chest against me sent sparks of heat from my breasts down to my toes. "You bring your bathing suit?"

"No..." I grinned. "I brought a bikini."

"Don't make me choke one of them brothas." I saw the desire burning in his eyes. "We can change after we eat."

I tilted my head and savored the kiss he gave. When he ended the kiss, his eyes met mine and searched. "How was your day? I missed you."

"I went to the mall with my sister. They should be here shortly." I couldn't tear my eyes away even to glance down at the watch on my arm. I was too busy staring up at him. "Did you ask me inside so you could take advantage of me?" I whispered.

"Something like that." The impact of his words robbed me of my breath just as he captured my mouth in a kiss that was soft and intoxicating. Leaning back against the counter, Howard drew me tightly in the circle of his arms. His tongue slipped inside, each stroke was confident and felt so familiar like we'd been doing this for a long time.

"Get a room."

Blushing, I turned in his arms to see my sister and Faze coming through the sliding glass doors.

"This is my house and it has plenty of rooms, including this one," Howard told them, then took his time releasing me. I didn't mind the least bit.

I looked at my sister and winked. She was rocking the red jumper showing off her thick shapely legs and pink painted toes in white sandals.

"Where do you want this?" Layla asked, holding a large bowl I knew held her scrumptious ambrosia salad.

"In here." I opened the refrigerator and made room on the bottom shelf.

Layla grinned. "Look at you. Already acting like the lady of the house."

I gave her a playful eye roll, but it did feel good. Everything felt good with Howard. I hoped it last. However, unlike my sister's wild imagination, I was taking things slow. She was probably already planning our wedding.

Howard reached for a pan of seasoned chicken wings and the four of us went outside.

The next few hours were fun. I wasn't at all surprised at how many people knew my sister and Faison. The Air Force world was small enough that people often crossed paths during their careers.

When I had stepped out in my two-piece, pink bikini with high cuts on the side, his eyes had burned with fire as he drew me in his arms and whispered, "I'm five seconds away from telling everyone to get the hell out so I can have you all to myself." He nuzzled my neck with light kisses. I giggled, and we watched several play water volleyball. One thing about the military, Airmen are competitive. Layla and I joined in, and we played a match against the men. Of course, we won, although they claimed they were being gentlemen and allowed us to win.

The deejay was an Airman—medically discharged after his ankle was snapped during a mobilization to Djibouti—who now hosted parties and worked the night clubs. He was rocking tunes for the grown and sexy crowd. As much as I complained about people still doing the electric slide, I was out of my seat joining the line. The celebration was fun, and the barbecue was delicious. My man had skills.

I pigged out on ribs and chicken wings and moved to a lounge near the pool after my second helping of ambrosia salad. Layla came and took the chair beside me.

"They demolished your salad," I told her. "I think Taylor had four helpings."

"Yes, either him or Howard." We both looked across the pool at them. Now that he was done cooking, they were all sitting around a table playing bones. "I told you his friends were fine."

"And single, too. Could you imagine seeing all six of them walking into a club? The women would lose their minds." I took a sip from a can of Sprite and looked over at Howard rising from the table so that someone else could take a turn. He was wearing red swim trunks and all his tats were on full display. He was truly gorgeous. I knew he was the host of Taylor's promotion party, so I couldn't expect him to spend all his time with me. And yet I was itching to touch him. Goodness. *There would be plenty of time for that later.*

I was in my chair dozing off when someone tapped me on the shoulder. I looked up to see Rein smiling down at me. "Hey you." I introduced her to my sister who was sucking on another rib bone.

"Hey." Layla waved.

"I would have been here sooner, but I've been running my mom around."

"No worries. Have a seat." I pointed to the empty one beside me.

Rein looked cute in a tie dye shirt and blue jean shorts. "You're wearing the hell outta that bikini," she complimented.

I had slipped a white cover-up over it. "Thank you. You swimming?"

She scrunched up her nose. "Nah, girl, nobody wants to see all this cellulite."

"Oh please. Men like seeing a little jiggle."

"Meeks, this here is a damn earthquake." We shared a laugh. Layla leaned in to ask Rein about her wooden sandals and the three of us started talking about fashion. We were discussing the new Savage X Fenty lingerie-line when someone caught my attention. I lowered the shades from my eyes and glared. Sauntering across the lawn in a white two-piece beneath a see-through cover-up, showing off glistening brown skin, without an ounce of fat in sight, was the mystery woman who'd come by the office looking to reset the pin for her ID card.

"No, she didn't," Rein mumbled under her breath. I caught her glaring in the woman's direction.

"Who is she?" I asked.

"That's Giselle Wade. She's a training specialist at the education center."

I should have known Rein would have the inside scoop. I turned to Layla. "That's the chick I was telling you about who's been texting Howard." I returned my gaze to Rein. "She also came by my office wanting her ID card unlocked."

"*Her ID*?" Rein rolled her eyes. "That chick knows where the ID office is. That was just an excuse to come and see what the competition looked like."

"Oh, hell no." Layla hissed.

I watched as Giselle strutted like on a runway. Hips swinging, ponytail bouncing. Pink diamond-studded glasses were on her face resting comfortably on her small nose.

"Does she and Howard have a history?" I asked even though the answer was obvious.

Rein shrugged. "I'm not sure. If so, it was either recent or
short lived."

"I can't believe he invited her," my sister cried.

Rein gave a rude snort. "Knowing Giselle, she invited herself. She's been looking for a husband since she came to this base." The way the male guests were looking and trying to get her attention, I couldn't understand how she managed to still be single.

"You better go get your man," my sister warned and nudge my thigh, urging me to get up.

"You know that's not how I roll," I muttered and yet I was contemplating snatching off my earrings and grabbing a jar of Vaseline. And as the words slipped from my tongue, I watched in slow motion as the skank walked up to Howard and kissed him on the mouth.

Red-hot rage swept over me and I sprung up from the chair.

29

HOWARD

"Yo, Howard. Look who's coming this way."

I turned in the direction Taylor's gaze shifted to see Giselle coming across the yard. Who the hell invited her?

"You want me to run interference?" Watkins asked.

If I didn't shut her down there was going to be trouble. I nodded then stole a glance across at Meeks and saw Rein sitting beside her. They were both looking my way. Damn.

Watkins tried to stop Giselle, but she brushed passed him. I walked up to her and saw the grin on her face.

"Hello, baby. I came to congratulate Command Chief Taylor."

I opened my mouth to respond, only before I could get the words out, Giselle kissed me.

"Whoa," I said and pushed her away from me. Not hard enough to hurt her, but enough to get her attention and make sure everyone knew I hadn't asked her to put her lips on me.

She had the nerve to laugh. "What's wrong, Howard? You're not happy to see me? You weren't saying that when I was lying in your bed."

"What?"

At the sound of Meek's voice, I swung around to find her standing behind me. Rein and Layla were with her. All three women had hands on their hips.

Meeks moved up. "Keim, you care to explain what the hell
this woman is talking about?"

I scrubbed a hand over my jaw and blew out a breath. "I have no idea what she's talking about."

Giselle gave a throaty laugh that irritated me. "Seriously, Keim? You're going to stand there and pretend I didn't bring you breakfast, and we haven't been sharing lunch?"

"Lunch, huh?" Meeks said before she turned her attention on me. Disappointment flickered in her eyes.

I was too pissed to think.

"I didn't ask you to bring me breakfast, and I was already in the shower when you came in my bedroom."

Meeks looked from her to me. "What was she doing in your house?"

"He let me in." The chick had the nerve to smirk.

"She came over with breakfast. That was two weeks ago." I shook my head. This was ridiculous. But I could tell by Meek's expression she wasn't buying it. I looked at my boys for help, even they looked skeptical. Taylor was shaking his head. I know. That's what I get for trying to be the good guy.

"Giselle, go home." I turned to Meeks. "Nothing happened between us." She looked like she wanted to believe me, but I had to give her more to work with.

"This is the same chick that came by my office asking about her CAC card," Meeks said.

My brow rose. This was my first time hearing that.

She said, "So, I guess what you were really doing was dropping by to check me out." It wasn't a question. Meeks moved toward Giselle, but I grabbed her around the waist and dragged her over to stand next to me.

"Day, baby, she's not worth it," I said. "I haven't been

with this woman since I've started dating you."

Giselle lifted a brow. "Seriously? I came to see you last week and brought you lunch from Chick Fil-A, your favorite." She looked across the lawn. "I bet Staff Sergeant Powers can collaborate my story."

It took everything I had not to knock the smirk from her lips because she had come into the building with lunch, and Powers had been there to witness her presence before I managed to get rid of her.

Rolling her eyes, Meeks turned and started to walk away. Taylor jumped out in front, blocking her path. "Meeks, wait. Howard may have his faults, but this chick ain't one of them."

I didn't know if I should thank Taylor or knock him out.

"He's right, Meeks. That's not his style... and neither is she," Rein added with an evil eye roll.

Layla gave a two-finger snap. "I know that's right."

All eyes were on us. Even the deejay had lowered the volume of the music until Taylor signal for him to play something and turn it up. Once Johnny Gill started singing, *put on your red dress… and slip on your high heels…,* I leaned in close to Giselle. This was a discussion I'd rather have in private, but she was the one who'd made this fiasco a public display.

"Giselle. This is my woman. And I told you the day you showed up at my house I was no longer interested in spending time with anyone other than my sweetheart. It's also the same thing I tell you every time you text my phone or show up at my job."

"Yass." Rein was grinning. She was such an instigator.

Giselle was wrestling with Watkins, who was trying to get her to leave. She yanked free from his grasp and moved toward me. "I don't appreciate you stringing me along."

"Did I ever make you any promises?" I asked her.

"Well, you did—"

"Giselle," Taylor voice boomed. "Bruh asked you a question and you're acting like a spoiled brat. Did he make you any promises?" He took a step closer, reached out, and brought a hand to her face, lifting her chin so she was forced to look at him. "Answer...the...question." He spaced the words out evenly. Reid and Cole raised their brows in puzzled amusement, me included.

"No," she finally responded with attitude.

"Didn't he tell you he was seeing someone?" Before she could speak Taylor held up a hand and said, his tone low and scathing, "And before you answer, get rid of the attitude."

She swallowed. "Yes." She was either nervous or turned on by Taylor's demeanor. Good, let her stalk him.

"Then why are you here making a fool of yourself?' Taylor asked.

"Because he didn't even give us a chance and I needed to make my intentions known."

I reached over for Meek's hand again. There was some resistance before she allowed me to lace our fingers together. I gave her a gentle squeeze then dragged her back over by my side. "Listen, Giselle. I'm too old for games. This woman is special to me and the only person who can fuck this up is me. So, I'm going to tell you one last time to stay the hell away from this house and my job, or I'm getting a restraining order."

Disappointment flashed in her eyes as she stood there.

"You heard what my man said." Meek's lips curled into a triumphant smile.

"Let's go, Giselle. I'll walk you out to your car." Taylor took her gently by the arm.

Giselle gave a sardonic look before she glanced from me to Meeks and said, "When you get tired of her, come see me."

"What the—"

Meeks dove but I caught her midair and brought her back down next to me. She tried to wiggle free and, as tempted as I was to let her go, I knew it was not the type of problem either of us needed. Besides, Giselle wasn't worth it. "Get her outta here!" I barked.

"C'mon, Giselle. Let's go," Taylor told her. As she turned around, he draped an arm across her shoulders and walked her across the lawn.

"What's up with those two?" Cole asked as soon as they were far enough away.

I just shrugged. I didn't care just as long as she doesn't bother me or my girl again.

I pulled Meeks into my arms. Leaning down, I kissed her then took her hand and led her into the house where we could talk in private. After I closed the door, I turned and took both of her hands. My gaze fell to her face. "I'm sorry about all that. I hope you believe me."

"I do believe you." She leaned forward and pressed her lips to mine. The touch of her mouth sent tingles of awareness and the urge to shout, *Damn, I'm proud to be a man!* through my soul.

When she drew back, I smiled and said, "Stay here with me tonight."

Her brow lifted. "Are you asking so I'll know she's not coming over?"

"No, I'm asking for the same reason I invited you to stay all week. The same reason why I invited you to this barbecue. I wanted you to see inside my world. Be around my friends. Stay at my house. I also want you to meet my daughter." I saw her stunned gaze before she burst into another beautiful smile.

"I would love to meet her."

I lifted Meeks off the floor, kissing her with everything I had, trying to show her better than I could tell her that she was special in my life. The only thing stopping the kiss from continuing was that we needed to come up for air. I reared back, stared at her breathing heavily, her lips moist and red from my kisses.

Outside, I heard a loud howl, and someone was shouting my name.

"What's going on now?" Meeks asked.

I heard more howling and a smile curled my lips. "Give me a second." I moved toward the front door where my boots were waiting and slipped my feet inside.

"Why are you wearing those?" She laughed when I returned to the kitchen. I probably looked ridiculous to her in swim shorts and combat boots.

I took her hand and winked. "You'll see. Come with me."

30

MEEKS

Taking my hand, Howard led me outside. As we moved across the lawn, I spotted Rein smiling. She signaled for me to come over and join her and Layla.

Howard dropped a kiss to my cheek then released his hold. "Go ahead while I get ready."

"Ready for what?"

Howard just smiled and jogged across to join the others. I walked over to Rein and my sister. They were both grinning, which meant they knew something I did not. There were several others that looked confused so that made me feel a little better, but not much. As we gathered around, I saw my brother-in-law also jogging across the lawn to join them.

"Would someone please tell me what's going on?" I snapped impatiently.

Layla winked and bumped her shoulder into mine. "Relax and watch."

I released a frustrated sigh then folded my arms and watched the guys get into formation. Three in a row. Cole, Reid, and Tell in the back. Watkins, Taylor, and Howard in the front.

Faison stood off to the side. He cupped his mouth and shouted, "Thetas, line up." Six more men joined the group until there were four rows.

"Thetas?" I murmured and caught Rein looking at me.

I suddenly, felt a heady rush of anticipation. We moved closer, and I looked over at Howard. He looked so sexy my heart fluttered.

"Atten hut!" Faze bellowed and the pack stood at attention. It was then that I looked down and noticed all twelve Airmen were in swim shorts... and green combat boots.

"Oh damn," I whispered under my breath.

"At ease."

On command, they all parted their thighs and clasped their hands behind their backs.

"Atten hut!"

All twelve displayed their military bearing, and there was nothing that I found sexier than a man who was disciplined and confident.

This is my pack. Howard's introduction echoed in my ear. And it finally all started to come together. The tattooed Greek letters on their forearms. These men were a brotherhood. A fraternity. A pack.

"Forward, march!"

The pack started marching in place. Left foot. Right foot. Shoulders back. Heads held high. Tatted-up bodies hard like steel. And all twelve dripping with sexiness.

"Halt!"

The group stopped. They thumped their boots in unison.

Faison shouted. "About face."

They all twirled around with precision.

"Right face." They turned to face the pool.

"Left face." The pack turned to face us.

"Forward, march!" This time instead of marching in place, the pack moved in a slow jog around the pool. Eyes in front, heads held high, still in formation.

Faison sound off in song, "I don't know what you want

to do."

"Go find my girl," they responded in unison.

Faison called cadences as they rounded the pool again and when they reached the original spot, he shouted, "Halt!"

Stomp. Stomp.

The men stood at attention, bodies now glistening with light sweat. My heart was pounding profusely. All I could think about was getting my hands on Howard and licking the moisture across his chest. They stood that way for several seconds and just as I was getting ready to look at Rein and my sister and ask what was wrong, a familiar tune blared from the speakers and everyone shouted.

To H-Town's *Knockin' the Boots,* the men began winding their hips, and the air crackled with excitement. What had me fanning myself was when they began incorporating military facing moves into the dance moves.

Grinding hips. Right face. Stomp. Winding hips. Left face. Stomp. Winding hips. About face. Stomp. Stomp. Back muscles rippled, arms were large and flexing with each movement. Even my brother-in-law had joined in, and my sister was screaming with excitement. She loved that man and it was obvious to all who knew her that the feeling was mutual. I felt like I was watching a remake of *Stomp the Yard* the way they were moving. And just as the song ended, the group did two hard stomps and the performance ended. The guests went wild with applause. Layla raced over and threw herself into her husband's arms.

My head whipped to the left. "Rein, *oh my god.* What was that?"

"It's a fraternity. Theta Lambda Chi. They're a military brotherhood of active duty Air Force, guard, and reserve. If this was a drill weekend, there would have been over forty members here. There are also chapters at Seymour Johnson, Keesler, and now at Dover Air Force Base."

"I had no idea. Other than college step shows, I've never seen anything like that before."

She winked. "Get used to it. They have parties all the time. They also do fundraisers to serve the community with brotherly love. You should see the turn outs at the car wash."

"With bodies like that, I can imagine."

Rein nodded. "We have a sorority as well."

"Really?" I was excited.

She smiled proudly. "If you're interested, I'll send you the link to the application."

"Yes, please." I caught movement and spotted Howard coming toward me. I drew in a breath and waited. Within seconds, he swooped me into his arms.

"Oh, my goodness, that was so dope. How come you didn't tell me about the brotherhood or the fraternity?"

He shrugged. "I figured I could show you better than I could tell you."

I grinned. "You showed me alright."

ΘΘΘ

Much later, while Howard said goodbye to his guests, I started the dishwasher. This was my kind of barbecue when everyone stuck around long enough to help clean up the mess before departing. My sister, Rein, and I managed to squeeze all the leftovers into the refrigerator and then wiped down the countertops and loaded the dishwasher.

"Okay, I don't even clean my own place this good." Rein was standing back with her hands at her hips looking at how spotless we had the kitchen.

I grinned because I couldn't have done it by myself. I didn't cook so, other than running the dishwasher, my kitchen stayed clean. "Next time you have a barbecue, I'll make sure to stay back and help you clean."

"Me, too," Layla chimed in. Over the course of the afternoon the two had realized they had a lot in common.

Rein reached for her purse and slung the strap over her shoulder. "Well, I've got a date with my new boo, so I'm out of here."

I waved, mouthed *thank you,* and watched her slide the door open and step outside.

Layla slipped off the stool at the counter. She reached for the to-go container she had made. "I need to get out of here as well. We need to pick up Maya and get her ready for bed." She looked over her shoulder at the men standing out in the yard. "Besides, you got work to do." She started winding her hips seductively like she was on a stripper pole. I was cackling like a fool. I followed her outside where Howard was still saying good-byes. My heart fluttered at the sight of him. After the performance, he had slipped into a t-shirt, but his boots were still on his feet. Loosely laced and sexy. I walked over and stood beside him, and he brought a hand around my waist and drew me by his side. It felt so good being with him, and even though he'd made our relationship known, I couldn't help thinking about Giselle and wondering what really went on with them. Did he manage to make her feel as good as he had me feeling? I knew it was my insecurity flaring up, but I just couldn't help but to think that maybe my time with him had been too perfect. The same as it had been with Dame. He'd had me so blind, I thought we were going to get married. All because I had lowered my guard and allowed him in, and my world shattered. Did I really want to take that chance again?

I thought about that until the last guest, but the moment we were alone my mind and body became putty all over again.

"I've been waiting all day to have you too myself," he confessed and took my hand in his.

I bit my lip and my gaze collided with his. His nearness made me tingle. I was grinning too much to respond. He led us into the house and closed the door, and then he was kissing me. My arms were around him and when he pulled me close and deepened the kiss, I went limp in his arms. He scooped me up and carried me to his room, then laid me gently down on the bed and lowered on top of me. We kissed and kissed some more and yet it just wasn't enough. I wanted more of him. A lot more. My body was begging to feel the slow burn that had gotten me caught up in the first place. The burn didn't allow me to think. Only feel.

I moved restlessly against him. "I want you inside me." My voice was rough, almost desperate. Howard looked down. His expression dark and intense.

"Then take off your clothes." Howard rolled away so I could rise.

I stood up from the bed and began a strip tease. I tried to incorporate facing moves like him and the pack, but we both ended up laughing.

"Okay, chill, let's get serious for a moment," I told him. I slipped out of my clothes and stood before him, naked, moistening my lips with the tip of my tongue.

His expression softened. "Damn, babe, you are beautiful."

"Yeah, I know," I said with a saucy grin, then pointed. "Now, your turn. Take off those clothes."

"You don't have to tell me twice," he said, chuckling, but wasted no time yanking his clothes off. As soon as his beautiful body was on display, I dove onto the bed. Howard rolled on top of me and took my mouth again. My brain turned to mush, and my body caught on fire. His hands were all over me, gently touching and caressing. I kissed him back harder, seeking his heat.

"I can't keep my hands off you," he told me.

"Touch away," I told him, looking into his eyes. Until his mouth settled over mine again. He kissed his way from my mouth to my cheek and traveled downward where I needed to feel him the most.

31

HOWARD

I kissed my way across Meek's shoulder, inhaling her sweet scent. I loved the soft moans escaping her breath, the sound vibrated through her body. The way her nipples responded to my touch let me know she enjoyed being here with me. And the mere thought sent heat through my body straight down to my dick. I would take her slow even though my erection was straining for quick release.

"You smell so fucking good," I murmured softly. I moved to her neck, raining small kisses, then up to her lips, meeting her tongue with mine. But I didn't stay long before I moved to her cheek and then to her ear, licking until she was breathing heavy. I was back at her neck and over to her shoulder, then I was painting a path with my tongue down the length of her arm and along her hand. I took her fingers into my mouth slowly, one at a time. And when I finally moved to place my head on her chest, my stomach did a slow roll. Hands caressed my back. Her palms gliding over me felt so sensual. Heat rushed through my body from every direction to center at my groin. I liked the way it felt, blood pushing through my veins in urgent need. The heat filled my cock until I felt ready to burst. We were no longer in a backyard filled with guests. Meeks was in my bed where I needed her. I lifted my head to stare down at her. She was beautiful. Her eyes were closed, lips parted, and her chest rose with every ragged breath.

Mine. Mine. Mine. Or rather she will be because I had made the decision that she was everything I was looking for in a woman. After tonight, I hope she understood that because I wasn't going away.

I knew she was afraid of relationships, especially with military men, but she was willing to give me a chance. As a man with integrity, I did not take that honor lightly.

I licked her breasts, my tongue stroking her nipples. "Look at how your body responds to me, Day. So fucking beautiful."

"Keim, please..." She squirmed beneath me.

"Shhh," I said against her wet flesh. "We've got all night." And I had plans to keep her up late. I kissed circles around her chocolate nipple, then moved to the other.

Her hands slid along my back and hips. I held my breath as her palm slid down over my butt, then up along the muscles of my back. I loved having her hands on me. Lifting the weight of her breast, my thumb caressed her nipple.

"God, I love when you do that," she purred.

So do I, but I like this more. I captured a nipple between my teeth and bit softly. She whimpered and moved beneath me. I released her, trailing kisses over the brown slopes. Fuck. Her breasts were beautiful. Supple and Soft. Nipples erect. So damn soft. I took my time. I felt her jolting beneath me. There were more whimpers, and she was driving me crazy. I was driving her crazy with my fingers and my mouth. She deserved patience and tenderness but that didn't stop the burning need to be inside her. I was better at showing her than telling her. I pulled her other nipple deep into my mouth, rolling it around with my tongue and the edge of my teeth, igniting a fire and causing her to arch off the mattress. Meeks responded to me. Her soft moans set my pulse pounding. I had known from the moment I had first laid eyes on her at the deployment briefing.

"You're mine," I told her, my lips against her soft skin.

The burn inside me was blazing. Burning me with urgent need.

I kissed my way down her body, my tongue caressing her flesh, causing her to flinch and moan some more. Meeks gasped and tightened her hold on my head.

"Keim." My name came out raw. Breathless. Sexy.

Smelling her essence, licking between her sensitive folds had become my new craving.

"Now," she commanded between gasps.

"Not yet," I whispered against her damp entrance. "I first want to make you feel good."

Using my tongue, I took a swirl. She was wet. Aroused. I savored her flavor. "You taste so damned good." I couldn't get enough of her unique taste. Using my fingers, I spread her open, feeding her. Appeasing her hunger. Driving her wild. I wanted her wild. I wanted her to want me so damn bad that she felt on the verge of insanity. I wanted her to be burning with the need to have my dick inside. I watched her expression. Eyes glazed. Lips parted. Softly gasping for air. The second she was crying out and her body jolted and pulsed, I raised her hips off the bed, and pushed into her tight heat.

"Fuck," I hissed and stretched to accommodate my girth. "So good. So fucking good." It took control to move slowly when what I really wanted was to spread her wide and feed her my dick, one inch at a time. I wanted it to be good for her, too, so I clinched my teeth and stroked. In...out...in...out. With shaky breaths in between. Dammit, she was slick, warm, and my erection felt so snug. Her pussy clenched like a fist wrapped so tightly around me. I closed my eyes just a moment. I had to stop and take several deep breaths in fear of this ending far too soon, but every cell inside was screaming for me to keep pumping my way to completion.

"Fuck..." Meeks started winding her hips, rocking upward. I started moving again except this time my pumps were harder and faster. It was just too good. Heat raced from my cock down to my thighs until they were scorching hot.

"You like that?" I asked, gritting my teeth as I moved faster and harder.

Her hands glided across my back, her fingernails delving in my flesh. "Don't stop," she begged. "Please, don't stop."

I withdrew and plunged, pushing through her core, feeling the flames engulf me. "Look at me," I told her, and when she opened her eyes, our gazes locked. I lowered my head until our mouths touched. Lips parted. Eyes watching. I stroked at a deep sporadic rhythm. I was pounding so hard, she was sliding across the bed and using her hands to brace her head from hitting the headboard. I couldn't stop. The heat had built. Meeks was moving with me, her body urging me to continue. I also saw it in her eyes, heard it in her raspy breaths. I kept on driving my cock between her legs.

"Harder," she said. "Don't you dare stop."

I noticed her head had reached the headboard, so I shifted off her and rolled her onto the side. Lifting her leg, I switched angles and plunged into her again. She tilted her hips, driving me even deeper. "Yes, that's it," she said with broken breath. She pulled her leg toward her chest, holding it with her hand so that I could focus my attention elsewhere. Reaching down, I found her clit and flicked it with my thumb. The way her body shivered, and the sound of her whimpers was overwhelming. I drove harder, giving us both everything we needed. I watched her face, waiting for that exact moment. And when her eyes widened with a gasp, I knew it was time. I plunged harder, intending to give her multiple orgasms. I spread her legs and drove deeper. She was crying out my name, and then a second one hit her hard and strong, this time taking me with her. Pleasure like I'd never felt before Meeks came into my life ripped through me, and then I was soaring. Pounding into her, racing toward release.

"Baby," I whispered, when I could breathe again. "Don't move. I want you right here in my arms with me inside of you."

She didn't answer, only breathed.

"And as soon as I catch my breath, I plan on making love to you some more." Her breathing started to increase, responding to me. A soft, breathy moan. "And again, in the morning." I planted kisses along the soft skin along her neck. "And once I've had my fill, I'll make you breakfast while you soak in the tub." She drew in another breath, her muscles clinched around me, milking me to the last drop.

"Soak?"

Holding her close to me, I whispered near her ear, "Oh, trust me. You're going to be sore. I have a healthy appetite and haven't got my fill yet," I whispered. I felt her lush body quiver and a soft moan slipped from her throat. My fingers traveled to caress her nipples. They were erect. Good.

Me, too.

32

MEEKS

The next few days could have been characterized as amazing.

We spent our days and nights together. If we weren't at work then we were with each other, laughing, talking, and sharing. We even played a few games of basketball at the base gym and I got a chance to spank that ass. But the sex… the sex was the icing on the cake. Explosive.

On Thursday, Howard had a full schedule of briefings, so I was on my own for lunch. I didn't mind because he was coming to my house later for dinner and dessert. Since I can't cook, the only thing on the menu was me.

At lunch, I decided to run over to Burlington and see what cute outfits they had on clearance. Howard was taking me to Myrtle Beach for the weekend. The shore was a great place to visit during the fall season. It was already the middle of September, and the weather channel was forecasting an early winter.

I pulled off the base and headed in the direction of the shopping center with Howard on my mind. Just thinking about him had me smiling. I loved the way he helped to ease the pressures of the workplace and focus on enjoying life. I sighed. But it wasn't easy. I had a meeting with Major Michaels this afternoon to go over the overages across the wing. Meaning she wanted a report of all positions that were double slotted—two Airmen sharing the same position—since the time limit was two years. Letters would be sent out to unit commanders to either move them from the slot or start the process for the Airmen to be discharged. It wasn't a grave concern for lower grade Airmen but for technical sergeants and above, having someone sharing your slot on the manning document stopped you from being promoted.

I pulled into the Walmart Neighborhood Market shopping center, and as I moved past Marshall's I spotted a vehicle that caught my attention. I stopped my car, grinned, and backed up. It was Howard. He was leaned back against the hood of his Navigator, arms folded looking sexy as hell in uniform. I don't think I've ever looked at a man and wanted him with all the air in my body. But each time I saw him, my chest burned so badly I could barely catch my breath.

A car was in the way, blocking the lane, so I circled around and planned to park in the spot on the other side beside his Navigator. As I drove around, I noticed something had his attention. My eyes followed the direction of his gaze. Abruptly, I slammed my foot down hard on the brake. Thank goodness no one was behind me.

What the—

I saw a woman climb out of a black Mustang and saunter over toward him wearing a tight, black, wrap dress. As I watched, a sensation settled at the pit of my stomach. The kind you experience when you see something you wished you'd never seen. The kind filled with disappointment and betrayal.

I knew she was there for him because he was leaned back, waiting. Only now there was a cocky grin on his lips. The woman was gorgeous with caramel-colored skin and curves all over the place. Her hair was light brown and cut short, and the style looked gorgeous on her. Increasing uneasiness filled my gut. I didn't want to believe what I saw, so I blinked and blinked again thinking maybe, just maybe since Howard had been on my mind, I had conjured his image. But after three blinks, the scene in front of me hadn't changed. Instead, it had gotten worse. She sauntered over to Howard in heels higher than I could ever imagine wearing without falling on my ass. However, she managed to move with the grace and experience of Queen B right over to my man. Or at least he had been my man before this moment. Now, I wasn't sure if anything I thought I had felt about him had been real or just a figment of my imagination.

As she moved closer, a smile spread across her face and that fool was grinning back like he'd just caught a fifty-pound bass on the end of his hook. Once she was standing close enough, the woman pressed a palm against his chest then leaned in and kissed him on the cheek. My heartbeat accelerated. I was ready to jump out the car and tell that skank to take her hand and mouth off my man. Only he wasn't mine. We'd never defined our relationship and, after today, we never would. Glaring, I started cursing under my breath. First Giselle. Now this. Was it ever going to stop?

And Layla wonders why I have trust issues.

Men couldn't be trusted. It had all started with my father and it never stopped. No wonder my mother was so bitter and hateful when it came to men.

I sat there long enough to watch Howard reach for his wallet and hand her several bills, and then I couldn't bear to watch anymore. Instead of going to Burlington, I turned around in the strip mall parking lot and headed back to work. No point in wasting money on an outfit I'd never wear. There wouldn't be any trip to Myrtle Beach for me.

During the drive back, I tried to strip the incident from my mind, but I just couldn't. Howard told me he was too busy to break for lunch and yet he had been in the parking lot with another woman. Lies. He knew her. She wasn't some random chick. They knew each other intimately. Shaking with outrage, I sped back to the base, but I had sense enough to slow down outside the gate. Otherwise, security forces would have been writing me up and reporting reckless driving and speeding to my commander.

Furious, I made it back into the office. Hayes sprung from her chair and tried to get my attention, but I held up my hand. "Give me a moment," I murmured because otherwise I was liable to snap out on someone. I stormed into my office, shut the door behind me, and stared. Was this really happening to me again? I swayed, trying to hold myself upright. Not again. I had put myself out there and once again I had gotten burned.

Dayana, when are you going to learn?

At this rate probably never.

I grabbed a water from my mini refrigerator and took a long swallow, trying to get myself to calm down. There was a knock and, before I could respond, the door opened. My stomach lurched.

"Did I just see you over near Marshall's speeding out of the lot?" Howard asked curiously.

"I'm surprised you noticed, being that you were occupied," I said over my shoulder as I walked back behind my desk.

"How could I miss you the way you burned rubber. I'm surprise your car still has tires," he joked as he stepped into my room and shut the door. I wasn't in a laughing mood. I collapsed into my chair, berating myself for having been so stupid.

I briefly closed my eyes and shook my head. "Now, I see what's really been going on when you claim that you're too *busy* for lunch."

His brow lifted. "What the hell is that supposed to mean?"

"Matter of fact, that's the same excuse you used when Giselle was bringing you lunch."

"Are you talking about Sherry? That's nothing to worry about." He leaned in speaking practically in a whisper.

I shrugged and tried to act like it didn't hurt, but it did. "You lied then and you're lying now."

"Lied about what?" Howard asked, moving closer to my desk until he was towering over me. "That was Sherry. My ex-wife."

And there we have it... The other shoe drops.

"You're still seeing your ex-wife." This was Dame all over again.

"Of course not," he said like I was the one being ridiculous.

I sat back on my chair, truly offended. "I know what I saw."

"And what's that exactly?"

In my mind I replayed her palm pressed against his chest, her lips on his cheek. That satisfied grin on his face. He wasn't about to make me think I was crazy. "So, if you aren't seeing her, why did you lie about lunch?"

"I didn't lie. I wasn't planning on going out, but she needed to pay for my daughter's driving lessons and, instead of waiting until Friday to pay child support, I told her I would just meet her during her lunch hour."

"And you couldn't have just Cash App'd her?"

Howard raised his brow again. "Why would I do that when she works only fifteen minutes away?"

"So, this isn't the first time the two of you have met for lunch." The words left my lungs in a long rush and I realized I sounded like that jealous girl again.

"Day, you're being ridiculous." He had an amused look on his face. Now he was going to be laughing behind my back. Probably even sharing with Sherry during pillow talk. Dammit, why did I go against everything I stood for? Letting him know I was jealous had been a bad idea. I hated to say it, but I should have kept my mouth shut and acted like it didn't matter, even though it does.

"No, I'm not ridiculous. I'm stupid for thinking that for once I had gotten it right. For letting down my guard, dating another man in uniform, and trusting him with my heart." A sob hit my throat, but I refused to break down in front of him.

Howard placed his palms on the desk and leaned in close. "Day, what the hell are you talking about? There's nothing going on between Sherry and me."

"That's what they all say," I said, and I noticed he flinched at the disgust in my voice.

Howard was quick to counter. "I say it because it's true."

I blurted out, "I saw her kissing you." My chest was heaving.

He dragged a frustrated hand down the length of his face. "You saw her kiss my cheek. She was thanking me for not being a deadbeat father."

"And because you saved the day, she couldn't resist kissing you." My tone was dripping with sarcasm.

"Sherry and I are friends. We were able to divorce and continue our friendship. What's wrong with that?"

I snapped. "What's wrong is I've been here before. My ex and his wife continued to be friends and stay connected because of their kids and, yet, it was never over. The more she needed him the more he was there until they finally decided to get back together."

"That's not happening with us. She's married."

I laughed grimly. "And that's supposed to mean something? Because it looked to me like she might be having second thoughts."

He chuckled. "Looking like what?"

His laughter pissed me off. Did he think I was some kind of joke? "I'm no fool. I saw the way the two of you were looking at each other."

"And how was that?" he challenged.

"Get out of my office." I spat the words at him.

He sighed. "Would you just relax and listen?"

"No, this is the second time. First Giselle, now this. I don't trust you." The only reason why I wasn't going off was because I was in uniform and my staff was right outside the door.

"I'm not like your ex because there isn't anything going on between me and Sherry."

"Dame said the same thing and yet he'd been lying."

Fool me once, shame on you. Fool me twice, shame on me.

Yeah, right. Not this time. "Just leave me alone."

"Fine, but we're going to talk later," he warned.

Who did he think he was talking to, one of his Airmen?

I lifted my head and stared him straight in the eyes. "We don't have anything to talk about."

Howard cursed under his breath. "Day, all men aren't the same."

As far as I was concerned, they were all liars.

"Mommy, why isn't my daddy coming to get me?"

"Dummy, I told you! All men are liars."

I shook off the memory and glared over at him. Howard's gaze softened and he shook his head.

"You have trust issues that you need to work out."

"I don't have trust issues. I just trust men with issues. *And* baggage."

Howard moved toward the door. A low growl rumbled his chest as he said, "This conversation isn't over."

It was for me.

33

HOWARD

Ain't that about a—

One minute I was enjoying spending every second of the day with the new woman in my life, and the next thing I know, I'm blindsided with a swift kick to the balls and falling hard on my big ass. Fuck… And it's all because my woman—because she *is* my woman—can't trust.

First, it was her issues with her ex-boyfriend and his wife, and then Giselle's sabotage attempts by sneaking into my bedroom, showing up at Meek's job, and her Emmy award-winning performance at Taylor's promotion party. Now those incidents, I could understand. However, seeing me in the parking lot with Sherry and accusing me of trying to get back with her... Now that shit was ridiculous. Meeks had some serious issues with trusting men.

So how is that your problem? I shook my head but left the subject alone.

I'd done everything I could from day one to not only tell her but show her my feelings and intentions. There had been no games or any other woman I was sharing my time with. Just her. Every moment of the day we had spent together, I made sure she knew I was a man of integrity, honor, and valor and that should have counted for something. Dammit.

I stormed angrily across the parking lot toward my office. To hell with my SUV. I'll get it later. I needed to walk and cool off before the discharge briefing at fourteen-thirty. With each step, I replayed the event in the parking lot. Yes, Sherry had kissed me, and maybe I had been grinning quite a bit. But anyone who knew us knew my relationship with Sherry was strictly platonic. Over the years, we had gained mutual respect and set out to be the best damn parents we could be. Sherry was one hell of a mother, and I loved her for it. She was firm when she needed to be. Growing up, she had lived in an abusive home and had made a promise from the moment she found out she was carrying Ava that our children would never experience that kind of pain or neglect. Instead, our daughter would know every single day just how much she was loved, even after we had to get in her ass for something sneaky, she tried to do. Sherry and I were friends. That was it.

I scrubbed a frustrated hand down my face and drew in another long breath as I remembered Sherry pressing her hand to my chest. Maybe that's what Meek's saw. Hell, she was complimenting a brotha. Said she hadn't seen me look this relaxed and happy in a long time. Sherry had always been a touchy-feely kind of woman, but it was just who she was. I could, however, see how another woman would have a problem with it. But Meeks being unreasonable and not giving me a chance to explain, now, that was unacceptable. Conflict and disagreements happen in all relationships, but I had hoped when the time arose that we would have been able to work through them together.

You were wrong.

Now I had to prove myself. Guilty before proven innocent. That's how people with trust issues think. They sit back, waiting for you to do something to fuck it up.

I crossed the street, raised my hand, and saluted an officer. The more I thought about Meek's behavior, the angrier I became. The signs were all there, and yet I chose to ignore them because I'm always looking for a challenge. In fact, I couldn't blame anyone but myself. When Meeks resisted and said she didn't trust men in uniform, I should have backed away. Any other man would have taken it as a sign that they didn't need the headache of a woman with trust issues and hang ups about dating servicemen. Only there was a problem with that scenario. Unlike the other women, Meeks attracted me on so many different levels, so I felt she was one challenge I couldn't resist.

Nothing worth having comes easy, my father always used to say.

But a woman's lack of trust in her man, that was a different ballgame. Trust issues was a battle I wasn't sure I could win. I didn't want to have to keep proving myself, and yet, as I neared the Maintenance Group, I reminded myself that when I set off down this path, I knew what I was up again. I then asked myself, was she worth the fight? And an answer came to me without hesitation.

Hell yeah.

Pulling my shoulders back, I stepped into the building. We were far from over.

34

MEEKS

"Day, you're being ridiculous."

As soon as he was gone, I called Layla. But after hearing her response to my ranting, I wished I hadn't.

"I know what I saw," I whispered impatiently into the phone.

"But maybe it's not what you think," she said it as if I was the one who was being ridiculous. "Why didn't you just listen to what the man had to say?"

"Because I already did that with Giselle. I'm not going to keep going through this," I responded with attitude, sucking my teeth for good measure.

"Giselle was just some random chick he's done with. This woman was the mother of his daughter, but you didn't give him a chance to explain so..." She purposely let her voice trail off.

"You're no help."

"I can't help you, Day. You either trust the man or you don't. But Keim is right, you do have trust issues."

"What? I can't believe you're siding with him."

Layla groaned. "All I'm saying is exes can be friends."

I took a long, deep breath, shifting on the chair in agitation before speaking. "I don't know if I can get with that."

"Well, you don't have much of a choice because everyone has a past, including you," she pointed out.

Startled, I looked up to see my commander standing at my office door. "Layla, I have to go." I ended the call and sprung up from my chair.

"As you were," Major Michaels commanded and waved her hand dismissively. I returned to my seat and shifted my eyes to the papers in front of me.

"I've pulled the overages. Now I'm working through the list. I should have the letters for you before COB today."

She nodded and stepped closer. "Can you email me the manning document?"

"Yes, ma'am. I'll do that right now."

She approached me and leaned over the desk. "I have the group commander breathing down my neck about a promotion package. He wants to promote one of his Master Sergeants."

I raised an eyebrow knowingly. "Are you talking about Thomas?"

Her almond-toned face became very serious. "Yes, she has the time in grade and time in services, and they are ready to promote her."

"Yes, but she's an overage."

She nodded. "Right, and double slotted with Haley. So, they want to move Haley out that position and into another just so they can promote her."

I paused, frowned, and said, "But according to the Air Force Instruction, we aren't allowed to do that."

"Correct." She winked. "You let me handle that."

I watched her leave my office and smiled because I had mad respect for Major Michaels. She wasn't going to be pushed into doing anything she didn't find ethical.

I went back to work and refused to waste any more time thinking about Howard. What could he tell me that I hadn't already heard or seen? But no matter how much I tried to focus on my work, I couldn't get the image out my head of Howard and Sherry together in the parking lot. I replayed every second trying to see things through Howard's eyes to determine if maybe I had made too much of something that really had been innocent. But I thought the same thing about him and Giselle. How long would it be before it happened again? Also, Sherry was his daughter's mother, so if Howard and I continued our relationship I would be subjected to seeing him and her together. I wasn't sure if I could deal with that.

I ended up leaving work early and, instead of heading home, I decided to check into a hotel. I knew if I had gone home, Howard would have been at my door demanding that we talk, and I couldn't bear it. I was weak, and with one glance I would have given in and would have ended the evening lying on my back with my legs in the air. I wasn't willing to be that girl again.

Howard called, but I ignored him. I needed time to think. I needed to sort out my feelings. Layla was quick to point out that I always assumed the worse, so I needed to figure out why. However, instead of thinking, I spent the evening crying and trying to figure out why I couldn't get it right. Was I really that insecure? Dame, Howard, and the countless many before them… What was wrong with me?

No more men in uniform.

No more men with ex-wives and children.

I said it once and I'll say it again. That was my mistake. That was the problem. I didn't stand by my decision. My word didn't mean shit. Instead, I got all caught up in looks and charm and found myself swept up emotionally again when I should have known it was too good to be true.

I left the hotel long enough to grab a bottle of gin, then I went back and drank until I passed out. I woke up the next morning looking a mess. Even a hot shower didn't help. Luckily, I had a clean uniform in my office closet. I made it in early, grabbed my gym bag, and headed to the ladies' locker room. No amount of make-up was going to help my swollen, red eyes. I would just have to blame it on seasonal allergies. By the time I made it back to the office, my team was in place.

"Good morning, Senior Master Sergeant Meeks," Hayes greeted. "I brought in some Krispy Kreme donuts, so help yourself."

I smiled because I had a feeling she knew I'd had a bad day yesterday since her desk was the closest to my office.

"Thanks, Hayes. A donut sounds wonderful right about now." I went into my office and put my things away in my closet, then reached for my coffee cup, and headed back out on the floor. While the coffee brewed, I spent a few minutes with my team, making sure everything was okay with them both personally and professionally, and seeing if there was anything, I could do to assist them. I was grabbing my second donut when Major Michaels arrived. She was wearing a pink Nike gym shirt and shorts. The beads of sweat on her forehead signaled that she had just finished running. She ran along the flight line a few days a week.

"Good morning, everyone," she said.

As always, my team used proper customs and courtesies when greeting her. She acknowledged them individually before returning her gaze to me.

"Senior Master Sergeant Meeks, you and I need to go over the discharge tracker together. I have a meeting with the Wing Commander and JAG this afternoon."

I nodded. "Yes, ma'am. I'll have it to you this morning."

"Thank you." She reached for a donut and within seconds was in her office with the door shut.

I turned to Hayes. "I need to see that tracker this morning."

"I'm on it. The command support staff and I updated it on Monday, so it's current."

She was the bomb. The wing was determined to have all the members sitting on our manning waiting discharge for numerous reasons—attendance issues, fitness failures, and medical issues—released from their unit as soon as possible. Medical had to be reviewed by a board, so that required a formal process, but for the other members, that was just a step-by-step process that legal needed to make sure had been followed before they could be discharged. We had two members from the FSS who were on that list. One hadn't passed a fitness test since basic training, and the other had so many unexcused absences that it was in the best interest of the wing to let him go.

I went to my office, and it wasn't until I sat down in my chair that I remembered Howard being there in my space, larger than life and full of fire.

Ugh…I missed him.

I shook my head, pulled my shoulders back, and got to work. I was reviewing the discharge tracker when Rein came by sipping a bottle of alkaline water.

"I hope your morning is better than mine," she said. "I've been doing a full body cleanse since the weekend and I'm craving bacon."

I looked up and grinned.

She studied me then raised an eyebrow, "Meeks, is Howard keeping you up all night, because you look like you haven't been getting any sleep. Although, that could be a good thing."

I sighed. I guess my mood was written all over my face. "No, I just have a lot on my mind."

"What's wrong?" she said, her concern genuine.

I couldn't even use the seasonal allergy lie, instead I gave a dismissive wave of my pen. "I don't want to talk about it."

"Yes, you do. Any time someone says, 'I don't want to talk about it,' what they are really saying is, 'Girl, I got problems,' so go ahead and spill." She grinned. "I promise it will make you feel so much better."

She didn't have to push. I didn't have many female friends and typically kept my personal business personal with the exception of my sister, but I needed a friendly ear.

I swirled around in my seat and, in a low voice, I told her the story. By the time I was done, Rein had an alarmed look on her face.

"I can't believe he did that, especially with Sherry," she whispered.

"You know her?"

She shook her head. "I know *of* her. Sherry broke his heart, and the only thing between them is Ava."

"I know what I saw." I know I was being stubborn, but I didn't care.

Rein frowned. "Do you think that maybe you misunderstood what you saw?" She held her hand up to stop me from interrupting. "Now, hear me out. I'm not taking sides, but what I am saying is that just isn't his style."

"So, you think I made it up?" I asked, getting defensive.

"Of course not," she replied in a rush of words. "I just

feel like you need to talk to him and give him a chance to explain."

I rolled my eyes. I should have known she would take his side.

"Think about it. There's no way he would have come out and let everyone know you two are together if he wasn't crazy about you." She shook her head. "No way would he jeopardize what you two have to be with Sherry."

"She's beautiful."

Rein threw her hands up in the air. "So are you."

I glared. "And your point is?"

"My point is...talk to him. I hate to see you so miserable. He's a good man."

So was Dame and that didn't stop him from going back to his family.

"Please, just fix it before it's too late," she advised.

It felt good to relieve some of the tension that had been sitting on my shoulders. "He's probably pissed at me."

Rein threw her hand in the air again. "He'll get over it. The important thing is that the two of you talk."

I felt myself relax a little. I don't know why, but I felt like there was hope. Maybe it was something I had known all along, but with her saying as much it gave me the excuse and maybe even the courage to talk to him.

"Okay, I'll think about it."

"You need to do more than think about it," she suggested and then rose. "Let me get out of here before I reach over and snatch that sinful-looking donut from you."

Smiling, my eyes perused her. "I don't know why you're starving yourself. You look good."

"I want to look better than good." She walked around my desk and hugged me like a true friend would and then left my office.

After Rein was gone, I thought about what she had said and decided that maybe she and Layla were right. I needed to talk to Howard. Maybe I was making more of this because I had been hurt so many times before.

I finished the report and went into Major Michaels's office to discuss and approve. Once she signed off on the routing sheet, I walked over to the wing commander's office. I needed the exercise. I arrived to find Master Sergeant Robyn Rice behind the front desk. She was the wing staff's executive assistant. We chatted for a few moments, and then I exited the building and made the decision to walk over to the Maintenance Group to speak with Howard. I couldn't resist the smile on my face at the idea of being able to see him. I was even hoping we could work things out, and mentally I could let the situation go and move on.

I crossed the parking lot and headed toward Hanger 13. As I drew closer, I felt a tingle ricochet from my head to my toes. *Admit it, Day. You can't wait to see Howard.* Yes. I confess. I couldn't wait to see him.

While I was coming around the building, a red sports car passed me and pulled into a spot a few spaces from the wing commander's and parked at an angle that would prevent the car in front to get out.

"Ignorant," I mumbled under my breath. When the door opened, a pink stiletto and a shapely leg stuck out the car. I looked up and drew in a long breath when I realized it belonged to Giselle. She climbed out, straightened the front of a form-fitting black dress, then reached down for a green folder before shutting the door behind her. She looked gorgeous. I tried not to feel intimidated, but who was I fooling. I stopped walking and started to turn away but not before she saw me. She gave me a once-over with a slight chuckle and a two-finger wave before she sauntered into the building, shaking her head.

Rage filled my lungs while I turned around and stormed back to my office.

35

HOWARD

I was about to lose my damn mind.

I'd been calling Meeks, leaving messages on her phone, and I still wasn't getting any response. I believed in allowing a woman her space, but this right here was ridiculous. I hadn't expected the silence to last so long. Yesterday evening I had even found myself driving over to her place, hoping if I had shown up on her door unannounced, she would have answered, but she wasn't there. I had a feeling that might have been intentional. Yep. Dayana Meeks was avoiding me.

I heard throaty laughter outside my door and cringed. My eyes shifted to find Giselle posing in the doorway.

"Hey, handsome."

"I thought I asked you not to come by my office anymore."

"I'm not here to see you. I have a meeting with Lieutenant Colonel Tennison." She grinned and stopped me before I could speak. "Relax. It has nothing to do with you. We are going to discuss continuing education opportunities for the group. I want to increase enrollment across the wing."

I wasn't the least bit threatened by her speaking to my commander. "I'm glad you found something you're passionate about."

Laughing, she sauntered into my office like she owned the space. "I could have been passionate about you if you weren't so fickle."

I stared until she shyly dropped her head.

"Seriously, I want to take this opportunity to apologize to you. I didn't mean any harm." She shrugged and fluffed her hair. "You can't blame a woman for trying."

"He might not mind your games, but I do." At the sound of the low raspy voice, my eyes zipped back over to the door and groaned when I spotted Rein. She strutted into my office with complete attitude. "You need to leave," she told Giselle, who looked slightly intimidated by her presence.

"Well, Keim..." Giselle paused to clear her throat. "... I have an appointment, so I better let you go." She looked from Rein to me again. "Again, I hope you can find it in your heart to accept my apology." She turned and was careful not to bump into Rein, whose eyes followed her until she was out the room.

"*That's* why you're in the doghouse," she barked the moment we were alone.

I frowned. "Rein, what do you want?"

"I came to give you some advice." She walked over and dropped down in the chair across from me.

"And what would that be?" I asked sarcastically.

"Stay away from her." She gave me attitude right back. "Giselle's messy."

I shrugged and asked, "I'm trying. What do you want me to do? Get a restraining order on her?"

"That's doesn't sound like a bad idea," she murmured amusingly.

I heaved a sigh. "Rein, I'm sure you have work to do."

"Oh, relax." She gave a dismissive wave then lifted a plastic bottle in front of her face. "I'm on lunch and since

I'm detoxing, water is all I have until dinner."

"Poor thing." I didn't even bother to hide the sarcasm.

Grinning, her lashes dipped over her eyes. "Listen, I like seeing you and Dayana together, so fix it."

"I'm not the problem."

Her eyes widened. "Then, what were you doing kissing your ex?"

"I wasn't..." My voice trailed off as I scrubbed the length of my face with my hand. Rein was waiting for me to give her all the juicy details and that shit wasn't about to happen. "Listen, I already told Day nothing happened. She's either going to believe me or she isn't."

"With that attitude, she never will," she muttered.

I frowned.

Rein narrowed her eyes at me as if she already knew exactly where I was going with this. "Dayana is miserable without you."

That got my attention. I sat up tall in the seat.

"And I know you're miserable without her, so quit being stubborn and go work things out."

I didn't bother to deny it. "I will."

"Why not now?" I guess she read my look of dismissal, because she said, "You can't take a break?"

I chuckled because Rein was truly a pain in the butt, but also a good friend. "Yes, I guess I could go out and stretch my legs."

36

MEEKS

On the walk to the office, it took everything I had to maintain my military bearing. It was over. I couldn't believe it, but my relationship with Howard had ended.

By the time I made it back to the Mission Support Group, I had replayed that smirk on Giselle's face so many times I was ready to go find the skank and scratch her eyes out. And to think, I had just been seconds away from making a fool of myself. I didn't care what anyone said, I was done.

I headed straight into my office and closed the door behind me. I removed a carton of yogurt and tried to eat while I worked, but it stuck in my throat. I had a retirement interview at fifteen-hundred-hour with a member to determine how many good years he had before he submitted his package to Air Reserve Personnel Center for review. I took several deep breaths trying to clear my thoughts.

Sergeant Hayes had prepared the spreadsheet Major Michaels had requested, but before I submitted anything up the chain of command, I liked to verify that the information was accurate. I wasted enough time thinking about Howard. Plenty of time to cry about him later. I wasn't going to make the same mistake I had made with Dame, allowing our relationship to jeopardize my career.

I was conducting my review and had pretty much let the incident slide from my thoughts when I heard Hayes out in the lobby say, "She's in her office." I knew *she* had to be me.

I assumed my appointment had arrived early, so when I heard a knock at my door, I replied, "Enter." I looked up from my laptop and froze when I spotted the command chief standing in my doorway. He wasn't in uniform, otherwise I would have popped up out of my seat and given him his respect, even though I wasn't quite sure if I had any left for him.

"Carlos," I said softly.

Dame's lips slipped into that signature grin of his that was borderline cocky. "Hello, Day." Not waiting for an invitation, he stepped into my office. I found myself staring into his gorgeous gray eyes that were so piercing they'd left me breathless on several occasions. His butter-bean brown complexion was accentuated by chiseled cheekbones, a wide nose, and sensual lips that I remembered feeling on my own lips and other parts of my body. *Except for the place I had craved the most.*

After shaking off the initial shock, I said, "What are you doing here?" Last time I had seen Dame I was still at Whiteman Air Force Base, Missouri. It was our family day weekend, and he had been with his wife and kids.

"I'm here for a few days attending a leadership training. I thought I'd drop by and surprise you."

Well, I was surprised.

"Have you had lunch yet?" he inquired.

My eyes strayed down to my phone. It was after one. "No, I haven't." It wasn't a complete lie. "I had some yogurt."

"How about I take you to lunch? I remember there used to be this great Italian restaurant right off base."

I nodded. "Lopez's. Yes, it's still there."

He grinned some more. "Good. Let's go. I'd like to catch up."

I hesitated, asking myself why I was considering going out to lunch with him. He already broke my heart when he decided to go back to his family. But then I decided the last thing I wanted was for him to think I was holding a grudge. Nope. I wanted to show him I had moved on with my life and he no longer mattered. Besides, I was curious to hear what he had to say.

"Sure. I can't say no to free food."

That got a chuckle out of him and the familiar rumble caused a stir at the pit of my stomach. I removed my ID card from the machine, then reached for my purse and hat and followed him out. I noticed my staff watching, but it was none of their business.

"I'm going to lunch," I said to no one in particular and followed Dame out the door and over to a Volvo he had rented.

We were quiet most of the ride. It was strange riding in the car beside him again. This was something we used to do all the time, disappear in the middle of the day and go to lunch, or head to my apartment for a chocolate snack. Only there would be no romp in the sack this time. Dame wanted to talk, and I was ready to listen and make sure he was aware I had moved on.

Once at the restaurant, we were immediately seated, and then we ordered. I loved the Italian salads but today I felt in the mood for the special, which was spaghetti. After our waitress brought us both a cola, I looked across the table and caught Dame looking at me.

"What?"

"You look good."

I shivered. "How am I supposed to look? Tore up? Depressed?"

"No, not at all," he replied in a husky voice that dreams were made of. "I'm just saying you look really good. Beautiful. I tried to keep that image of you in my head, but my memories didn't do you justice."

I couldn't resist the smirk.

"How's it feel being the force support squadron superintendent?"

I grinned because he knew this was what I had wanted at Whiteman, but I'd been passed up twice for promotion.

"It's dope. Lots of work, but I have a great commander here. She fights for her people, so I respect that. I do a lot of hand holding around here, but you know the deal."

Dame laughed. "Yes, I do. It's never a dull moment. We're getting ready for our next rotation and we will have another group deploying in a few months."

"I'm surprised they let you out."

"Me, too," he drawled. "But I needed this training. Been trying to attend this conference the last two years they've offered it. Air Combat Command rarely has any seats, but this time I got lucky."

"Good for you." I knew he was doing everything he could to make it up to National Guard Bureau and get an assignment at the Pentagon.

"How does Layla like having you close to her?"

I took a thirsty sip and was surprised he'd remembered my sister's name. "She loves it. It's great being near family again." I took another sip. "Like you told me, family is important."

Dame's expression grew serious. "Listen—"

I jumped in before he could say it. "Look, let's not dwell on the past. I understand why you did it. You had to do everything you could to make your marriage work.

I'm no longer mad about it."

"I wish you were mad." His sinful mouth curved into a wolfish grin. "In fact, I was hoping you still missed me. At least a little bit. You stopped responding to my text messages."

Lowering my lashes, I murmured, "I needed to get on with my life." Uh huh. I'd never tell him I missed him, even when I did. "Let change the subject."

"No. Let's not," he urged.

It took a moment for the meaning to register. His demeanor shifted to its usual commanding presence as he squared his shoulder and held his head high.

"What I'm trying to say is… hold up." Dame reached inside his pocket, pulled out a folded sheet of paper, and handed it to me.

I unfolded and looked down at it. I gasped. She'd filed for divorce.

My gaze snapped up to meet his.

"It's mutual this time," he said solemnly. "We tried to make things work but decided that we're only going to be hurting the kids by trying."

My heart was pounding while I tried to regain my composure. "Whatever happened to, 'I'll do everything to fight for my wife and my kids'?"

"I've already moved into my own apartment in Warrensburg."

I held out the papers, returning them him and didn't know what to say. I had waited two years for this moment and, now that it was here, I didn't know what to say or how to feel. Was it too late for us?

I could only maintain eye contact for a split second before Dame reached over and took my hand in his. "I want us to start over."

I snatched my hand away. "I don't think that's a good

idea."

"I think it's a perfect idea. I love you, Day. That's never changed. I want us to work through this because I know we can. We had something good. You have to admit."

Yes, what we had was almost too good to be true, which was the problem. It had all been a lie.

Like your relationship with Howard.

My gaze returned slowly to his face. His eyes studied my face, causing me to feel hot and suspicious of him.

Dame leaned toward me, dropping his tone to match mine. "Are you seeing someone?"

I hesitated because I was not sure if I wanted him all up in my business. "I've been dating." Well, at least that was true since after what I saw this afternoon, I wasn't sure anymore.

"I don't see a ring, which means I still have a chance. I had your heart once and I want that back." His eyes perused my face and neck, lingering over each feature.

I swallowed to say, "What makes you think I want that?"

His gaze returned slowly to meet my eyes and a hint of a confidence lingered on his lips. "Because you loved me, and I can see in your eyes that a part of you still does."

He was making me sick with that pretty-ass smile of his. He knew his words were working on me, and he loved it. Frowning, I leaned back in the booth, needing to put some distance between us.

Dame stared at me, until his brow lifted as he said, "So you're not going to say something?"

I stayed quiet, refusing to feed his ego.

He dragged in a long breath before releasing to say, "I'm here until next week. I want a chance to fix this thing between us. That's all I ask for. If you give us a chance, I can get us back to where we need to be."

Oh my, he was trying hard, I thought as I stared at his broad shoulders and penetrating, gray eyes.

"You still love me, and I know I love you. I want a life with you. I want to make you my wife."

I laughed, surprising myself. "The problem is you already have a wife." I hated that I sounded bitter, and I was not trying to go there.

"I meant what I said. I'm sorry for everything I put you through. But I'm not going to apologize about the way I feel about you."

He started to say something else, but I held up a hand before he could respond and blurted, "I'll have to think about it."

"Well, at least you didn't say no," he said with a lazy smile and wagged his eyebrows.

I used to love when he did that and couldn't help but laugh. He was staring and I couldn't even look at him anymore. And at that moment, I didn't quite understand what I was feeling.

Could my life get any more complicated?

37

HOWARD

As soon as Rein left, I was prepared to head over and take Meeks to lunch, but my commander caught me in the hallway and had me in his office for over an hour talking about some random shit.

Dude, find yourself a new woman. That's what I wanted to tell him, but I knew I couldn't. Besides, I understood his pain. I had been there with Sherry. Also, the last few hours without Meeks had me feeling the pinch at my gut. Nope, I didn't want to end up onboard that ship again. I was prepared to fix things with Meeks.

I headed over to the Mission Support Group. She and I were going to talk. I was going to get her to listen even if I had to plant my butt in a chair inside her office for the rest of the afternoon. I pulled into the parking lot and walked toward the rear of the building. I spotted a Volvo pull in and Meeks got out. A grin curled my lips because my girl was looking fine. Her hat was tilted low so I couldn't see her eyes from the distance, but there was no mistaking the ruby red tint to her luscious lips and that dazzling smile made everything below my waist start to stir.

I headed her way, but, as I walked up to the car, I noticed a dude behind the wheel. Our eyes locked, and I would have been blind not to see the triumphant grin on his face before he pulled away. My gaze shifted over to Meeks, who stood at the door and waited.

"What's up?" I said. "Who the fuck was that?"

Hard defiance tinted her eyes. "Really? How can you question anything I do?"

"Because I can," I barked, knowing just how ridiculous I sounded. "Now I'm going to ask you again, who was that?" I didn't care if I sounded possessive. The thought of that dude sniffing around my woman was making me crazy.

"A friend."

I stepped closer. "What kind of friend?"

I could see the challenge in her eyes. "*My* friend," she replied, and turned and walked inside the building.

I followed. "Is this some kind of game?" I said whispering, trying not to yell in the hallway, but I was pissed and didn't bother hiding it in my voice.

Meeks snapped her head in my direction. "I should be asking you the same. I come by your job to talk and I see Giselle walking her narrow ass into your building," she spat without slowing her pace.

Damn. I didn't even bother to explain because the expression on her face told me she wouldn't have believed it anyway.

I grabbed her wrist. "I asked who was in the car."

She stopped walking, looked in my direction, and rolled her eyes. "Not that it's any of your business, but that's my ex-boyfriend."

"The married one?"

She jerked her hand away. "The soon to be divorced one. They filed for divorce."

"What does that have to do with you?"

She gave me a strange look. "Nothing but it made me

realize I need time to think."

I leaned toward her and whispered, "Think about what?
Getting back with him?"

"No," she whispered back and then paused before adding, "But between Giselle and Sherry, and now Dame, I need time to think." She was avoiding eye contact and my gut told me her decision had very little to do with Giselle and Sherry and more to do with her ex.

"Take all the time you need." By the look on her face, I think she was curious about my choice of words but didn't comment.

I turned and walked back to my Navigator. There was nothing else to say. I'm not begging a woman. No matter how much I wanted her, Meeks needed to decide. She needed to choose me.

I peeled out the parking lot pissed. Her ex? Was she fucking kidding me? She was ready to throw away everything we had all because she saw me talking to my ex-wife in the parking lot. I shook my head. Nah, I don't believe that for a second. I wasn't about to start apologizing for every move I made. Nor was I going to keep explaining myself. Hell no. I needed her trust, and if she couldn't give me that then we were wasting each other's time.

I got out the SUV and headed toward the building with rage filling my veins. I pushed the door open, removed my hat, and stuffed it angrily into my pocket. I had a meeting in half an hour and didn't need this. I needed to get my game face on. I rounded the corridor toward my office to find my pregnant UDM standing there. Happy for the distraction, I gave her a sincere grin. She was one hell of an NCO.

"You're back. How was your appointment?" I asked.

She'd left for her monthly checkup.

"The baby and I are doing fine." She was beaming with joy the same way Sherry had when she was pregnant with Ava.

"Good." I signaled for Garvin to follow me into my office. Her timing couldn't have been more perfect. "Have a seat. What are you working on today?" After she began explaining, I added, "Make sure you're training Washington and delegating some of your assignments."

"Yes, Chief. I have been," she replied, then the smile slipped from her lips. "I dropped by to let you know Senior Master Sergeant Woods broke his ankle out on the track this morning."

"Fuck," I muttered under my breath. The damn overachiever was probably out there showing off again.

"Medical just DAV coded him in the system. He won't be able to participate in the exercise."

"Dammit." A deployment availability code in the system meant he wasn't going anywhere until medical released him. I reached across my desk for the roster of participants.

Garvin leaned forward. "Chief, I need to know if we can replace him or, do I need to submit a shortfall?"

"Let me see who the XO is." I scanned the list. The executive officer was a second lieutenant. That meant Woods could be replaced with one rank above his. Tapping my finger against the page, I took a moment to contemplate what I was getting ready to say before I replied, "No, no shortfall. We're going to replace him." I met her eyes. "I'll fill his slot."

A distraction was just what I needed. Meeks said she needed time to think, well, so did I. My being away for a few weeks would either make or break us.

38

MEEKS

Much later I was at home, sitting out on my back deck, thinking about the things Dame had said while we had lunch. He was right. We used to have something that was good, but I was in a new place in my life and had met a man that made me feel things I didn't even know I could feel for someone else. Didn't that count for something? There were so many pros and cons I could raise about the two of them. Dame was supposed to be my past and Howard my future. Now shit was all fucked up and I couldn't think straight.

"Damn you both." I picked up the glass in front of me and gulped down what was left of my second glass of red wine. I didn't want to call Layla, but after an hour of staring off into the neighbor's backyard, I decided to share my situation with her despite the expected backlash.

"*He's what*?" she shouted at the end of my spiel. I went back in the house and brought the entire wine bottle outside with me. I poured myself another glass.

"He showed me the divorce papers."

"Oh, my goodness."

"I know, right?"

"What are you going to do?" she asked curiously.

I sighed. "I don't know. That's why I'm calling you."

"Uh-uh, I'm not getting in the middle of your love triangle."

"But I need some big sisterly advice." I was desperate.

"All I can tell you is that you need to follow your heart. What that is, only you know." There was a pause. "I thought you liked Howard?"

"I do." In fact, I liked him a lot.

"But you love Dame."

"I used to." I still do, but it wasn't the same. What I felt with Howard was so different from the relationship I'd had with Dame. We had an energy I couldn't bring to words. It was the uncertainty that had me spooked.

"Well, how do you feel about Dame now that you know he'll soon be single?" she questioned. Goodness, she was so nosy, but then I did call asking for her advice.

"I don't know." And that shit bothered me.

"Then that tells me your feelings for him have changed."

I agreed. That much was true.

The tone of Layla's voice said she was pleased so I was surprised to hear her say, "Well if Dame's going to be here then I guess you need to see if the chemistry is still there."

"And what about Howard?"

"I guess you'll have to tell him the way Dame told you when he decided to go back home to his wife and make it work."

I recalled him saying, *"Day, baby, I have to find out if we can still make our married work."*

Hell no. I know what that shit felt like.

"It isn't necessary. Howard and I aren't in a committed relationship." At her silence, I continued. "I told him I needed time to think. What I do with that time is my business." But even as I said it, my heart wasn't into it. I was crazy about Howard. I liked him so much that if I knew we had a chance without other women popping in and out of his life, I would have told Dame to kick rocks and go home to his wife. But I wasn't sure anymore. After seeing Howard with his ex-wife and then Giselle walking into his office after he'd promised me in front of all his friends their relationship was over, I didn't know if I was willing to risk my heart. It was the same thing again. Another man in uniform lying.

"You love living on the edge," Layla replied with a snort. "I don't see how single people do it these days. Thank the Lord I'm married."

I hung up more confused than ever about my life. I was divided in two directions, and I didn't know which way to go. Part of me wanted to believe the old saying about the bird in the hand but the curious side of me began to wonder. What if? What if Dame had never gotten back with his wife? Would we have married? I had been happy back then. I had loved that fool's dirty draws until he ripped my heart out, but he had felt bound by duty to go back home to his family. I understood it had been the noble thing to do, but it did nothing to help ease the pain I had been feeling.

I went to my room and lay across the bed thinking of all the time Dame and I had shared. All the time and energy I had invested into our relationship. Now he was really getting a divorce and was free to date whomever he wanted and available for another woman to swoop in and sink her claws in him. But could I ever love him that way again? That's where the what if came in. His marriage was over. Maybe we could make it work this time, but was that really what I wanted?

I felt a stab of guilt because now there was someone new in my life who was helping me to love life and give relationships another chance. He wasn't married with small children. Howard was funny and cocky and so damn arrogant at times, but he was sexy, and his dick game made my toes curl like a ballerina. He pursued me like a tiger in the forest on the hunt with relentless determination. He wanted me, and he made his presence known. No hiding in the bushes waiting to pounce. Nope. His intentions to claim me were clear. And yet even knowing all that, the unknown, the "what ifs" about him and his ex-wife and that skank Giselle was wearing me down and refused to go away.

"I meant what I said, Dayana. I want you."

I wanted Howard too, but I was frightened and didn't know what to do.

39

HOWARD

She still hadn't called.

Ever since I'd walked up on Meeks with her ex-boyfriend, I hadn't been able to stop thinking about seeing the two of them together. I needed some idea of what was going on before I went out of my fucking mind.

"Man, you got somewhere you need to be?"

I looked up from the sofa over at Chief Master Sergeant Denver Tell, sitting in the recliner across from me. "Why you say that?"

"Because you keep looking down at your phone," he said with a grin.

I needed to know what the fuck was going on. I squeezed the beer bottle in my hand so tightly my knuckles went white. "I'm expecting a call." At least that was the truth.

His brow rose. "You know the expression about a watched clock never ticks?"

I cleared my throat to regain my resolve. "I see you got jokes this evening."

Tell laughed as he reached for another buffalo wing on his plate and dipped it into ranch dressing. While we watched the game, I remembered the afternoon at the City Center when I'd asked Meeks about her past relationship.

Our conversation replayed in a continuous loop in my head.

"I wanted all of him. Not part of him."

I took another angry swallow of beer. Was Meeks trying to play a brotha?

I know what I saw, and that dude wanted her back. He was smiling in a way that made a man want to confront another and find out why he was all up in his woman's face.

After seeing them together doing whatever the hell that was, I went back to my office. When I left my meeting, I tried calling Meeks. Her phone went to voicemail, and I hadn't left a message. I needed to talk to her, not some recording.

Tell had invited me over to his apartment to watch the game, but my mind was focused on my phone that still hadn't rung.

"How'd your date go with that new chick?" I asked, trying to shift my focus.

"Alana?" he scowled. "She was looking for an ID card. She got the wrong one baby BABY," he added in a bad Notorious B.I.G. impersonation that caused us to chuckle. It was good seeing him laughing again. Just last year, Tell was still mourning the loss of his wife. They'd been married ten years when she'd left on what he thought was a business trip to Colorado Springs. She was killed in a skiing accident while on vacation with her lover. After her death, he wouldn't allow anyone to get close and tried to hide the pain behind sarcastic wit, but I saw through the façade.

"Daddy, can I have some water?"

I looked over to see my goddaughter, Samantha, standing in the entryway. Dark mahogany skin, deep dimples, and large brown eyes that were going to win the hearts of a lot of little boys. Yeah, right. They were going to have as much luck as Ava.

Tell's face instantly melted. "Sure, ladybug." He put down his plate of wings, then rushed over and scooped up the five-year-old in his arms, causing the miniature replica of his dead wife to erupt with girlish giggles. I felt a lump in my throat at the sight of them. Tell may not have time for serious relationships, but nothing stopped him from being a good father to his daughter. Nothing or no one was that important.

My cell phone vibrated, startling me. I picked it up from the coffee table and smiled when I saw a message from Meeks.

Can you come over?

Sure, I could, only what had taken her so damn long? I couldn't help but wonder if her ex had been at her place. Just thinking about it pissed me off. I decided to wait before responding. I wasn't a yes man waiting for her to summon me.

After Tell took Samantha back to bed, he returned to the living room smiling.

"You're good with her," I told him.

He nodded. "Yeah, I know."

"But she's going to get to that age where she's going to need a woman around."

"Ain't nothing I can't handle."

My gaze snapped to his. "You planning to be at the store buying tampons?"

His brow rose.

"And bra shopping?" I should know.

"Whoa, I got plenty of time for all that." He chuckled and shook his head.

"Kids grow up fast. I remember when you were learning how to change her diaper." I finished the beer in a gulp. "Sam needs a woman in her life. Time for you to stop playing and get serious so she can have a mother."

"Didn't I hear your phone chirping?" Changing the subject was the sort of thing Tell did when he didn't want to discuss his personal life.

"Yep." I rose. The moment of truth would soon be at hand. "I'm going to see my woman."

Was our relationship over?

Fuck that. We weren't even close to done. We'd just begun.

ΘΘΘ

It was after ten when I knocked on her door. Meeks kept me waiting and I knocked again. What was she doing? On the phone talking to him? My fist clenched and unclenched. This was my fault. I kept trying to tell myself I wasn't ready to define our relationship. *What the hell were you waiting for?* I was wrong. I had claimed her the second I had met her. She's mine, dammit.

I finally heard soft footsteps, and then the lock turned. When the door opened, I tried to control my jealousy.

"Hi," Meeks said shyly.

There she was standing in front of me. Beautiful. Wearing a long t-shirt. No bra. Her nipples were prominently on display. Had he seen them, too? I clenched my teeth at the thought. Had she allowed him to take one into his mouth and taste? Damn, I was acting jealous again, and that was not my style.

Meeks stepped aside, and I moved into the house. The scent of her sweet perfume smelled good, but it wasn't the same familiar fragrance; instead, it was a new scent. Sweeter and more alluring. *Why the change?* I wondered.

The thought did absolutely nothing to simmer my uneasiness.

"Come on back so we can talk." She signaled for me to follow her into the living room. She was barefoot. Her ass bounced with each step. The hem on the shirt teased me with thoughts of what was underneath. And I intended to find out.

"Day," I called after her.

Meeks stopped and turned around. I saw her look at me and then swallow.

"We can talk later," I told her. "Take off your shirt."

I almost expected her to refuse. But instead she bit into that juicy lower lip of hers and nodded. Her eyes never left mine while she dragged the fabric over her head and tossed it away. No panties. I figured as much. Standing there in the middle of her living room, I stared at her breasts, then all her other curves. I unbuttoned my shirt, then slipped out of my clothes until I was also naked. Slowly, Meeks started walking backwards, batting her incredibly thick eyelashes, and the look she was giving took my breath away. Images flooded my mind of the great sex that usually followed her flirting. I was fueled by jealousy and a possessive need to be inside her. I closed the short distance between us, and when I reached her, I swooped in taking her lips in a hard, controlling kiss. I knew I was being rough, but I didn't care, and she didn't seem to mind. I was communicating nonverbally that she belonged to me. I kissed her mouth, exploring, licking, nibbling, and then biting her softly. First her mouth then her cheek and neck. I drew her up into my arms and captured a nipple in my mouth and suckled and squeezed and bit her, leaving marks, claiming my territory.

I started for the stairs, practically taking them two at a time as she clung to me. Legs wrapped around my waist.

Her nipple still in my mouth. I couldn't get enough of the feel of her warm flesh. I flicked the tip with my tongue, causing her to moan my name. Once we reached her room, I lowered her onto the bed. The sheets were rumpled. The bed was unmade and images of her in bed with her ex brewed its ugly head again.

"Were you with him tonight?"

"Wh—"

"Were...you...with...him?" My tone was harsh and even.

Her eyes widened. "No."

"Good answer. Now get down on your knees."

Without hesitation, she lowered onto the floor. I had my dick in my hand waiting, wanting, anxious to receive. Meeks didn't make me wait. She started at the tip, taking it first between her lips before sliding it deeper into her mouth. She replaced my hand with hers and I allowed her to do what she did quite well. Fuck, it was hard to remember why I was angry. Her head bobbed back and forth as she took me deeper while her other hand massaged my balls, warming them up for what was to come. Her eyes met mine as she sucked faster, and I slipped deeper inside her mouth. She did that swirling move around the head with her tongue that made me go wild. Making me harder and angrier. Because all I could think about was if she had just done the same with him. Those were my lips. The only cock she should be sucking was mine.

I dragged her up and pushed her back onto the bed. "Open your legs." I covered her body and spread them even wider. I didn't even give her a chance to prepare before I was burying myself inside her. Oh Damn… She didn't need preparing. Meeks was wet. The soft release of air between her lips sent me wild. I drew her legs up around me, fucking her. I was practically growling with each deep penetration.

"Please," I heard her say.

"Please what? Stop? Say it." It pained me, but I was no fool.

She started rotating her hips and moaned, "Please, don't stop. Fuck me."

She looked so beautiful lying beneath me, head thrashing around. How could I stay angry? Easy, I looked away. I wasn't ready to let the situation go. She hadn't offered any explanation. I turned her over onto her stomach, and with her body flat on the mattress I laid on top of her, immobilizing her and entered her from behind. Her head was turned. Her left cheek flat on the mattress. I nibbled on her earlobe as I sent my cock deep, penetrating her again and again. She tried to move, but I wouldn't allow it. Instead, I pounded harder this time. "You told me to fuck you, so I'm going to do just that and show you what you'll be missing."

"Missing? What are you talking about?" she asked, but I provided no answer. We would talk later.

"Hush. Lift up." I reared back taking her hips with me. I pushed inside her and started moving in a deep, determined rhythm.

"Ooh, that feels sooo good." Her praise was a soft whisper.

I slipped a pillow beneath her, raising her hips higher and putting that pretty pussy on display and her ass in the air. I wasted no time plunging inside hard, again and again until she was whimpering softly and begging me not to stop. My dick worked her until she was sliding across the bed toward the headboard. Before she reached it, I slid her back to me, lifting her ass up just the way I wanted her. I didn't stop. I kept thinking about what her ex wanted with her. He was back to claim what was mine, and I was determined to take out my frustrations and leave my mark on her. Meeks was crying out my name, singing praises. Begging me not to stop even when I felt her pussy take my dick in a vice grip and she was coming. She felt so warm, and the feeling of being inside her was so good it wasn't long after that I was pinning her back down on the bed again. I grabbed onto the bars of the headboard and used it as leverage as I drove deeper. Her body answered to me. She was screaming with ecstasy as I howled my own release.

I lay there on top of her only shifting slightly to the left to allow her air to breathe but my cock stayed buried inside her. I wasn't ready to let her go. When our breathing slowed neither of us spoke. Instead, I wrapped my arm around her. Meeks clung to my flesh and we drifted off to sleep.

When I finally woke up, she was gone, and I was lying in the bed staring out at the moon that lit up the bedroom. I wasn't sure where my phone was. Probably still downstairs on the floor with my clothes, so I had no idea what time it was. My body told me it wasn't long before I would have woken up anyway. I rolled out of bed, made a quick pit stop in the bathroom, then headed downstairs in search of her. When I reached the bottom of the stairs, I spotted her standing in front of the window staring outside. She didn't turn around, but I knew she'd heard me. I walked over to her until my cock was pressed against her ass. My hands were against the glass on either side of her face. Glancing over her shoulder, she gave me a sad smile before looking out the window again. I could tell she wanted to talk but didn't know how. Too late. I was not interested in hearing what she had to say because I could tell it was going to be nothing but gibberish. I don't do gibberish. I wanted fact. Words that were straight to the point. Honesty, not wishy-washy. And she was titter-tottering on the fucking fence. Damn, the jealousy was back, but so was my hard dick. She felt it moving against her soft round ass.

"Howard, I—"

"I don't want to hear it. Come back to bed."

She made no motion to return to her room, which was fine. I don't think I could have waited that long. I lifted her hips and pushed my dick inside her again. I heard the soft sigh, air that was warming the window. Holding her hips, I began pumping her feverishly. The way I was fucking her, what the hell was there to even think about? I was determined to put something heavier on her mind than the shit she was contemplating.

"Raise up on your toes," I instructed her, then I gave her no room to leave. No space to move. Her naked body pinned between the glass and me. The beige sheers hanging from the curtain rods were the only things saving the entire complex from seeing what it looked like to be fucked in the wee hours of the morning. The big question was, which one of us was being fucked? Bending my hips, I pumped her from a different angle and brought one hand around to stroke her clit. I felt the fire burning, but I wasn't ready yet to stop. I wanted her pussy so sore that she'd be still feeling me days after my departure.

I pulled out long enough to turn her around. Dayana's eyes were wide and dark with what looked like fear and desire. I lifted her and lowered her down onto my cock and walked her back to the wall and leaned against it. I pounded in her forcefully, fucking her the way she had asked me to, the way her whimpering was begging me to please her. With my arms, I spread her legs wider and penetrated her even deeper.

"Watch me fuck you," I demanded.

She lowered her head and I watched the expression on her face. The desire was building in her eyes. The sight of my dick going inside that sweet, wet pussy was so overwhelming. No matter how hard I fucked her, her body responded to me. Her head lifted and our eyes locked. Her pussy clenched around me, and Meeks was crying out my name. I pumped even harder, holding her hips and dragging her up and down the length of me, slamming her back against the wall then dragging her to me again until I exploded. Even though I was done, I kept her their pinned against the wall, her legs up and over my arms, spread. Her juices surrounded me. I wanted to hold onto this moment for as long as I could. To make sure she didn't forget. Hell, me either. Not that that was even possible. She was in my soul. Hell, Meeks had my heart. Just admitting that pissed me off even more.

A phone rang. It was Drake's ringtone. Our eyes met again. But hers were searching, silently pleading with me to understand. I was pissed off and yet I released her. When she reached for her phone and looked down at the screen and hesitated, I knew it was him. Dammit. I wanted answers, but I was going to wait until she got off the phone to get them.

"By the way," she said, her eyes meeting mine. "While you were upstairs, Giselle called." She rolled her beautiful eyes, pressed Talk on the screen and walked away.

40

MEEKS

"What did he want?" Howard asked the second I returned to the room. He didn't have to say his name. I knew who he was talking about.

"To talk."

"Talk, huh? Is that all he wanted?"

He was going to make me say it. After the way he just fucked my brains out, how in the world was I going to say that? "Let's not make this about him."

"Then, what's it about?"

"It's about trust."

His brow rose. "And what did you come up with?"

I didn't hesitate before saying, "Why is Giselle still calling you?"

"How the hell should I know? I told her to stop calling me."

"And yet she hasn't stopped." I blew out a frustrated breath. What a way to fuck up a great morning. "I think we both should take some time to think about what we want."

Howard laughed. "Let me guess. You want to take a break so you can see him."

This conversation wasn't going at all how I'd planned it. "Listen. H—"

"I'm not interested in games." Howard walked away and started putting on the clothes he'd left on the floor last night. Oh, what a night.

I had to explain things to him a little differently this time, to make sure he understood how important this was for me. "Look, Keim. I'm not playing games. I like what we have. I like it a lot. I just don't like the way I act around you."

"And how is that?"

"Insecure," I mumbled. "That's not easy for me to admit."

"Day, since we've been together, I've done everything I could to show you how much I care about you. I've even announced to my friends that you are the only woman I want in my life, so I don't see what the problem is."

"The problem is I feel like you have too many other women in your life. Regardless of the relationship, they're still there."

He shook his head. "I can't change that. My life didn't begin the day I met you."

"And neither did mine. I know when someone is trying to get with my man."

"Oh yeah, well, I know when someone is trying to get back with my woman. I saw the way that dude was looking, like he'd just won the fucking lottery." His eyes met mine in a hard stare. "Let me guess, he asked you to give him another chance."

I just stared.

"Don't tell me you're thinking about letting him break your heart again."

I shook my head. "No, I'm just trying to figure all of this out. I've had my heart broken so many times. I don't know if I'm willing to take that chance again with anyone."

"What does that mean for us?"

I took a deep breath and searched his eyes. I needed him to understand. "It means I need time to think and figure out why relationships always leave me feeling so insecure."

"So, this isn't about your ex?"

I shook my head. "No, it isn't about him, but seeing Dame made me realize that before I can be serious with anyone, I need to figure out who I am and what I want."

He didn't look happy. "I'm leaving tomorrow," he finally said.

"What?"

"We had a last-minute swap out. Bailey is doing everything she can to get me ready to leave in the next forty-eight hours. She deserves an award for that."

Bailey had left me a message to call her. Now I know why. "I'll make sure to submit her for one."

He put one leg back into his jeans and then the other. "Are you going to tell me why he was calling you?"

He was not going to let it go. "Breakfast." I shrugged. "A second chance."

Howard gave me a long, hard stare as he yanked the shirt over his head. I reached down for my own t-shirt and put it on.

"I'll take it by your silence that you're considering it."

"I don't know what I want at the moment."

"Hmmm, interesting." There was no mistaking the sarcasm in his voice.

"What is that supposed to mean?"

"What that means is I'm surprised to hear you're considering giving him a second chance."

Now he was putting words in my mouth.

"What the hell have we been doing the last few weeks…passing the time?" he asked.

I met his eyes and shook my head. "No, not at all. I care a lot about you."

"I hear a *but* at the end of that sentence."

I shook my head. "There's no but. I just need time to think."

"Take all the time you need," Howard said, but I could tell he didn't mean it. He didn't mean it at all.

"I love what we have," I confessed.

"If you did then you wouldn't need time to think."

"That's not true." I followed him out the room. He stopped and swung around.

"The mistake I made was by not defining what this is." He used his fingers to point at me and himself. "This we developed between us." He reached out and dragged me to him and gave me a rough kiss, lining his long, hard body against mine, pressing me into him, and overwhelming me. "Let me make myself clear. I want you. Mind, body, and soul. There. I've put my feelings out into the universe, but you've got to want the same. I need to know that you want me to pursue you. I told you, once you do, I'm coming for you hard."

"Please, I—"

Holding up a hand, he cut me off. "We'll talk when I get back."

"No, I don't want you to leave before we've had a chance to talk." I had to get him to understand but he wasn't having it.

"Tell me when I return."

I couldn't believe what he was saying. This was why I liked him so much. I rushed over and kissed him hard on the lips, then drew back and gazed up at him. "Will I see you before you leave?"

"We'll talk when I get back." I took that as a *no*.

I watched him leave. What he was saying was the best way to leave things. I didn't want to say something I might later have to take back, and I didn't want him to make any promises. I needed to get this thing with Dame over with for good first. Close that chapter. I also needed to figure out why I had such a hard time trusting. Until I did that, there was no way I was going to be able to give my heart and soul to anyone.

41

MEEKS

Two days later, I drove over to Hangar 9 to watch the team leave. Bailey was doing accountability and bags were being loaded onto a C-130. I stood far enough away so I wasn't seen. One hundred and sixty members were leaving. Backpacks were on their backs. Duffel bags were being weighed and loaded onto the plane as I watched. I always felt a strong sense of pride when I witnessed the men and women serving beside me dedicate their lives to our country.

The flight line was a no-hat zone, so it was easy to spot Howard. Since he was the most senior NCO, he was the troop commander. I swallowed and remained frozen in place as I watched him walk toward the plane with so much lazy, sexy confidence that a warm, delicious feeling slid down my spine. Once he reached the top of the stairs, he stopped, slipped the bag from his shoulder, and stood to the side while the others made their way across the flight line. One by one, the team boarded. Howard waited outside the door and greeted each with a handshake and a smile. Goodness, he was such an amazing leader. No wonder his Airmen had mad respect for him.

As the last member boarded, Howard turn his head and my heartbeat quickened. Even though I couldn't see his eyes, I knew he was looking at me. I drew in a deep breath and stared. I couldn't stop looking at him. Little pulses sparkled, and my heart raced.

"Senior Master Sergeant Meeks, I didn't know you were coming over."

I whipped my head around at the sound of Bailey's voice to find her standing behind me. "I decided to come and see them off."

"The PDF line went well; everyone was present and accounted for," she said excitedly.

"Wonderful," I whispered. The personnel deployment function line was the final check for deploying Airmen to ensure all paperwork was correct before deploying. "Is there anything you need me to do to help?"

"No, ma'am. I'm going to wait until the aircraft leaves, then I'll go up to the office and depart everyone in the system before I head to lunch."

"Okay, I'll see you this afternoon."

As soon as she left, I looked back at the plane. Howard was gone. The door to the aircraft was closing. Not seeing him didn't do anything to stop the ache of missing him. The memories of his body over mine...inside of me. I had hoped to see him yesterday before he left, but he hadn't return any of my calls. Howard was a man of his word.

We'll talk when I get back.

That meant I had less than four weeks to get ready.

I made it back to my car when my cell phone rang. Dame's number popped up on the screen. I took a deep breath and pushed the number on my steering wheel to answer the call.

"Hey, Dame."

"Hey, baby."

I remembered the way his terms of endearment used

to keep me wet for him but now the words did nothing for me. In fact, it felt off. Maybe because I never expected to hear him refer to me that way again.

"You have plans for this evening?"

Yep. I planned to spend the evening feeling sorry for myself.

I buried my face in my hands and released a slow breath before saying, "I guess I do now."

"One of the officers in my class mentioned there's a great place near the Coliseum with live jazz." There was no mistaking the excitement in his voice.

"Yes, with a saxophone player."

"So, you heard about it too?" He didn't wait for an answer. "Sounds like you want to go."

I lifted my head and nodded, even though he couldn't see me. "I do." The two of us had always liked jazz clubs. "I've heard it's a great place to go." *And I thought I'd get a chance to share it with Howard.*

"Good. How about we have dinner first?" When I didn't respond right away, he added, "I want to spend every second I can with you."

"Sure. Dinner sounds great."

I went back to the office and completed my work for the day. Every few minutes I caught myself checking my phone, hoping for a text from Howard that never came. I told myself to let it go and focus on the evening ahead. I had plenty of time to sort through our relationship later.

On the way home, I stopped at the commissary and picked up groceries. I also grabbed a bottle of red wine. Once at home, I pulled off my ABU top and retrieved a bottle of water from the refrigerator, took a seat on the couch, and unlaced my boots. I flicked on the television and watched an episode of *Flip or Flop* while I unwound. Where was the excitement I used to feel knowing I was going to spend the evening with Dame? Instead, I felt so relaxed and uninterested. I preferred spending my evening binge watching. Sure, I was looking forward to seeing him, but I couldn't quite put my finger on it, except to say the only one I had been thinking about this afternoon was Howard. I missed him.

Get it together!

In the next few weeks I had to get passed my insecurities and figure out what I wanted from Howard. But tonight, I would focus on Dame. I had to know for sure if what we had was over before I could move on and start a new beginning.

After the thirty-minute episode, I poured myself a glass of wine then went upstairs to get ready for dinner. I turned on my iPad and listened to iHeart radio. I took a hot shower and by the time I shut off the water, I was humming to myself. I was determined to have a great evening. At one time, I had been hopelessly in love with Dame, so spending time together would help to understand what my feelings were and if Dame was part of the reason why I was so afraid of opening up my heart to someone else. Only this time, it would be different. Dame had gone back home to his family and had given it a try for the sake of his children, but now knew they had been hurting the kids by trying to stay together. If I put thoughts of Howard aside and kept reminding myself, I would remember and understand this was our chance to find out. The problem was my heart was saying one thing while my mind had already headed in a different direction. I drew a sigh and pushed the uncertainty away. I had to figure it out. One way or another.

I found a red dress that required a racerback bra. I slipped on a black one with matching panties then slid the dress over my head. Staring into the full-length mirror, I grinned and liked what I saw. The material clung to my hips and looked amazing over my ass. At the back of my closet were a pair of black strappy sandals with three-inch heels. They were perfect to complement the dress. I was ready to drink, laugh, listen to music, and maybe even dance.

Once my makeup was perfect and my favorite scent of Escada was applied to my most intimate parts, I went downstairs and poured another glass of wine and waited.

Dame was right on time.

I opened the door to find him looking amazing in a gray dress shirt, starched black slacks, and gray combat-style boots. I drew a deep breath and immediately the familiar scent of Dolce & Gabbana Light Blue cologne filled my nostrils. The smell brought back so many memories.

"Hi," I said, and suddenly felt shy.

"Hello, beautiful." Dame leaned forward and pressed his lips to mine. The kiss was familiar and nice, but there were no sparks.

"You ready to go? A brotha is starving."

I smiled. "Sure. Let me get my purse." I stepped away and grabbed the small bag from the console table. "I'm ready." I locked the door. Dame took my hand and laced our fingers together. It was something that we used to do all the time and it felt natural. He led me to the Volvo and assisted me onto the passenger's seat before he walked around to the other side.

Relax, Day. You know him. And now he's free.

I watched as he walked around the car toward the driver's seat.

But he isn't Howard.

I shook off the thought. The last thing I wanted to do this evening was compare Howard to Dame. One man didn't have anything to do with the other. The only common denominator was me.

Dame slid onto the driver's seat and shut the door. Once his seatbelt was in place, he turned and looked over, meeting my eyes. "What do you have a taste for?"

I shrugged. "I'm flexible. What do *you* want to eat?"

"I'm thinking barbecue."

"Barbecue it is."

"You know of any place in particular?"

I smiled. "Yes, actually I do." I gave him directions and leaned back against the soft leather. While he drove, Dame reached over and laced my fingers with his.

"I missed you," he confessed and brought my hand to his lips to kiss it. "I didn't realize how much until I walked into your office the other day."

I smiled and remained silent because I didn't know what I felt or what to say at this point. Dame didn't seem to notice. His phone rang. I looked over to see him glance down at the screen then silence the ringer.

"Do you need to get that?" I asked and felt that familiar feeling of uneasiness squeeze at my chest.

"Nope. The only person I'm focused on this evening is you." He sent a smirk my way, which I tried to return, but in my mind, I was replaying all the times his phone rang and it was his wife needing him to come home.

"I want to spend this time getting to know you again," he added, taking his eyes off the road. "I want to hear about everything that has happened in your life since you arrived on the east coast," he said, reminding me that we used to share everything.

"Nothing to tell. Not really. I moved here and settled in. Spending a lot of time at work or hanging out with Layla and Faze."

There was a pregnant pause before he said, "You seem

a little distant. Have you met someone special?"

I knew that question was going to come eventually. "I think so."

He hesitated before asking, "Do I need to be worried?"

"It's too soon to tell," came out my mouth before I had a chance to stop it. I gave him a weak smile. Now Dame was going to think my hesitation had to do with him, and that wasn't completely true. The problem was Dame was very competitive. Like Howard, he loved a challenge.

"You and I... does this feel awkward to you?" he asked, taking his eyes briefly away from the road.

I nodded and decided to be honest. "It does. Just a little."

"That's understandable. It's been awhile. But what we had was so powerful I have no doubt that we can get that back," he said confidently.

I wasn't so sure. I learned a long time ago that people cross paths but that didn't mean that they were meant to be in each other's lives forever. We all served a purpose. Maybe I had been in his life to get him to cherish what he had with his wife, or maybe I had been there to show him what he had been missing. I don't know. I just don't know.

He headed toward the restaurant, and as soon as we pulled into the parking lot, my nostrils were filled with the scent of smoked meat. Goodness. Memories of my first time there came flashing back at me. It was so intense I realized coming here had been a huge mistake. This was my place with Howard. Not with Dame.

I faked a smile when he came around and helped me out the car. He took my hand and escorted me towards the door. This was such a mistake, but I was going to just go with it. We were escorted to a table and immediately glanced over the menu. I suggested the potato salad, and Dame was game. We also ordered the baked beans, brisket, and wings.

We talked and I noticed how hard he was trying to rekindle what we once had. I wished I could feel the same way. I felt like a fraud trying to recreate something that no longer existed, but I refused to accept that. Not yet. Dame and I experienced a love that I never thought I could experience with anyone else. He had been all that and then some. Or at least he used to be. Had I really changed that much?

We arrived at the jazz club just at the start of the first set.

There was a line, but I was happy to see a grown and sexy crowd dressed to impress. My dress was perfect. Dame stood beside me with a hand low at my waist. He paid the admission fee and we walked inside. The club was huge with bar height tables and chairs that surrounded a large dance floor. The stage was close to the front of the building, so there really weren't any bad seats. The club was already crowded. Most of the patrons must have arrived for happy hour and stuck around. Dame found a table in the middle of the room. He took my hand and led me through the crowd, and I couldn't help but wonder if any of Howard's friends were here and would see us. It was dark in the space and yet I scanned the area. I was being ridiculous. I didn't have much time to worry before we were seated. Within minutes, I forgot all about being seen and found myself captivated by the performance. I loved jazz, and the quartet was phenomenal. And when the female saxophone player moved up to the microphone, Dame and I looked at each other and grinned. We used to go to the historical district of Vine Street in Kansas City for Jazz and barbecue all the time. It had been our thing. By the end of the first set, his arm was draped across my back possessively.

I leaned in closer so he could hear me over the sounds of the DJ who was playing Raphael Saadiq during intermission. "Oh, my goodness, that was amazing."

"Now *that's* the smile I've been waiting to see," he said, grinning. I stared up into Dame's eyes and felt something hot and familiar. And scary.

"Would you like something to drink?" His lips brushed my earlobe, and I realized how intimate this was getting.

"Sure. I'm going to the ladies' room." I didn't really have to go, but I needed a little distance between us for a few minutes. I slipped off the stool and headed toward the only obvious place for the restrooms, which was at the rear of the club. I hadn't gone three feet before the men started staring and throwing compliments as I passed. I could feel their eyes burning a hole in the back of my dress as I sauntered toward the rear. There was a single bathroom, one for the men and one for the women, which meant I had to stand and wait. I walked up to the door to see a woman in a hot pink dress and black rhinestone stilettoes ahead of me. She swung around, and it took a moment for me to realize who was standing there. I think it was the long, dark wig.

"There you are," she exclaimed and grinned.

"Rein?" It was a question because at this point, I wasn't sure. She could have had a twin sister I didn't know about.

"Yes, Day, it's me," she said like it should have been easy to recognize her.

My eyes traveled the length of her. "What—"

"I'm out on a date." she said by way of an explanation.

"And?" I said because I wasn't following her.

The door to the bathroom opened and as soon as a short, round woman with a fabulous short cut departed, Rein dragged me inside with her and locked the door.

"Don't tell me you brought me in here to watch you pee?" I'm just saying.

"No, I brought you in here so I could hear about your date."

My brow rose. "My date?"

"Layla told me."

Of course, she did. "You two have gotten pretty chummy." I walked over to the mirror and took in my appearance as I said, "I wouldn't really call it a date, but I am out with my ex."

I caught her reflection. Rein scrunched up her nose. My eyes traveled up to the Tyra Banks-looking wig on her head. I whipped around. "Wait a minute. Aren't you on a date?"

She blinked her faux lashes. "Yes, I'm out with Matthew."

I started waving my finger like it was a magic wand. "What's up with this look?"

She shrugged and looked into the mirror, and I noticed she was wearing blue contacts. "I'm not ready yet for him to know who I am and what I look like."

"What?" I exploded with laughter. "Are you serious?"

"Absolutely. I do it all the time. Once I feel that the relationship is going somewhere then I'll tell him my real name."

"What a minute… he doesn't even know your real name?" I shook my head. "I thought he was sweet, and you really liked him?"

She took her time before admitting, "I do, but it's always that way in the beginning. I'm waiting to be sure."

"'Goodness. And I thought I was bad."

"I'm just smart." She released a deep belly laugh that was surely fueled with a sprinkle of insanity, and I joined her. My girl was bonafide cray-cray and, for that reason, I liked her even more.

There was a hard knock at the door.

"I'll be out in a minute," Rein yelled loud enough to be heard over the music.

"So, what's up with you and this guy? I saw you walk in, but I was waiting for the band to break before I came over. By the way, my name is Montana tonight."

"Really, Blue? You told him your name is Montana?" I asked wide-eyed.

"It's my middle name."

Blue Montana Rein. I don't know what her mother had been thinking, but I liked it.

"What happened with you and Howard?"

"We are taking a break. Between Giselle and Sherry, I don't know how much more I can take."

"Ooh, speaking of Giselle…" She purposely let her voice
fade. "Oh hell… Sorry, boo, but I might as well use the bathroom while I'm in here." She moved over to the toilet, and I mumbled under my breath and turned around.

"You must really feel comfortable around me," I said.

"Chile, yes. You're like the sister I've never had. Even Layla and I talk on the phone at least once a day."

Gossiping about me of course.

I reached inside my purse for my lipstick. "What were you about to tell me about Giselle?"

There was another hard pound.

"We're coming. Hold your horses," Rein voice boomed.

I laughed. This was a side of Rein I hadn't seen before.

"Anyway, I heard that Lieutenant Miles filed a complaint against Giselle."

I swiveled around just as she flushed the toilet. "For what?"

"Stalking," she said, eyes dancing with mischief. She then moved over to the sink.

"Are you serious?" I nearly jumped out of my skin when I realized she'd said Giselle had been stalking someone else. I needed to sit down. "Hell, I might as well go, too." I took a seat waiting for the juicy details.

"Apparently she had been stalking him the way she's been doing Howard. Showing up at his house…his job…blowing up his phone."

I was shaking so bad I could have peed on myself. "This sounds like a *Lifetime* movie."

"Tell me about it." Rein reached over for a paper towel, then turned around and leaned against the counter as she spoke. "I was told the two of them used to date, but it didn't last long because she's crazy. You already know Giselle doesn't know how to take no as an answer. Miles had moved on and was dating a registered nurse. Giselle started stalking and pretending something was still going on between them. I
heard the nurse got sick of it and left Miles."

"Damn." The same way I had reacted with Howard. I couldn't help but wonder if that had been Giselle's intentions all along.

I handled my business, flushed, and moved over to the sink. I noticed Rein watching me.

"I don't know why you're trying to act like you don't care when I already know you do." She gave me that same annoyed look I got from Layla sometimes.

"I never said I didn't care." In fact, what I felt for him was more than that. That's what frightened me.

"Just don't end your relationship with Howard because of that psycho."

This time there was a closed fist knock; the way the police do when they're about to bust down the door.

"Let's go."

Nodding, I reached for a paper towel and followed her out the room where we were met by the angry expression of a beautiful, light-skinned woman in a shimmering black dress who we both ignored.

I couldn't believe how stupid I had been. Howard had been telling me the truth and yet I refused to believe him. Regret spread through me like a virus, slowing my steps. The mistake might cost me any chance of gaining his trust again. The realization hit me in a rush to my gut. While Rein headed to the left side of the club where her date was seated, I grabbed onto the edge of the bar and took several deep breaths while I pulled myself together.

"Beautiful, you okay?"

I felt a hand on my elbow and looked up and down at a short, older man with a receding hairline. There was concern in his eyes, along with that predatory gleam.

"No, I'm fine. I tripped on my shoe." I gave him a smile that said thank you, but I'm not interested before heading toward the table. As I made my way, I saw Dame with his head down texting away on his phone, and the feeling of uneasiness returned. Goodness, would I ever be able to get past that feeling? As soon as he saw me, he completed the text and put his phone away.

"I was getting ready to come looking for you," he said, smiling. I spotted a glass with gin and orange juice waiting for me. I took the seat beside him and immediately reached for the drink.

"One of the guys from my warrior leadership course is here. I told him we didn't mind sharing our table with him and his date."

"No, of course not," I managed between sips.

The rest of the show I couldn't concentrate. Instead, I thought about what Rein had just told me. Howard tried to tell me, but I refused to listen. Was I really that insecure? As I listened to the music I began to wonder if maybe I had made a big deal over nothing with him and his ex-wife. Ugh… Why couldn't I have just believed Howard?

After the show, I faked a headache and asked Dame to take me home. On the ride I was quiet. I had so many thoughts going through my head and so many questions that I couldn't answer. Dame's phone vibrated, and I was instantly on edge and quick to assume the worse. Why was it so hard for me to trust? When he pulled up to my townhouse, he started to shut off the car, but I reached over at stopped him.

"The porch light is on, so you don't have to get out," I said.

"Okay, I hope your head feels better." There was no mistaking the disappointment in his expression.

Leaning over, I pressed my lips against his, then leaned back, staring into his eyes while I caressed his cheek. "Thank you for a wonderful evening."

"The first of many," he whispered against my mouth. He kissed me again, this time deepening the kiss. I allowed it, and yet there were still no sparks, just that old familiarity. I was the first to draw back.

"I'll call you tomorrow," Dame told me.

I nodded, stepped out of the car, and made it into the house. Sleep wasn't going to come easy.

42

MEEKS

"I'm going back inside to talk to your mother," I told Mya.

"Okay." She jumped off the swing and rushed over to climb the stairs of the slide. I shook my head as I watched her. If I could find a way to bottle up all that energy, I would be rich.

Faison was cutting the grass at the far end of the yard. I waved at him and headed back inside. My sister was finally off the phone.

"Hey, sorry about that. It was one of the moms at Mya's school. We're planning a huge fundraiser next weekend." Since she was a stay-at-home mom, she was always participating in events.

"I don't know where you find the energy after dealing with Maya all day."

"Day, you're only as old as you feel." She reached for an oven mitt, moved over to the double oven, and removed a large breakfast casserole.

"That looks good."

She grinned. "Of course, it does."

My sister loved to cook, which was one of the reasons why immediately after buying the three-bedroom house, she had the kitchen renovated. Now, the room had stainless steel appliances with a commercial-sized stove, dark cabinets, and gray and white Quartz countertops. The large island was the central focus of the space and surrounded by silver barstools. I moved to one and took a seat.

"Rein told me she saw you last night."

I raised a brow. "In one of her costumes."

Layla laughed. "She told me about that, too."

I laughed right along with her. "That girl is crazy."

She walked over and turned off the oven, then grabbed two bottles of from a large side-by-side refrigerator and slid one over to me.

"Thanks."

"So, what brings you over here this early in the morning?"

I glanced down at my watch. "It's ten o'clock."

"For a Saturday, that's early for you." She was glaring at me like she was my mama. She took a seat on the stool across from me.

I popped the cap on the bottle and took a long, thirsty drink. "I needed someone to talk to."

"How was your date last night?" Layla asked but I could tell by her expression, my big sister already knew where the conversation was headed.

I shrugged. "It was okay. Dame is still the same person."

"But you're not."

"I don't know if that's it or if I just don't want to travel down that road again with him."

She nodded. "Well, that's understandable."

"I don't know if we could ever get that back, and part of me doesn't want to try anymore." Leaning forward, I placed my elbows on the island. "Every time his phone rings, or I catch him texting, I have flashbacks of that bullshit I went through with him and his wife. I don't know if I want to go through that again."

"Do you love him?"

I hesitated. "I love him, but I'm not in love with him. If I was, I would be willing to do whatever it took to get back to what we used to have."

"What does he say?"

"Dame wants to try, but I don't think that's even possible now."

Layla looked stunned, but that didn't stop her from probing. "And, why is that?"

"Because I'm at a new place in my life. I've moved on and met an amazing man."

I caught the grin before Layla brought the bottle to her lips and took a swallow.

"I don't want to go back to what we used to have. It just doesn't fit into my new life. I don't miss that. I don't miss Dame, at least not in that way."

"Wow. You have changed a lot from that sniffling cry baby that was calling me every five minutes."

"Don't make me throw this bottle at you," I teased.

"So, where did you leave things between the two of you last night?" I saw that curiosity in her eyes.

"I kissed him goodbye and went inside."

"Wow, you really are over him."

I nodded. "Yes, I am."

I could tell she was proud of me. I was proud of me, too. "But I think part of the reason why I am over him is because I am too afraid to go back down that path. I didn't like the woman I had become. I went from needy and desperate, to bitter and insecure. I don't want to be her anymore." I swallowed. "I'm afraid I'm headed down the same path with Howard."

"You know who you just described, right?"

"Yes. Mama. And that's what scared me. I don't want

o be her," I said, downing the rest of my water. "All we heard for years was the bitterness. '*Military men ain't shit,*' and '*Look at your father and the way he abandoned us.*' All of the resentment and hateful words about how he'd treated us."

Layla hesitated before saying, "I know you hate when I say this, but I think Mama's to blame for a lot of what you're feeling."

"Daddy is just as responsible," I said in protest.

My sister drew a breath and knew better not to go there. We've had so many disagreements over which parent was to blame that over the years we decided to just agree to disagree. "You really need to talk to him."

"And you really need to talk to Mama."

Her gaze held a challenging gleam. "I will if you will."

I flinched, stung by her words. "What? Are you serious?"

Layla gave a dismissive wave. "Yeah, yeah. This has been going on long enough. But the same goes for you. You have to confront Daddy about your hurt. It took months of therapy for me to figure that out."

Frustration and fear twisted my insides. "You're right. I don't want to lose Howard because I'm afraid to trust. And if that means talking to Daddy, then I'll do it, but I'm not making any promises. I just need to understand."

"I think you made a wise decision."

I went to open my mouth and then closed it. I wasn't so sure.

43

MEEKS

While I watched the entrance, I sipped my second cup of horrible, watered-down coffee. Goodness, even after I mentioned it to the waitress and she made a second pot, it didn't get any better. I drew a breath, filling my nostrils with the scent of burnt toast and bacon. Reaching for the sugar, I added more to the cup and took another sip and cringed. *Oh well.* Since I hadn't come to the diner for the coffee, I decided to let it go and gather my thoughts. The bell over the door rang and my heart rate galloped in anticipation before I spotted a short, petite woman and a child step into the small establishment. Growing impatient, I glanced down at my watch and scowled. I'd been sitting in the corner booth at the back of the hole in the wall in Glenn Burnie, Maryland for over thirty minutes. Ever since my arrival, I begun to doubt my reason for coming. Panic tightened my chest. What the hell was I doing?

"You ready to order?"

My head snapped up to look at the waitress standing there with a hand propped at her hip, tapping her foot impatiently. This was the second time she'd asked me, and it wasn't her fault I was still waiting.

"Sure. Can I have some raisin toast?"

She frowned. "That's it?"

I raised my mug. "And more coffee."

She scribbled on the pad then ripped off the page and headed toward the counter. Obviously, she was having a bad day. Probably a lot of small orders and low tips. I would have to remember to leave her a generous donation.

I was looking around at the wooden tables covered with blue vinyl tablecloths and the nostalgic décor on the walls when I heard the bell again. My head whipped toward the door and this time my breath stalled because I saw my father, Harry Jackson, coming through the door. He stepped in and scanned the room, and his eyes widened when he recognized me. A grinned curled his lips as he made his way through the maze of tables to where I was sitting. He wore blue jeans and a royal blue shirt that showed that, even at sixty-five, he was still in great shape.

"Dayana," he said, smiling nervously.

I tried my best to return a grin, but I couldn't even fake the way I was feeling. Shock was at the top of my list. I rose and didn't make any attempt to move in any way that wasn't necessary. My father walked over and embraced me in a strong hug while my arms remained at my sides.

"It's so good to see you," he said. The breath I had been holding gushed out as he squeezed.

I reared back and stepped out of his embrace. Collapsing back down onto my seat, I signaled for him to take the one across from him. The waitress wasted no time coming over. While she took his order, I stared at my father over the rim of the cup.

I could see why my mother had fallen in love with him. He had smooth, dark berry skin and eyes that were copper and identical to mine. His curls were closely cropped, Army-style, and he had an intriguing scar that bisected his upper lip. He was handsome with a precision cut beard and mustache with only minimal gray.

Once the waitress left, my father shifted on the seat and placed his hands on the tablecloth. Awkwardness filled the booth. I twisted my hands nervously in my lap.

"Thank you for calling me. You have no idea how long I've been waiting for this chance to talk to you." The intensity of his gaze as he studied me had warmth blooming in my stomach. There was no way I was falling for that. We both had waited a long time for this moment…but for different reasons.

"The only reason why I'm here is because I have to let the past go, so, I can move forward with my life."

His gaze remained steady. I was quite sure he would agree. "I would like that. It's time we talked and put everything out in the opening." My father was grinning like this was a family reunion or he'd finally found his long-lost daughter. Neither was the case. He'd always known where I was and how to reach me. Hell, he and Layla talked a few times each month.

I raised my hands to the table. Before I could open my mouth, the waitress returned with his coffee and refilled my mug. As soon as she was gone, my father cleared his throat and said, "So where would you like to start the conversation?" He reached over and covered my hand with his. Startling heat of familiarity swept through me. I snatched my hand back so fast I smacked myself in the chest.

"Listen, this isn't a reunion. I only came here because I need answers."

Leaning forward, he said softly, "What kind of answers?"

"I need to understand why you lied to my mother all those years."

He looked surprised. His eyes widened and my father stared before he finally lowered the coffee mug and folded his hands on the table in front of him. "I won't make any excuses for my relationship with your mother, but I never lied to her."

"You're lying," I cried, outraged that after all this time, he wasn't going to be honest.

I watched my father looking around and I realized I was talking loud enough to have all the customers in the diner in our business. I lowered my voice, but the ice remained. "Mama told me you promised to leave your wife."

"Day, I was a young, black man who had just been commissioned as an officer in the United States Air Force. That was huge back then." Despite the pride, he shook his head. "I had married my college sweetheart and was having regrets. I came back home wishing I was single like all of my buddies." He paused as the waitress arrived with a stack of toast for me, and bacon and hash-browns for him. I doubt I would be eating more than a slice of bread to settle my stomach. I was suddenly nauseated.

"I was on TDY to Whiteman when I met Rhonda."

A conversation played in my mind of Mama telling me how she had met a handsome officer at a party. She said it was love at first sight. At least for her.

As if he's read my mind, Daddy replied, "I fell in love with your mother."

I met his eyes. "Then why didn't you leave your wife?"

He gave a strangled laugh. "Because April found out she was pregnant." His gaze locked with mine and he looked as if he was begging for me to understand. I didn't.

"Then why didn't you leave Mama alone?"

"I tried." He dragged a hand down his face. "But Rhonda was like a drug."

I nodded knowingly and mumbled, "Mama used to say you were like a shot of tequila. She loved the feeling she had when she was with you regardless of how bad you were for her."

My father smiled and for a moment he appeared lost down memory lane. I pulled him back.

"What I don't understand is why you strung Mama along when you knew she was crazy about you?"

"Dayana, I tried to end things with Rhonda and do right by my wife and my son, but I couldn't stay away. Everything that was missing from home, your mother filled that void." His voice was filled with frustration.

I took another sip of my coffee and remembered how Dame used to tell me I checked off the boxes of everything missing in his life. I also remember begging him to be with me and the struggle he had of feeling torn in two directions.

"Once your mother found out she was pregnant with Layla, it was too late." He sighed and reached for a slice of bacon.

I took a bite of my toast, but it stuck in my throat. I had to gulp down cold coffee before I was able to speak again. "Mama said you promised her that eventually you were going to leave your wife, and that's why she kept waiting." I tried to act like I didn't understand, but I did. I, too, had been that girl with Dame.

He sadly shook his head. "Dayana, I never asked her to wait."

"But she did and then she got pregnant with me." There it was. The bitterness in my voice.

"Yes, she got pregnant with you." Warmth painted his lips. "By then Dillon was five and I was stationed at Hurlburt Field, Florida. We flew up right after you were born and spent the weekend at your house. I didn't realize how inquisitive Dillon was until we arrived, and he began asking so many questions. I was so afraid my wife would find out my lie."

"You told Dillon Mama was your cousin," I said and shoved my chin out.

There was regret in his eyes, but I wasn't falling for it. Mom told me about that day when my older brother came to the house to meet me. The brother I was too young to remember. "And even after all of that, Mama waited." I took another sip of coffee and watched him sitting there, shoulders slump with remorse.

"It was wrong. I know that. If I wasn't married, I would have made Rhonda an honest woman and we could have all been a family, but I couldn't. I didn't mean for any of it to happen the way it had, but I was in the service and I wasn't willing to risk my career by my commander finding out I was having an affair." He looked so broken that I almost felt sorry for him because I knew what he was thinking. Mama never told me, but her younger sister, Roxy, had been visiting one summer and spilled the drama.

Mama had caught a plane to Florida and knocked on the door of the Jackson's apartment with me on her hip and Layla holding her hand. She had confronted the other woman and by the time my father had arrived home from the base, the two women were sitting in the kitchen eating cookies while Layla and Dale played, and I slept. The real Mrs. Jackson made it clear her husband would support his children and give them all the benefits they were entitled from the military, but the relationship between Mama and Jackson had to end. She added that if she ever found out he and Mama were still messing around, she would ruin his military career. I think that's when Mama mentally broke down because Aunt Roxy said Mama was never the same again.

Daddy would call to check on us and even made plans for Layla and I to come and spend summers with him and his family. I remember being six, and then seven, and even eight, excited, telling all my friends I was going to spend the summer with my father and brother in Florida and, yet, each year it never happened. I was so hurt. When he promised to come to my tenth birthday, I didn't believe him because I just didn't trust him anymore, but there he had been. By then, Daddy had been Major Jackson and proud of all that he had achieved. He talked about the big house that he had in Alexandria, Virginia and showed me pictures of my brother and my two younger sisters. I asked him if I could go with him.

"Not this time, baby."

"But why?" I cried. "Why can't I go with you?"

He shook his head. "Day, you're too young to understand."

He had bought presents, and Layla and I stayed with him at the hotel that night. I remember hoping that he would surprise us in the morning and tell us we were going with him. Only we checked out the hotel and he took us home. I cried for weeks and refused to take any of his calls. It went on like that for years. He would show up, spend a day or two, and then he was gone again. He left us all—Layla, me, and even Mama—hoping and wishing for so much more. He sent me cards and even showed up for some of my track meets in high school, and he had been there for my high school graduation, but by then I told myself I hated him. I hated what he had done to Layla, me, and Mama. And she never let us forget it.

"To this day, Mama hates men. She's bitter and angry and has absolutely no trust when it comes to relationships," I told him.

"I know." He sighed. "Somehow your mother always knew where I was stationed and then, out of the blue, I would receive a call from her."

I never knew that.

"She would rant and rave and cuss me out for days, and then suddenly the calls would stop. Time would pass and then the calls would start again."

"She's never married. Any time she met someone nice she would end the relationship because she doesn't trust men." I felt tears threatening my eyes. I shook my head, trying to hold them back while I was hit with a cruel punch of memories. "Now here I am, feeling so unworthy of love. I'm insecure and needy." I blew out a long breath. "I'm afraid I'm going to end up just like her." My words caused his eyes to widen in alarm, but I continued.

"I have spent my life not trusting. Especially men in uniform. Mama used to say, 'Military men can't be trusted,' and I believed her. Especially since I'd had several failed relationships with servicemen. Most of them were lying about another woman and just couldn't be trusted."

"Day, I'm so sorry. I wish things could have been different. I wanted you and Layla to be a part of my life and get to know your brother and your twin sisters."

"Well, we would have if you hadn't cut us out of your life." At the blank look on his face, I continued. "Why did you make so many promises to me? Do you know I used to have my bag packed weeks in advance, sitting right next to my closet door?"

"Day, I—"

I was so fired up I cut him off. "I would brag to all my friends I was going to Florida to spend the summer with my dad and my big brother. And then you wouldn't show up. I was so humiliated I would hide all summer so my friends wouldn't see me." I could still remember the pain of feeling abandoned that spread through my vein like a virus. "Do you have any idea how much that hurt me?" My voice had elevated again when I noticed the other patrons looking our way.

"Day, I don't know what Rhonda told you, but I asked to keep you girls every summer. Your mother wouldn't let us have you."

"Us?"

"April and I."

I rolled my eyes at the mention of his wife and bit into the hard toast.

"Sweetheart. April stopped me from seeing your mother, but she never stood in the way of me seeing my girls."

I shook my head dismissively, trying to hold back the memories that had tormented me for decades, but they continued to play in my mind like a scratched vinyl record. "Please don't lie to me anymore."

Reaching over, my father covered my hand with his. My eyes snapped up to meet his, only this time I didn't pull away.

"It's true, Day. Every summer we made plans to have you and Layla, and every summer your mother refused to let you come."

"That's not true," I spat defensively.

His expression was calm. "I'm not lying. Your mother was…" I could tell he was trying to choose his words carefully. Good choice. Despite our faults, I was very protective when it came to my family. "After April found out about your mother and I and I ended the relationship, your mother became very bitter. I'd send her child support checks; she'd send them back. I would call, she would tell me you weren't at home. I'd make plans for you girls to come spend the summer with us and she would say yes, and then a week before it was time for me to pick you girls up, she'd change her mind."

This couldn't be real. I sat there in disbelief.

"I asked Rhonda why, and she told me, 'The girls and I are a package deal.'"

The words flowed through my chest and registered. How many times had I heard my mother speak those exact words on the phone with her girlfriends regarding guys she dated and dumped?

All or nothing. My girls and I are a package deal.

"April and I both tried to talk to her, but she refused to listen. When I threatened to go to court for visitation, she threatened to report my adultery up my chain of command."

I heard what he was saying and yet I still didn't want to believe it.

"Do you remember that summer you were at your Aunt Georgia's house?"

My eyes widened. How could I forget? It was the first time Mama ever let us stay with her. "Yes, I remember. Mama and Aunt Georgia got into a fight—" I stopped and eyed him suspiciously. "How do you know about that?"

He swallowed. "I was the reason why they got into it. Georgia asked to keep you girls that summer just so that I could get two weeks with you."

I replayed that day in my head. I would never forget it. "I had no idea what they had been fighting about. I just remember Mama punching Aunt Georgia in the mouth and them fighting in the front yard. One of the neighbors called the police."

Daddy nodded. With his shoulders slumped, he looked defeated. "Somehow your mother found out what your aunt and I had planned. She drove back to Memphis to pick you both up."

I remember we were so sad. The entire ride back to Missouri, mom was on a tirade. We never saw my aunt again.

"Aunt Georgia died that fall in a car accident." I remembered going to the funeral and Mama fainting at the church. For weeks she wouldn't speak to anyone, including us, but once she did, she blamed Layla and me for Aunt Georgia's death. I never understood why.

All this time. Layla tried to tell me, but I refused to listen. If only I had known. If only I had tried to listen. I hunched my shoulder and wanted to disappear underneath the table.

"Listen, I don't want to point the blame because I made a lot of mistakes and wish I'd handled things different." His voice had softened.

I looked up to study my father's face. His eyes were warm, unshed tears were in the corners waiting to fall. He cleared his throat, blinked, trying to push them away so he could speak.

"I would like a chance for the two of us to start over, if you'll let us."

Daddy and Layla had squashed their issues years ago, but I had been too stubborn, hurt, and afraid of what mama would say. Layla never cared what Mama thought, which was why the two of them bumped heads all the time.

"I—"

"Day, honey. You're already here. Please just stay through the weekend. Let's spend that time talking. April wants you to come to the house. Dale would like to see you. I'll even get the girls on the phone." He squeezed my hand while his eyes and voice pleaded with me to finally give him a chance.

Wasn't that the reason why I had come here, to find answers? Now that I had them, the horrible truth kept repeating inside my head. I shook the thoughts away.

"I can't make any promises, but I'd like to spend the weekend trying."

Daddy sighed and smile. "That's all I need."

44

MEEKS

I'm glad I had taken leave on Monday. That allowed me the opportunity to wait until after rush hour to check out the hotel and head back to Virginia. I wished I could say that everything was wonderful. Nope. There's still a lot of healing to be done. Even surrounded by family, I still felt the resentment. I saw the life that my brother had—the opportunity to live with both a mother and a father—and the jealousy returned. I talked to my sisters on the phone and heard about the excitement in their lives, and I was envious. Even April was kind, but I resented her the most because if it wasn't for her, maybe my parents would have gotten married and the life my siblings had could have been my life.

Daddy and I talked and spent most of the time alone, just the two of us. He allowed me to yell and cry and was always ready with open arms to hold me. It was going to take time to undo all the years of hurt and resentment, but I was on a path of recovery and I was going to continue no matter how difficult the journey. I owed it to myself. No matter how broken and insecure I felt, I was worthy of love.

I had made it as far as Richmond when my phone rang. Mama was calling. I mentally prepared myself for the verbal beatdown I was about to endure.

I pushed Talk on the steering wheel. "Hello, Mama."

"I just heard some disturbing news from your sister."

I guess that meant she and Layla were now back on speaking terms.

"What is that, Mama?"

"That you drove to Maryland to see your father." She didn't even give me a chance to speak. "Please tell me you're not that damn stupid."

I cringed and felt like that little girl again, curled up on the bed broken and alone. "I'm not stupid. I wanted to talk to him."

She cackled. "You're beginning to sound like your sister. After all he's done to you and to me, why would you even do that?"

"Because he's my father, Mama, and I had so many unanswered questions."

"I've always been honest. I told you everything you needed to know, so what could he possibly tell you that I couldn't?"

I didn't answer.

"And no matter how you spin it, Dayana, he abandoned you. He's never been there for any of us. I told you that."

"That's not what he told me."

"And you believe that bastard over me?" She was appalled.

"Mama, I'm not sure what I believe anymore. All I know is that I have issues I have to work out. Issues that are affecting my relationships. I don't know how to trust. I can't seem to have a relationship with a man."

"What did I tell you? Men can't be trusted. I taught you a long time ago the only person you can trust is yourself and God. Everyone else will disappoint you."

Uneasiness settled in my stomach. The same way it always did after one of her lectures. I had heard this my

entire life and she had me believing that there was no such thing as trust until you verified. All these years, I had endured her ridicule
and humiliation.

"Mama, I can't continue like this. It's affecting my life. I want a husband and children. I want to be happy."

She gave a harsh laughed that sent a chill racing down my spine. "Happiness? There's no happiness, especially not with a man. The only happiness you'll ever find is within yourself." She was only partly right. I needed to learn how to first be happy with me before I could ever find happiness with anyone.

How could I have been so stupid all these years to allow myself to be so insecure and empty inside?

"Mama, I'm going to have a relationship with my father and I'm going to fix my life. But you've got to change, Mama. You can't spend the rest of your life allowing this bitterness to eat you up inside. Look at what it's done to your life. In fact, look at what it's done to your girls."

There was silence on the other end, only heavy breathing.

"Dayana, I better go. I'm watching *Maury* and they're getting ready to reveal if this fool is the father or not. I'll call you later."

The phone went dead and I drew a breath. She would never change, but that wasn't going to stop me. I scrolled through my contacts and called Layla.

"Hey, Day."

"I talked to him," I announced.

"Good, I'm so happy." Layla sounded relieved. "I talked to Mama."

"I know. She just called to cuss me out."

There was a silent pause while I thought about all the

years we had endured the wrath of Rhonda.

"Day, I tried, like I promised. But I'm not ready yet to fix my relationship with Mama. I don't want that toxic behavior around Maya." Her voice was filled with frustration.

"I agree. I don't want Maya exposed to that bitterness." No child deserved that. "April and Daddy invited me up for the holiday."

"Are you going to come?" I could tell she was holding her breath with anticipation.

I blew out a shaky breath. "Yes, I'm going. I'm looking forward to seeing everyone."

"I'm so happy to hear that," she squealed. "We're planning to drive to Maryland as well."

"One big happy family," I sang while brushing tears away from my eyes.

"We can be. We just have to want it bad enough," she told me.

I paused for a moment, her confident words had rattled me, but I pulled it together and straightened my shoulders. "I was calling because I wanted to know if your therapist is taking any new patients."

"Yes, she is," she was quick to say.

I hesitated for a second before admitting, "Good, then I'm going to need that number."

"Wonderful. I'm texting it to you now."

45

MEEKS

I pulled up at my townhouse, reached for the bag of groceries off the back seat, and started for the door.

"Dayana?"

My head whipped around to see Dames coming my way. *Oh damn.* Despite the surprise, he looked handsome in his uniform, starched and stiff the way he'd always worn it.

"Hey," I greeted. "You been sitting out here waiting for me?" I asked innocently.

"Yes, since you haven't answered any of my calls, I decided to come over and see what's going on."

He was right. Since the night we had gone out to the jazz club I'd been avoiding his calls.

He stepped closer. "Day, I haven't spoken to you all week. What's going on?"

"I went to Maryland to visit my father," I explained.

"Your father?" His brow rose with surprise because he knew the story of our relationship, or at least the version my mother had planted in my head. "Oh damn, how did that go?"

I signaled for him to come inside the house. I moved to the kitchen and Dame followed. "Actually, my visit with my father went well." I put my groceries away while I gave him the Reader's Digest version of my weekend.

"Wow, that's deep. I'm happy the two of you finally had a chance to talk and work things out." Dame had taken a seat at my island. I was standing on the other side, directly across from him.

"I was thinking you were avoiding me," he said and chuckled like that possibility was ludicrous. It took a moment to realize I wasn't laughing along with him. "Wait… What's going on?"

"Dame, I've been doing a lot of thinking these last few days and I've realized something."

"What's that?" he asked cautiously.

"That relationships have their season."

He looked a little taken aback, but asked, "What does that mean?"

I drew a breath. "It means that just like the weather, relationships aren't always meant to last forever."

"Okay…" His voice trailed off while he studied my eyes. "I'm trying to understand what you are saying."

"I'm saying that I'll always love you, but our season has passed."

He countered with, "Why? I love you and you love me, Day. We can make this work. I know we can."

"I'll always love you, Dame." There was no denying that. "But we had our time, and now our season is over. My heart has healed. I was hoping there was still something there between us, but it's too late."

Leaning forward, Dame crossed his arms on the countertop as he said with a confident smirk, "Babe, you just need time. If you transfer back to Whiteman, we can make this work."

"I don't want to come back." I huffed defensively because once again it was all about him and his career. For a spit second, I thought about my father and his unwillingness to risk his career to see his girls. *Don't go there.* The healing process had begun, so I shook that thought away and pushed my shoulders back with confidence. "I love it here. I've started a new life." I swallowed. "I've met someone who I want to give my heart."

His brow launched up his forehead. "Wow, what the hell do you think I'm doing? I'm offering you my heart."

"And I gave you mine and you smashed it," I reminded and met his hard glare head on. "Do you have any idea how hard it was for me when you took your wife back?"

Dame dropped his eyes and didn't even look at me when he said, "You know why I did that."

"Yes, I do. You made your choice and I respected that, now respect the decision that I have moved on. It's time for you to go home to your children and allow me to start my new life."

Dame left shortly after. Kissed my cheek and reminded me he would be around one more day if I wanted to talk. But we both knew I wasn't going to call. Like I told him, our time had passed.

After he left, I showered, then changed into shorts and a t-shirt and caught myself smiling in the mirror. It was over. All this time I'd been holding on wondering what if. Now I knew. My life had changed. I wanted more. Deserved something greater. I just had to believe as my sister reminded me. Instead of waiting for a referral, I had contacted Military One Source and they immediately scheduled me to see a therapist. My first session was on Thursday. I was both scared and excited.

Reaching for my phone, I scrolled through my text messages until I found Howard's. I then sat there reading through every text we had exchanged since we'd met. The messages told a story of a man who was so into me. A man whom I doubted his sincerity. Was it too late? Not knowing was driving me crazy.

When I read the last text message from him, my chest ached.

Baby talk to me.

I had ignored the message. Too angry over seeing Giselle at his job to listen to anything he had to say. I drew in a long, shaky breath. Somehow, some way, I was going to fix things between us. I just need a chance.

We'll talk when I get home.

That's all I kept thinking about. What I was going to say and how I was going to say it. I had made a mistake. A terrible mistake. I hoped that during my uncertainty I hadn't ruined everything we had. I don't know what would make me even think that he wasn't the one or think I missed what I had with Dame. One date with my ex had cleared that up for me. I cared so much about Howard. If I was honest to myself, I'd admit that I loved him.

I quickly sent him a text message.

Can't wait to talk when you get back. Miss you.

I hit Send before I could change my mind. I didn't expect to hear back from him; however, I wanted to make sure my intentions were known. I didn't want Howard to have any doubts in his mind I wanted to be in his life.

Now I needed to work on me and wait.

As I lay across my bed and reached for the remote control, I felt more at peace than I had felt in months.

46

MEEKS

Over the next two weeks I threw myself into my job. There was plenty of work, so that was easy to do. I was in the office before the rest of the team, and then the last one to leave every evening. It helped pass the time and I'd hoped it would leave me less time to think about Howard, but that was a lie because he was always on my mind. Major Michaels had eased off a little so the mood in the office had calmed and we were able to breathe just a little bit without feeling micromanaged, especially me. I brought in a cake for my team, thanking them for all their hard work. I even let them leave early on Friday to start their weekend.

Over the weekend, I took my niece shopping for her Halloween costume. She wanted to be the princess in *Frozen*, so we searched four different stores until we found her size at Party Central. Afterwards, I took her to Surge and the two of us bounced around on trampolines like jumping beans for an hour. We had lunch and ice cream at McDonald's, and then it was time to take her back to her parents.

"You need to stop spoiling her," Layla scolded as we walked through the door with several bags in our hands.

"Who else do I have to spoil but my Maya poo," I told her and laughed.

"I had the best day ever, Aunt Day," Maya squealed.

"Thank you, baby." I turned to Layla and stuck out my tongue after Maya dashed down the hall to her room.

She rolled her eyes and laughed. "Okay when she becomes a teenager and acts a fool, I'll be sending her to your house."

I left the bag on the sofa and followed Layla into the kitchen.

"I baked an apple pie. You want some?" she asked although she was already reaching for the knife.

"You know you don't even have to ask." My sister made one of the best apple pies I'd ever tasted. I took a seat and waited as she grabbed two small plates and silverware and moved over to the table.

"I think we also need ice cream," she added and headed over to the refrigerator.

Once we had everything, Layla lowered onto the seat across from me. We were both quiet while I cut a big piece of pie.

Layla stabbed a slice of apple then look up at me. "How's therapy?" she asked, sounding almost afraid to ask.

I looked up from eating ice cream and nodded my head. "It's actually going well. I like Christine. She really listens and helps me to figure out things on my own instead of trying to give me all the answers."

Her shoulders sagged with relief. "That's good."

"Yeah, I think so. I know it's going to take time. Can't undo years of damage in a few hours, but I'm seeing her twice a week unless I decide I need more or less."

"I'm so happy for you." She suddenly stopped smiling. "Have you spoken to Mama?"

I rolled my eyes. "Yes. She called and wanted to talk about a purple mattress she'd seen on TV that she wants to order. The conversation was going fine until she asked me if I was coming home for the holiday. When I told her I was planning to spend Thanksgiving with Daddy, she hung up on me."

"Good old Mama," Layla said with sarcasm.

I nodded and put another spoon of ice cream in my mouth. "Mama will just have to get over it. I'm no longer living my life by her rules."

"Good for you."

I ate my pie in silence before looking over at my sister again. I could tell she wanted to ask me something. "Go ahead and say it."

She smirked. "When does Howard get back?"

"Wednesday," I responded in a shaky breath. "I'm so nervous."

She waved off my concerns. "Relax. It's going to be okay. Just open your heart and be honest with the man with how you feel. And *trust* that he's got you," she added.

Her words caused me to shiver. I couldn't wait for him to get home. He never responded to my text. Although I wasn't surprised, the uncertainty was driving me nuts. I hoped he felt the same way.

ΘΘΘ

It was after six and a good time to end the day and head over to Hangar 5. The buses were scheduled to arrive at nineteen-hundred-hour. I made a trip to the ladies' room to make sure I had everything in place, then I hopped in my car and headed over. The parking lot was full, and I spotted families carrying balloons. Husbands were holding flowers. I contemplated going over to the Base Exchange to grab something but decided it was too late for that. I was just going to come with honesty on the table.

I was so nervous; I hadn't been able to eat all day. Instead, I'd been waiting and watching the clock. Now the moment of truth had finally arrived.

I walked across to the hangar where there were two F-15s parked, one on either side of the large structure. Between the aircrafts, folding chairs had been lined in rows. A bandstand stage had been assembled. The executive officer was at the podium checking the microphone. I waved and walked over to Bailey, who was talking to one of the unit deployment managers. All of them were ready to take accountability for our team.

"You all set?" I asked her, trying to smile, but it was so hard considering my stomach was twisted up in knots.

She nodded. "Yes. The reception should be short this evening. The UDMs and I will take accountability as they depart the buses, and then everyone will stick around long enough for the wing commander to say a few words before being dismissed."

"Sounds like you have it under control."

"Yes, ma'am."

We spoke for a few more minutes. I spotted Rein and headed over her way. Her eyes lit up when she saw me. "Are you excited or what?"

"Or what," I replied with a rude snort. "But we'll see shortly."

Reaching over, she squeezed my shoulder. "It will be fine."

I hoped so. I wasn't sure but decided I could show Howard better than I could tell him. I hoped that was enough.

We both walked over and helped Airman and Family Readiness set up cupcakes with icing in red, white, and blue on a long table. A few of the first-term Airmen were handing out small American flags. The band had arrived, and the crowd grew with loud laughter and chatter that echo around the space.

"They're coming!" I heard someone shout.

My heart took off in a fast sprint and, within seconds, two large charter buses pulled inside the gate. The garage doors were lifted, so the vehicles were in clear view at the entrance where they parked. I practically held my breath waiting for the doors to open and then, one by one, they departed the vehicles. Thunderous clapping started. Others were waving their flags and cheering them on. Nervously, I moistened my lips while my eyes shifted from one bus to the other, watching, waiting as they departed all in uniform with backpacks on their shoulders. Wives raced over to their husbands. Husbands walked over to greet their wives. Children were squealing and jumping up and down while screaming "Daddy!" or "Mommy!" Tears began to blur my eyes as I stood back and watched it all, feeling a sense of pride that never went away. My gaze shifted again to the bus on the left and my heartrate skyrocketed.

Chief Master Sergeant Keim Howard stepped off the bus.

I couldn't move. All I could do was stand there and look at him. Taking in his gorgeous face and his large, masculine uniform-clad body standing large and in charge. He was taller and hotter than I remembered. Freaking sexy. His eyes scanned the space, and when they landed on me, they locked with mine. My pulse quickened, and even over all the chatter I heard my heavy breathing.

Howard licked his lips and mouthed, *Come here*.

Without hesitation, I headed his way. I was done playing games and was ready to show him I was ready for everything he had to offer me. I couldn't tear my eyes away. Everything and everyone seemed to fade as we stared. Howard stood with a rigid stance; legs slightly parted. Hands behind his back. He watched as I approached, eyes blazed with unmistakable masculine appreciation. I forced myself to slow my steps as I tried to remember my military bearing, but I wanted to run into the circle of his arms. Instead, I walked up to him until the toes of our boots were practically touching. Tilting my head, I gazed up and shivered as his eyes roamed over me. When he met my eyes again, his gaze was hot and searing.

"Hi," I croaked.

A hint of a smile curved Howard's sexy mouth. "Hello, beautiful."

Pleasure worked its way down my spine as I breathed, "Howard—" Before I could formulate my words, he cupped my face with his hands, lowered his head, and slanted his mouth over mine in a kiss.

47

HOWARD

I'd spent the last few weeks doing a lot of thinking about my life. The decisions I'd made and all the consequences. I guess that's what you do when you have a lot of time on your hands. And I needed that. It helped to figure out what was important in my life and the shit I could do differently.

Although my anger wasn't burning like before, there was still that feeling of resentment about Meeks not trusting me. But as I saw things through her eyes I started to understand. That didn't mean I liked it. It just meant I understood that she had a right to her own feelings. One thing I knew for sure was I wasn't letting her go, not over some dumb shit. I loved her. That was something I figured out. The longer I was away the deeper the ache in my chest. I wanted to reach out and call her, but I made myself wait. And after twenty-seven days without seeing my woman's beautiful face or hearing her voice, I knew there was no way in hell I was ever letting that happen again. The second I stepped off that bus and saw her, my first thought was, *"I need to taste her."* I swooped in and crushed her lips with mine, stealing her breath. Meeks' mouth was soft and warm and the kiss deep and slow as I tried not to devour her in public. There would be plenty of time for that later after the uniforms were off and we were alone, and yet, where the relationship went from here depended on what happened in the next few minutes.

That's if the wing commander ever got done with his speech and everyone tossed their flags in the air. Geesh. You would think we'd just come back from serving six months in Afghanistan. Instead I spent less than four weeks babysitting a bunch of Airmen, including the two knuckleheads that decided to steal a Humvee after-hours and ended up wrecking it. My eyes traveled over to the pop-locking trio that I made sit on the row beside me.

As soon as we were dismissed, I reminded those two they needed to report to the group commander's office first thing in the morning for disciplinary actions. I said a few words to the rest of my team, then went over to the side where Meeks was waiting. The sight of her standing in the crowd as I departed the bus had my stomach in knots. And at that moment I knew I had made the right decision about waiting to talk when I returned.

After getting my duffel bag off the bus, I followed Meeks out to her car, tossed my bags in the back, and we climbed inside. She didn't start the engine and neither one of us spoke for a long time.

"Is he gone?" There, I got right to the point.

"Yes. He left a few—"

"Is he *out* of your life?"

She blew out a breathy voice. "There's nothing left between us. You have to believe nothing happened—"

I held up a hand. I didn't want the details. I never wanted to know. Although, I'm not going to lie it was a relief to hear that nothing had happened. I don't like to share. All I cared about right now was that he was gone. "How do I know it's over?" I asked just because I felt like asking.

"You have to trust me." Her answer was unacceptable.

"Just like you trusted me with Giselle and Sherry." I still heard that bitterness in my voice.

She said softly, "You are right. The way I treated you was wrong. I know that now. But you must believe there's nothing going on between Dame and me. I made that perfectly clear to him."

"But how do I know that?" I repeated. And maybe I was being an asshole.

"Because I don't feel about him the way I feel about you."

I shrugged. "You say that and yet you believed what you wanted to believe and didn't allow me a chance to explain."

She swallowed and gave a jerking nod. "You're right, and—"

"Hold up. I'm not finish," I said. "You cut me out of your life and treated me like I had absolutely no integrity or honor when it came to being your man. As far as you were concerned, I was guilty before I had a chance to prove I was innocent. Day, that's not how relationships are supposed to work. If there is no trust, then we have nothing."

Meeks nodded and folded her hands in her lap. "You're right, and I'm sorry."

I cupped her chin, turning her head so that she was staring up at me. "I believe in fighting for what's mine, but my woman has to be willing to fight for me as well. She's gotta trust me."

"I know and I'm sorry." She swallowed. "What does this mean for us?"

"What do you want it to mean?"

She searched my eyes and I felt her body tremble as she said, "I love you."

My heart nearly flew out my chest at her confession, but I tried to tamp it down. "You say you love me, but you didn't come to me when things weren't right. You didn't give me a chance to explain. Instead you left me looking like a fool while you're out at the club with some other m—" I stopped because I was venting my frustrations and I hadn't planned on letting her know one of my boys saw her at the jazz club and reported it back to me.

Staring into my face with tears in her eyes, she whispered shakily, "I'm sorry. I don't know what more I can say to you. All I can do is try to show you."

I bit my lip so I wouldn't smile. "Am I your man?"

She nodded. "Yes, Howard, you're my man."

My eyes traced her beautiful, pink lips and then lowered to her slender neck where I leaned forward and stroked her warm flesh with my tongue. The air between us sizzled with awareness. No woman ever turned me on so much in my life. "And you're my woman. I don't take loving a woman lightly."

She drew back. Her lips parted and eyes widened as she whispered, "You love me, too?"

I lifted my gaze and nodded. "Hell yeah. What do you think this was all about?" I chuckled. "I don't act this crazy over just any woman."

She turned on the seat and practically leaped over onto my lap.

"Damn you, Howard." Her hand lifted to my chest. She gave a half-hearted attempt to push me way, then curled her fingers into my ABU top, gripping a fistful of fabric. "You had me so worried I lost you," she murmured, her voice brushing over me like heated silk. "I missed you so much."

"And I missed you." I slid a hand behind her head and dragged her mouth to mine, slipping my tongue between her lips with slow, languorous strokes. A low rumble vibrated my chest. Tasting. Sucking. Licking. No matter what I did, it wasn't nearly enough. It was all I could do to keep from lifting my hips toward her, into her. Remembering we were still sitting in the parking lot; I drew back before I did something crazy like drag her onto the backseat of the vehicle.

I stroked her cheek. "Babe."

"Yes?" she whispered, breathless and panting.

I licked my lips, still tasting her. "I don't want us to get to this point again. You have to trust me. I don't know if you noticed or not, but I'm the man in this relationship, which means I'm commanding this ship."

She gave me a look of wry amusement and withered on my lap. "Yes, baby. You"—she kissed my mouth—"are"—she kissed my bottom lip—"in"—she parted my lips—"control." With a sigh, she slipped her tongue inside.

I deepened the kiss and felt my body heating in ways that were better served at home. I growled into her mouth, "Let's get out of here. I need to make love to you… Now." I kissed her once more then hopped over into the driver's seat and hurried home.

Other Books by Angie Daniels

Feinin' *Big Spankable Asses Anthology*
Seduced into Submission- Curious
Seduced into Submission – Serve
Seduced into Submission – Obey
Seduced into Submission – Bound
Time for Desire
Beg For It
Talk a Good Game
When It Rains
A Delight before Christmas
Love Uncovered
When I First Saw You
In the Company of My Sistahs
Trouble Loves Company
Careful of the Company You Keep
Misery & Company
Intimate Intentions
Hart & Soul
Time is of the Essence
A Will to Love
Endless Enchantment
Destiny in Disguise
The Second Time Around
The Playboy's Proposition
The Player's Proposal
For You I Do
Before I Let You Go
In Her Neighbor's Bed
Show Me
Any Man Will Do
Coming for My Baby
Strutting in Red Stilettos

Running to Love in Pink Stilettos
Say My Name
Put Your Name on It
Every Second Counts
A Beau for Christmas
Do Me Baby
Naughty Before Christmas
Claiming What's Mine
Wicked Pleasure
Wilde & Sexy
Wilde about Her
Stilettos & Mistletoes
All I Want
Fire in My Soul

About the Author

Angie Daniels is a free spirit who isn't afraid to say what's on her mind or, even better, write about it. Since strutting onto the literary scene in five-inch heels, she's been capturing her audience's attention with her wild imagination and love for alpha men. The *USA Today* Bestselling Author has written over thirty novels for imprints such as BET Arabesque, Harlequin/Kimani Romance and Kensington/ Dafina and Kensington/Aphrodisia Books. For more information about upcoming releases, and to connect with Angie on Facebook, please visit her website at angiedaniels.com.

Printed in Great Britain
by Amazon

24798302R00179